When This War Is Over

Elaine Blick

Strategic Book Publishing and Rights Co.

Strategic Book Publishing and Rights Co.
12620 FM 1960, Suite A4-507
Houston, TX 77065
www.sbpra.com

ISBN: 978-1-62516-930-3

Book Design: Suzanne Kelly

With gratitude to my parents, Freda and Harold Blick, who met in Salisbury, England, and married there at the outbreak of war, in September 1939.

To Joan & Brendan
Love from
Elaine.

Preface

When I came to the end of NO WHITE FLOWERS, PLEASE I knew I had to write a sequel. After all, my chief character, Rhoda Pritchard, was only nineteen at the end of the book. My mother's life provided the inspiration for WHEN THIS WAR IS OVER, but as it is a novel I have not kept rigorously to the facts of her life and I would not like readers to regard it as biographical. For instance, the character of Lawrence is purely imaginary.

I had some difficulty in finding a title for the new novel until one day I was clearing out a drawer and found a letter written by Mum to Dad in 1943 when he was in the army. Immediately I knew what the title of this new book should be. I quote excerpts from the letter which was six pages long:

> *"My darling,*
>
> *I loved your letter this morning. I read the 1st instalment on the way to the office, and kept the last half for a quiet pause. It brought you so close dearest. There is a precious bond between us now—something so precious that I am anxious that nothing shall spoil it. It's wonderful to be one of the loved ones and to be wanted—one can feel pity for those who have never known this great gift....*
>
> *When this War is over, dear, we will build our home again, and make of it a lovely place, where happiness and love abide, and with God's help we won't let anything come into it which will spoil its peaceful atmosphere. Our little Elaine shall have pleasant happy memories of home.....*

There is still that something in the air which is like winter. Can you understand what I mean? It's the feeling one has when walking over the downs, or over heather-strewn moors—something exciting yet mellow- maybe it's the autumn tang in the air, and perhaps that's it in a nutshell....

Will close now my dearest- I could write lots more but had better stop. All my love to my sweetheart—I do love you Harold—more than I can ever tell you.

Freda"

I found the thoughts expressed in this letter very touching but what was most remarkable was the fact that it turned up at the very time I was writing my novel. Surely this was more than coincidence!

Salisbury and the village of Laverstock are the setting of the novel and mean a lot to me as I was born in Salisbury and we lived in Laverstock until I was five, when we moved to New Zealand. My earliest memories are connected with Salisbury and it will always be 'home' to me.

As I was researching the background of the thirties and the events leading up to the Second World War I was struck by how narrowly we in Britain escaped being invaded. The D Day evacuation was rightly hailed by Churchill as miraculous and he pulled no punches in telling the British people the blunt truth about the seriousness of their position. I am thankful that we had a God-fearing king on the throne at the time and a fearless leader like Winston Churchill. I am truly grateful to them and all those servicemen and women who laid their lives down for their country. Thanks to them we have our freedom today. I hope all those reading this book will feel as I do, profoundly grateful to the previous generation.

28th May 2013

Acknowledgements

I would first like to thank Mrs. Ansie Downs for her unstinting help and guidance to me in correcting this book. She not only proof-read the manuscript but checked times and dates so that there should be no discrepancies. I am very grateful for her able assistance. I am also appreciative of the help of Dr. Mary Tucker who read my manuscript and made worthwhile suggestions. She was willing to be consulted at any time about the medical conditions of certain characters. Without her help I would have made some serious gaffs. Then there is my friend Pauline Stansfield who always takes an interest in my writing and gives honest and constructive advice. I appreciated her willingness to read my manuscript also. Thanks also to my friends at Clarks Beach, Dorothy and Jim Johnston and Molly and Henry Hall who patiently listened to me read various chapters to them.

Last of all, I must mention the help I have had through the internet and the different websites that gave valuable information on World War 2. It is wonderful at the touch of a key to be able to access such a wealth of material.

CHAPTER ONE

It had been a long weary day and I was thankful to be on the bus at last. Hannah had insisted we climb to the top deck, and tired as I was I didn't have the heart to refuse her. After all, trailing round the shops was tiring for a child of two and a half. I glanced down at my shopping bag. It seemed pathetically light and yet how much queuing had been involved to buy these few items. There were more shortages than ever this second year of war. Still, we were better off in Salisbury than in many other cities. London was being bombed night after night, whereas air raids were intermittent in Salisbury, usually after the German bombers were returning from a night raid on London and wanted to lighten their load before flying back across the channel.

These thoughts flitted through my mind as I looked across at the other red buses standing at the station. There seemed quite a number of them this afternoon, full of tired shoppers like myself.

"Mummy, can we have bread and butter for tea when we get home?" Hannah asked eagerly.

"Yes, dear, and we can have as much butter as we like today because Granddad sent us a fresh supply from New Zealand."

My mouth watered at the thought of the huge lump of butter that had arrived yesterday. I would cut it up into smaller portions and give some to Miss Nugent and to Joan and there would still be plenty left for us.

I glanced at my watch. It was now five to three so the bus should be leaving the station in five minutes.

It was warm and drowsy up here on the top deck and I found my eyes beginning to close. I was just drifting off when a loud insistent wail jerked me awake. An air raid siren at this time of day! Surely there must be some mistake. Perhaps the mechanism had been triggered accidentally and it would stop at any moment.

Our bus started up suddenly, nearly pitching Hannah and myself into the back of the seat in front and simultaneously, as if by some hidden signal, all the buses pulled out of the station, setting off in different directions. As soon as our bus rounded the corner it gathered speed and swaying dangerously, hurtled along one of the main roads leading out of the city.

I put my arm protectively around Hannah, fearful that at any moment she would be thrown across the aisle or hurled against the seat in front of us.

"What's happening?" I shouted to the middle-aged woman in the seat opposite.

"We're driving out to the country—anywhere. It doesn't matter, just so long as we get out of the city," she shouted back. "The bombers could attack any moment."

"Are we alright, Mummy?" asked Hannah anxiously and looking down, I saw her eyes were wide and frightened.

"Of course we are, darling. The bus driver knows what he's doing," and I drew my little daughter closer to my side.

In no time at all we were out on the road leading to Old Sarum and as we sped along the quiet road past the ancient hill fort, I had a sudden vision of walking up its slopes one Sunday afternoon before the war. That seemed to belong to another age, as remote as Old Sarum itself.

Now we were out in the country, passing lush fields and mellow farmhouses of red brick with mossy roofs. Cows looked up as we careered past, then bent their heads lazily to tug at the grass. It was a sleepy summer's afternoon and it seemed madness to be tearing along like this.

What was that? Above the sound of the bus engine was another noise, one we had all come to dread, the sinister 'crump crump' of a German plane, quite different from the sound of the Spitfire or Hurricane. It seemed to be getting closer. I peered through the window. The plane was still some distance off, but I could just make out the distinctive red circle of the swastika on its tail. Yes, the plane was definitely following us. My heart was thumping wildly. I had heard of planes shooting at civilian targets. Without further thought I threw my arm around Hannah and dragged her to the floor throwing myself across her. "It's alright, Hannah!" I shouted, as the child struggled beneath me.

The next moment a window behind us shattered and there was a loud crack as a bullet embedded itself in the side of the bus. Then followed another and the air was full of noise, the loud roaring of the engine overhead and the report of bullets. The bus was careering from side to side and swaying as though at any moment it would overturn. Time ceased to exist.

Then suddenly it was over. Slowly the bus came to a standstill and in the distance was only the faint hum of the departing plane. I lay for a few moments then stood up shakily and looked down at my daughter lying curled on the floor.

"You can get up now, darling," I whispered. "The plane's gone. We're quite safe." Bending down I gently lifted her and she threw herself into my arms sobbing. I held her close, whispering comforting words and caressing her head. So occupied was I with the frightened child that at first I did not hear a man's voice calling from the front of the bus: "Jerry's gone! Everyone all right here? Anybody hurt?"

Looking up, I saw the driver standing at the top of the stairs, his roughened countryman's face concerned as he gazed along the aisle.

"What's wrong with the little girl?" he asked, coming over to us.

"She's just badly frightened."

"Enough to scare anybody. Nasty devil to fire at civilians. All part of Jerry's plan. Scare the daylights out of us so we cave in. Won't work though. Just make us more determined to fight back."

He lifted his head to examine the windows where the glass had been shattered.

"A close shave that. You'd have copped those bullets if you'd been sitting up. I suppose you all got down on the floor."

The lady in the seat opposite us nodded her head vigorously. "Naturally," she said. "I'd like to charge Hitler with my dry cleaning bills. Fairly ruined my new suit lying on that filthy floor."

The man laughed. "Just be thankful it's only your clothes that are damaged, my love," and turning to the passengers at large he announced cheerfully, "I'll make my way back along the road and pick up the route to Laverstock, where we were going before we were so rudely interrupted."

"Are we going home, Mummy?" asked Hannah, who had been listening closely to all this.

"Yes, dear, and we will have bread and butter and a nice cup of tea." Something like normality descended on us at the mention of these homely items and I felt Hannah relax against me.

When we pulled up at our usual bus stop it all seemed so perfectly ordinary it was hard to realise that, less than an hour before, we had been in the middle of a waking nightmare.

As soon as we were indoors I cut some thick slices of new white bread and spread them lavishly with butter and raspberry jam. Then I poured us both a cup of tea, mainly milk and hot water for Hannah. Companionably we sat down at the kitchen table with our plates and cups in front of us. Before we had a chance to eat there was a sharp rap on the door.

"Who can that be?" I said. "Could have waited till I'd drunk my tea."

I hurried out to answer the door, expecting that Joan had called by to collect her butter. Instead a telegram boy stood there holding out a yellow envelope to me. My heart jumped in my chest and I felt winded.

"Is this you?" he asked, pointing at the name on the envelope.

"Yes," I managed to say and took it from him.

When he was gone I remained standing at the open door turning the envelope over and over in my hands. I felt deathly cold and my teeth began to chatter. Telegrams meant one thing only in wartime. I had to sit down and nerve myself somehow to open it. Returning to the kitchen I was vaguely aware of Hannah, munching on her bread and butter. I sat down on one of the kitchen chairs, letting the envelope slide onto my lap.

"Mummy, you look funny." Hannah's voice was alarmed.

"I'm fine. Don't worry, darling. I've just had a bit of a shock." I tried to steady my voice.

"Why don't you open that letter?"

The matter of fact question, asked with childish simplicity, was just what I needed to bring me back to reality. Why indeed, didn't I open the letter? Better to know the worst than wait in this torment of suspense.

With trembling fingers I tore open the envelope. The word "Missing" jumped out at me.

This was the word every wife of a serviceman dreaded. Yet missing did not necessarily mean dead. It could mean that my husband had been taken prisoner. I struggled to hold onto hope, although despair very nearly overwhelmed me. Hannah was watching me curiously. I must not let her see my fear.

"Everything's all right, dear," I said. "Get on and finish your tea."

CHAPTER TWO

That night I sat at Hannah's bedside until she was asleep. Looking down at the smooth untroubled face and the small hands lying limply on the coverlet I wondered at the miracle of sleep. I knew there would be no escape into oblivion for me tonight. The same worrying thoughts kept chasing each other in circles through my brain until I could bear it no longer. I had to find distraction, anything to take my mind off my fears.

Stiffly I got up and tiptoed from the room, pausing at the door to look back at the sleeping child. Then I crossed the passage into the tiny sitting room and wandered over to the bookshelf. Perhaps there was something here I could read that would demand concentration, a book of poetry perhaps or even history. My eyes flicked over the titles: Keats, Dickens, a history of New Zealand; they all seemed irrelevant. I was about to turn away when I noticed an old exercise book of mine tucked in a corner on the bottom shelf. Idly I pulled it out and it fell open at a page that was dated, Sept 20 1931. I had written this ten years ago, the day I first came to Salisbury. I began to read, smiling at the artless expression of the girl I had once been:

Today marks the biggest change in my life so far. I have moved right away from everything I have ever known in coming to Salisbury. When they told me at Birmingham Infirmary that I had to leave general nursing because of my health I thought it was the end of everything. Then I saw an advertisement in the Nursing Times for a psychiatric nurse at Laverton House, a private hospital in Laverstock, Salisbury. I applied and, hey presto, I was accepted. Today I travelled down by train from Bristol and here I am writing this in the room I share with one of the other nurses, Joan Russell. I think we are going to be good friends, although she is two years older than I am—she is twenty-one, but that doesn't seem to matter.

I sat down in my favourite easy chair curling my legs under me. As I read on, it all came back vividly; that quiet Saturday afternoon when I arrived at Salisbury railway station and stepped onto the platform with my shabby suitcase. Just momentarily I had felt a pang of loneliness knowing there would be no-one to meet me outside, but fortunately when I went through the turnstile a taxi cab was waiting by the kerb. The driver asked me cheerfully where I wanted to go.

"To Laverton House, please. It's a private hospital in Laverstock," I replied hesitantly.

"Oh aye, I knows it. Hop in, miss, I'll take you there."

He gave me a rather peculiar look. Perhaps he thought I was a patient. I had a quiet smile to myself and leaned forward to see as much as I could of the streets we were passing through. On either side were half-timbered Tudor buildings with steep gables and small leaded windows. To my eyes, accustomed to Bath where everything was built on regular and classical lines, Salisbury looked quaint and medieval. As we swung out of one of the narrow streets I looked back and gasped, for there, like a finger pointing to the sky, rose the cathedral spire. It seemed almost ethereal as it hovered above the city and it inspired in me a sense of awe. I think from that moment I fell in love with Salisbury. In some strange way I felt I had come home.

Very soon we left the city streets behind and were out in the suburbs. As we approached the outskirts of Laverstock I noticed all the signs of a new housing development, with rows of small modern bungalows on either side. I felt a stab of disappointment that we had left behind the old world atmosphere of Salisbury.

However, the taxi drove on past the new houses and along several tree-lined streets before entering a cul de sac where large houses were set back in spacious gardens. In front of us was an entrance opening onto a gravelled driveway.

"Here we are, Laverton House," announced the driver, turning off the road.

I had an impression of a large country house, built of warm red brick with ivy covering most of the front. Manicured lawns, with flower beds on either side of the drive, completed the effect of a gracious country home and I felt like a guest arriving for a weekend house party.

The driver commented, as he lifted my suitcase out of the car, "Lovely old place, isn't it? What kind of work will you be doing here?"

"I'm going to be a nurse."

"Are you indeed?" and he raised his eyebrows.

After I had paid him, he touched his cap and drove off slowly. I paused for a moment wondering why he had seemed surprised. Perhaps I did not look the type to be a nurse in a mental hospital. In many people's minds it conjured up the picture of a female prison warder, with a large bunch of keys at her waist, ready to clap patients into a strait jacket. *At least I don't fit that image*, I thought as I picked up my suitcase. I studied the building before me. It was certainly nothing like my picture of a mental asylum. Curiously I approached the door and pressed the bell. The door was opened by a smart looking maid in a black dress with a frilly white headband in her hair. She looked at me enquiringly.

"I'm Rhoda Pritchard. I've just come down from Bristol by train. I think I am expected this afternoon."

"Come in, Miss Pritchard, and I'll fetch Matron," and with that she disappeared. As I waited I looked around the vestibule noting the touches of comfort and opulence in the furnishings. I was just wondering whether to sit down in one of the leather chairs when a door opened and a woman came towards me smiling, her hand outstretched. She was short and dumpy with a round face and mild grey eyes.

"I'm Matron Dunne," she said with a faint Irish brogue. "Welcome to Laverton House, Miss Pritchard. I hope you are going to be very happy here. I think you will find it rather different from a general hospital," and she smiled. "You've travelled down from Bristol today haven't you? I expect you would like to freshen up before you come to tea, which will be in half an hour's time. I'll get Millie, our maid, to show you to your room."

She went through a door at the side of the vestibule and a few moments later Millie returned. She offered to take my suitcase.

"No, I can manage thank you." The girl shrugged and indicated the wide curving staircase in front of us.

"Your room is two floors up, Miss. It's a bit of a climb."

It certainly is, I thought, as I followed the slim black figure up the stairs to the second landing.

"Your room is along here. It's number six," and Millie pushed open the door. I stood for a moment gazing into a room that could easily have been fitted out for a country house. From the floral carpet to the blue satin drapes at the sides of the tall sash windows, everything was comfortable and well appointed. Two beds were set well apart on opposite sides of the room with a couple of easy chairs between them and against one wall was a dainty bureau.

"It's a nice room, isn't it?" remarked Millie glancing around her.

"Yes, it is. Rather different from what I expected," I replied, thinking back to the cramped cell I had shared with Iris in the Nurses' Home in Birmingham.

"Well, if you don't need me I'll be off. Tea is in the dining room at five."

"Thank you, Millie. I suppose the dining room is on the ground floor."

"Yes, just to the right of the stairs."

When she had gone I sank into one of the easy chairs, content just to sit and absorb the restful atmosphere of the room. It seemed that everything about Laverton House was going to be different from what I had experienced at a general hospital and I felt a momentary pang for the bustling activity I'd been used to.

Don't be silly, I told myself. *You're lucky to have been sent to such a comfortable place,* and I seemed to hear Aunty Edith's voice saying, "Luck doesn't come into it. There's no such thing as luck. It's providence."

Whatever it was, the fact remained that only a few months before I had nearly died while I was nursing on the fever ward at Birmingham Infirmary, yet now I was well enough to go nursing again, even if it was only in a mental hospital. A sigh escaped my lips as I thought back to those busy days on the wards, when even the most unpleasant jobs could be turned into a joke, especially when I giggled over them afterwards with the other nurses. Then there was Iris, my room-mate and best friend. What fun she had been and what confidences we had shared.

I glanced curiously around the room. There was no evidence of anyone else occupying it; not even a brush or comb on the dressing table. Feeling a bit like a spy I crossed over to the wardrobe and opened the door. There I saw a row of dresses and coats all neatly hung up and shoes arranged in order from slippers to boots. The clothes and shoes took up one half of the wardrobe while the other half had been left empty. Whoever she was, the other occupant of the room was scrupulously tidy, not like the harum scarum Iris who left her clothes wherever she happened to step out of them. I smiled at the memory.

I heard a small cough behind me and started guiltily. A tall girl with glossy black hair cut fashionably short was standing in the doorway observing me, a quizzical expression on her face.

"Hello, I presume you are my new room-mate," she said and smiled slightly.

"Yes, I'm Rhoda, Rhoda Pritchard."

"And I'm Joan Russell. I only heard you were coming yesterday so I cleared some space in the wardrobe. Actually, I came back early. I was going to be away until tomorrow. That would have given you time to settle in. Sorry."

"Oh that's alright. I'm glad to meet you."

There was a pause as we studied each other. I noted Joan's pale skin, which was almost translucent, and her clearly defined features. Without being pretty she was what people would call attractive and refined looking. Only her mouth spoiled her. It was downturned and rather sulky. I wondered what she was thinking about me.

Joan smiled suddenly and all trace of stiffness vanished from her manner.

"I'll just get my coat off and show you where everything is, Rhoda. I suppose nobody thought of taking you on a tour of the place."

"Well, no, but I did find out from Millie where the dining room is."

"We've still got half an hour before tea, time enough for me to explain the layout of the house, then after tea we can go for a walk through the grounds."

She turned out to be a clear and succinct guide and by the time we went into the dining room, at five o'clock, I felt quite familiar with the house.

The dining room was pleasant and spacious with French doors at one end opening onto a wide lawn. About eight tables, each seating four, were arranged so that there was plenty of space between them. Only five of them were occupied, although all were laid for tea. As we entered, several of the diners looked up and smiled pleasantly at us. Joan led the way to a table at the end of the room where there was a view of the garden and yet was far enough away from the other tables for our conversation not to be heard. She seated herself at one side and indicated the chair opposite her.

"This way I can tell you about everyone without them overhearing," she smiled across to me. "Now you see that group in the far corner by the potted plant? They are the old-timers. They've been here from the year dot, in other words since the hospital was taken over by Dr. Hall."

"When was that?"

"Oh, about fifteen years ago, I think. Dr. Hall bought it when it was a rambling old country house and turned it into what you see today. He and Dr. Branson run it together, although Dr. Hall is mainly concerned with admin and the financial side of things. It's Dr. Branson who looks after the patients."

"It's fairly unusual for patients and staff to eat in the same dining room, isn't it? That would never happen in a public hospital."

"I suppose not, but this is a private hospital and Dr. Branson has quite modern ideas. He believes that mental patients should be treated as if they were normal. Laverton House is run along the same lines as a private hotel."

"What are they like, Dr. Branson and Dr. Hall, I mean?"

A strange look passed across Joan's face.

"Well, let me put it like this, they are as different as chalk from cheese. Dr. Hall looks the image of Gandhi, small and dark and rather sinister. Dr. Branson is a giant beside him."

"What are they like to the patients?"

"Oh, Dr. Branson is kindness itself, but Dr. Hall is only interested in what they bring in cash-wise."

Just then Millie approached our table wheeling a trolley, on which were sandwiches and a tiered plate of small cakes. We stopped talking and watched as she lifted these and a china teapot from the trolley onto the table. When she was gone we helped ourselves to a sandwich each and for a few minutes were silent as we ate.

I was the first to speak. "What kind of patients do they have here, Joan? The ones I have seen walking around look perfectly normal to me."

"Oh, they seem that way until you get to know them. Then you find out that they have all sorts of obsessions and quirks that make it difficult for them to lead ordinary lives. They simply need looking after, but they're not dangerous—we don't use strait jackets here—just in case you wondered," and she grinned. "I suppose they are a bit of an embarrassment to their families and so that is why they are happy to pay for them to be here. One of our patients is Lady Saddleton, a member of the Nightingale family, a great-niece of Florence. We call her Tuffy."

"And what is wrong with her?"

"Oh, she has an obsession about her weight. Thinks she's terribly fat. We have a hard job persuading her to eat. Apart from that she's a dear little thing."

"Will she ever get over that obsession, by careful nursing perhaps?"

"No, she's a chronic case, as so many of the old ones are."

"That's rather sad, isn't it?" I remarked.

"Not really," replied Joan airily. "They're happy enough and they are well looked after here."

"Tell me more about Dr. Hall, Joan, he sounds interesting."

Again a curious expression flitted across her face.

"Oh, he's alright. You'll meet him soon enough and then you can judge for yourself."

Joan was clearly being evasive and I glanced at her curiously. I was so busy watching her I didn't notice the girl approaching our table.

"Joan, do you mind if I sit here?" She looked across at me with a smile. "Hello, you're new here, aren't you?"

"Yes, I just arrived today. I'm Rhoda."

"And I'm Maisie."

"But my nickname for her is Fairy, for obvious reasons," interjected Joan, and as I looked at the girl's delicate colouring and long fair hair I could see how appropriate this nickname was.

It did not take long before we were all chattering freely and I experienced the same sense of easy camaraderie that I had known in the nurses' home in Birmingham. As Joan and I stood up to leave, Maisie turned to me.

"Have you seen around the grounds yet, Rhoda? They are quite extensive. I'll take you on the grand tour if you like, that is if you haven't anything more pressing to do."

I glanced at Joan.

"You go with Fairy," she said quickly. "I've got one or two things to do."

"Let's go then, Rhoda, shall we?" said Maisie, and as I followed her from the dining room I hoped she would shed some light on Joan's reluctance to talk about Dr. Hall.

CHAPTER THREE

I enjoyed my walk with Maisie through the grounds of Laverton House that afternoon. The trees were tinted with the colours of early autumn and a few leaves fluttered to the ground as we lingered on the rise of lawn gazing at the cathedral spire in the distance. So absorbed were we, that neither of us heard footsteps behind us and we jumped at the sound of a man's voice.

"Good afternoon, young ladies."

"Oh, good afternoon, Dr. Hall. I didn't hear you coming!" exclaimed Maisie.

"No, you were too busy admiring the view. And this is Nurse Pritchard I presume?" he added, turning to me. "You are from near Bath aren't you? That's a lovely city, though rather different from Salisbury. When did you get here?"

"Oh, just this afternoon. I arrived by train at three o'clock." I dropped my eyes, feeling confused in the presence of this man whose powerful personality seemed to reach out and swamp me.

There was a pause, then he said briskly, "Well, I'll continue with my constitutional and leave you both to enjoy the view." We watched him stride away, using his stick to swipe at some long grass.

"So that's Dr. Hall," I whispered. "He's exactly as Joan described him, small and dark and just like Ghandi."

"Is that what she said? Well, she knows him better than any of us."

"Why is that?"

Maisie raised an eyebrow. "You're new here so you wouldn't know that Joan is the favourite of the Halls. You could almost say that she is Mrs. Hall's protégé."

I listened carefully, absorbing this information.

"But surely it's not very professional of Dr. Hall to show favouritism to one of the nurses?"

"Oh that wouldn't worry him. This is his hospital and I suppose he can do what he likes."

"How does Joan like being singled out from the other nurses?" I said, remembering the slightly petulant look about her mouth.

Maisie looked thoughtful. "I think she is so used to it she doesn't really notice, though it must have come as rather a shock when she discovered she had to share a room. She's had that room all to herself for the past year, unlike the rest of us."

"I hope she won't resent me."

"No, Joan isn't like that. She seems to like you. Anyway, I got that impression at tea time."

As we walked back to the house I was more curious than ever about Joan's relationship with the Halls.

We were just about to go indoors when Maisie said, "Oh, by the way, some of us are getting together for cards this evening in the lounge. If you care to join us, Rhoda, you're more than welcome. After all it is Saturday night."

"I think I'll unpack and get settled in, but thanks anyway."

As I climbed the stairs I thought how familiar the house seemed already. It was hard to believe that I had only arrived that afternoon. At the door of the bedroom I hesitated. Suppose I were to disturb Joan? She had been used to her privacy for so long. I turned the handle gently and was relieved to find the room empty when I went in, although the smell of face powder suggested she had been gone only a short while.

I felt suddenly nostalgic for the small bedroom I shared with my sister Hazel in Paulton, and sinking down on an easy chair by the window, I sat and thought about those at home; Aunty Edith would be busy preparing for Sunday, probably making an apple pie, the boys would be playing with their train set and Hazel might be visiting one of her many friends in the village, hoping that her latest boyfriend would drop by.

I sighed. Their lives would be carrying on as normal while everything here was completely new and strange to me. Slowly

I began to hang up my clothes in the wardrobe, where Joan had considerately made space for me, and my thoughts turned to her and her relationship with Dr. Hall. I thought back to our chance meeting with him that afternoon and shivered at the memory of those penetrating dark eyes that had no kindly warmth in them. How could Joan feel comfortable in the presence of such a man? Mentally I shrugged and continued to unpack.

When I had finished I sat down at the dainty little bureau and made a diary entry in a new exercise book I had bought for the purpose. I had promised myself I would keep a record of each day so that my early impressions of Laverton House would not be forgotten, unlike when I was nursing in Birmingham and so busy I had not taken time to write a diary.

Having completed today's entry I took out my notepad and wrote a long chatty letter to Hazel. This contact with home made me feel better and when I glanced at my little bedside clock I saw it was nine o'clock already, not too early for bed after such a long day.

I must have been asleep for several hours when something woke me. It was probably the door opening, because in the dim light I could see Joan tiptoeing across the room. The luminous dial of the clock showed it was just after one o'clock. A few minutes later I heard her get into bed and shortly afterwards her breathing became regular. But while she slept I lay awake for a long time, my mind busy with all that had happened over the past twenty-four hours. Finally, I fell into an uneasy sleep.

When I woke it was morning and the sun was streaming into the room through the gaps between the curtains. I lifted myself onto one elbow and looked across at the sleeping girl in the bed opposite, huddled under the bedclothes. There seemed no danger of waking her so I got up and crossed to the wash basin. Looking in the mirror I saw that my face was white and there were circles under my eyes. At least, a little face powder would hide those.

It was Sunday and I wanted, on my first day in Salisbury, to go to a place of worship but I had no idea where the local Baptist chapel might be, so I decided to go down to breakfast and make enquiries.

Very few people were in the dining room and nobody that I recognised from the day before. I went to the sideboard and was helping myself to cereal and fruit when a girl came and stood next to me.

"Hello," she said, with a marked Irish accent. "You're new here, aren't you? I noticed you yesterday. How are you liking it?"

"Well, it's a bit early to say, but so far everyone has been very friendly. I'm Rhoda Pritchard, by the way."

"And I'm Ruth O'Reilly. Welcome Rhoda, to Laverton House, where it is often hard to tell patients from staff," and she grinned. "Sometimes I think they're saner than we are. Anyway, do come and sit at my table and tell me all about yourself."

Gladly I followed the girl to the end of the room and it was not long before I had heard all of her history. It seemed her parents had intended for her to enter a convent, but instead Ruth had managed to get right away from Ireland and her family by securing a position as a nurse at Laverton House.

I interrupted the flow by asking, "As you're a Catholic, Ruth, you will know where all the Catholic churches are in this area, but can you tell me what Protestant churches are near here?"

"Now let me see, there's a Church of England quite nearby, but I'm afraid I wouldn't know of any others. What denomination are you, Rhoda?"

"Oh, Baptist or Open Brethren, it doesn't matter which."

"I know who would be able to help you. Jim Davis, one of our male nurses, goes to a gospel hall. Look, there he is in the corner," and she pointed to a broad-shouldered youth with a shock of black hair falling over his eyes. "When you've finished breakfast I'll take you over to meet him."

Jim looked up in surprise as we approached his table. He scrambled to his feet and Ruth quickly introduced me to him. There was an awkward pause and then I said, "I understand you attend a gospel hall somewhere near here and I was wondering if you could tell me where it is and how I could get there."

"Oh that's easy. I go on my motor-bike and if you don't mind riding pillion you can come with me."

I had a quick vision of myself in my best clothes on the back of a motorbike and hesitated. "Well, that is very kind of you, but I was thinking more of a bus."

"Oh, there's no regular Sunday service from here, so you would have to walk. That's alright if you don't mind a five mile hike there and back," and he grinned. "No, you'd better come on the back of my bike. I promise I'm a careful driver."

I smiled back at him.

"Very well then, thank you, I will."

"Good, I'll meet you out in the drive at ten thirty. Wear something warm; it can be a bit chilly on the back."

As I left the dining room I found myself humming. This promised to be an interesting day.

"You seem happy," remarked Joan, glancing at me as I entered the room. She was sitting at the dressing table combing her hair.

"Yes, I've just had an invitation to ride pillion on a motor-bike to a church service."

Joan yawned. "You are devout. You wouldn't catch me going to church, except when I'm home, and then only because my parents expect it."

I felt sudden pity for this girl who spoke in such a world -weary tone.

"I'd better be off now. I arranged to meet Jim Davis at ten thirty," I said quickly, glad to have an excuse to escape from the room.

A few minutes later I was climbing onto the back of the motorbike, taking care to tuck my skirt firmly around myself so it would not blow up in the breeze. Once I was perched behind him, Jim kicked the engine into life. The bike leaped forward and I clutched at his waist. Jim laughed, but then he guided the bike sedately down the drive. When he reached the gate he turned up the throttle and the bike surged forward. I had a sudden sense of exhilaration. I felt young and free and gloriously alive as we roared down the country roads, but it was not long before we reached a small village and had to slow down. Jim drew up outside a plain wooden building which I recognised instantly as a gospel hall. A cluster of youths stood outside, rather like a herd of young steers I thought, and as Jim pulled into the kerb they moved forward, gazing curiously at me. I attempted to dismount as modestly as I could from the back of the bike.

"This is Rhoda Pritchard," said Jim addressing the group at large. "She's just joined the staff at Laverton House. Now make way, lads, we want to go in," and he beckoned me to follow him.

"Have you got a letter of commendation?" he whispered just before we entered the porch.

"No, we don't have them where I come from."

"I'm afraid they're a bit strict here. If you don't have a letter you'll have to sit at the back and you won't be able to take the bread and wine."

I followed Jim into the porch where a man was greeting all comers. He came forward with his hand outstretched and as I placed my hand in his I noted the firm warm clasp.

"This is Miss Rhoda Pritchard," explained Jim. "She has just joined the staff at Laverton House and only arrived yesterday. She usually meets with the Baptists so she doesn't have a letter of commendation."

"I see. Well, in that case, my dear, I must ask you to sit at the back." He spoke in a firm but kindly way and ushered me to an empty form at the very back of the hall. I sat down and after a pause Jim seated himself beside me.

"You don't need to sit back here," I whispered to him, but he merely grinned and handed me a hymn book.

Once the service commenced I was reminded of our gospel hall in Huntley, New Zealand, and I felt a stab of homesickness. Dad would still be going there, Sunday after Sunday, while here I was on the other side of the world. It was four years since I and my brothers and sisters had said goodbye to him in Auckland, yet the separation from him was still painful to me.

However, as I sat at the back of the hall this Sunday morning, I felt peace descend on me.

After communion an elderly man stood up and asked us to turn to the twenty-third Psalm. As I listened to the grand old words being read in his quavery voice, my mind went back to the time, a few months before, when I had nearly died of pleurisy and pneumonia at Birmingham Infirmary while I was nursing in the fever ward. As I was hovering on the brink of death I had been aware of the Good Shepherd guiding me through the Valley of the Shadow.

How strange and yet how significant that the twenty-third Psalm was being read on my first Sunday here. Surely this was God's way of showing me that he was still my shepherd and would be with me on this new path that had led to Salisbury.

After he sat down, somebody got up and prayed and then the service was over. Immediately, there was an outburst of chatter on all sides. Everybody seemed to be talking to somebody else and I suddenly felt very much an outsider. Even Jim had his back to me and was talking animatedly to someone I could not see. Suddenly, he turned around and said, "Hey Rhoda, this is Harold Blake. He comes from your part of the world, New Zealand isn't it, or is it Australia?"

"New Zealand," said Harold promptly and I noticed the slight inflexion in his voice that marked him as coming from there.

He looked directly into my eyes and I noticed that his were very clear and blue.

"What part are you from, Miss Pritchard?" he asked.

"Oh, Huntley, just south of Auckland," I replied automatically. "What about you?"

"My family come from Nelson, although I have spent most of my life in Malaya where my parents are missionaries, so it is hard to say where I belong."

At this point Jim interjected. "How amazing two New Zealanders should end up in a small place like this! You will have to get to know one another better."

I felt my cheeks grow hot but Harold merely smiled. None of us noticed the middle-aged man who had come alongside us, until he spoke.

"Well, Jim, aren't you going to introduce me to the young lady? I see you brought her on your motorcycle this morning, so would I be right in thinking she is working at Laverton House?"

"Oh, hello, Mr. Forster, this is Rhoda Pritchard and she has come to join the nursing staff at Laverton House. She is from New Zealand and I was just saying that she and Harold should have a lot in common."

"So they must and that is why I should like to invite you three young people home for lunch today." Turning to me he said, "Harold is a regular guest on Sundays and I know Mother is well prepared for a few extra at the table."

"Well, I accept and if Rhoda refuses she will have to walk back to Laverstock," said Jim with a laugh.

"I would love to come," I said quickly, smiling at Mr. Forster.

"Good, I will go and warn Mother that there will be three extra for lunch," and Mr. Forster left us.

CHAPTER FOUR

The Forsters' house looked as if it had originally been two cottages, now joined into one. Under the thatched roof the dormer windows were small with leaded panes, but on the ground floor, on either side of the door, were large modern plate glass windows which for some reason did not look incongruous. Walking along the flagged path I could see by the neatly mown lawns and the well weeded flower border that somebody lovingly cared for this garden.

Large tubs of red and pink geraniums stood on each side of the door, their cheerful colour warm and welcoming. Even the brass door knocker had been polished so that it reflected back our faces like a mirror.

At the first rap the door was opened by a little maidservant who could not have been more than fifteen. She ushered us into the lobby and Mr. Forster came bustling up behind her.

"Come in, come in," hc said, rubbing his hands and beaming at us. "It didn't take you long to find us, though you have been here once before I think, Jim. Now dinner will be a little while, so go on into the sitting room and make yourselves at home. Harold and Elsie are already here," he added, opening the door to the sitting room.

Then he hurried off, leaving us to enter the room which was large and comfortably furnished with deep armchairs and bright cushions. Harold stood up smartly and I noticed, almost subconsciously, that he was smartly dressed without being flamboyant, also that his moustache was neatly trimmed and his hair brushed smoothly back from his forehead.

"Hello once more, Miss Pritchard," he said formally. "Let me introduce Miss Elsie Sumner," and he waved towards the girl in the opposite chair who had remained seated since we came into the room. She acknowledged this introduction with a polite but distant smile.

Elsie gave an impression of cool elegance as she sat with her ankles neatly crossed beneath her long grey skirt. Her brown hair was caught up in a smooth chignon and her face was devoid of makeup, apart from a light dusting of powder over her nose and cheeks. Everything about her was understated, yet it was obvious to me that her clothes were well-cut and expensive.

Elsie looked up at Jim. "And how is life at Laverton House these days? We hear so many stories about what goes on there that it is hard to know what to believe."

"What kind of stories?" asked Jim. "You will be making Rhoda nervous. She only arrived yesterday to join the nursing staff."

"Oh, did you?" Elsie looked at me curiously. "What made you take up nursing in a mental home, of all places?"

"Well, it is rather a long story. I was in general nursing, but I had to give it up after a serious illness."

All three stared at me, but I was conscious mainly of Harold, as he leaned forward gazing at me intently.

"So mental nursing is a kind of second best?" he said thoughtfully.

"I suppose so." I was surprised at his perceptiveness.

I was about to ask him a question about his occupation when Mr. Forster appeared at the door and announced, "Lunch is ready. Please come through to the dining room."

As we went in Mrs. Forster was just placing a steaming bowl of potatoes on the table and when she straightened up I was struck by her similarity to her husband. They were both small and round and apple-cheeked, rather like a couple from a pack of Happy Families.

"Do sit down, ladies," said Mr. Forster. "You here, Miss Pritchard, next to Jim, and Elsie, my dear, you next to Harold."

Then he and Mrs. Forster sat down at opposite ends of the table. After Mr. Forster had said a brief grace, he began carving the huge joint of beef which oozed with meat juices and made my mouth water. Very little was said during that delicious meal and it was only after there was nothing left of the apple pie that conversation began.

"What brought you to Salisbury, my dear?" Mr. Forster asked me. "I think you said you came from near Bath. Would have thought there were plenty of private mental homes there."

"I suppose there are, but the doctor in Birmingham recommended I take a position in the south of England where the climate was more like New Zealand, so when I saw in the Nursing Times that Laverton House was advertising for staff, I thought I would apply."

"And you only arrived yesterday?"

"Yes."

"It is certainly amazing that you and Harold both come from New Zealand, although you have been here some years haven't you Harold?'

"Yes, I was sent to school here when I was eleven, with my brother Peter. My parents stayed on in Malaya where they are missionaries. Peter and I were born in New Zealand and my happiest memories are of staying in my father's house in Nelson. I haven't been back there since, but one day I hope to return."

He seemed to be speaking directly to me and I had a sudden vision of him as a small boy, cut off from his parents and living far from home in a boarding school. It was so much like my own childhood that I felt a tremor of sympathy for him yet from his appearance, there was nothing to suggest that he came from a deprived background. From his neatly clipped moustache to his smart sports jacket he looked every bit the young man about town. *Rather different from Jim*, I thought, who looked positively scruffy next to Harold, with his untidy hair and frayed shirt cuffs. Yet at the same time, there was nothing soft or unmanly about Harold.

I was so busy comparing the two I did not realise Mr. Forster was directing a question at me.

"How much do you know about our famous city of Salisbury, Rhoda?"

"Oh, very little, apart from the fact that it is very old indeed. It must be if it has a cathedral, I suppose."

"You are quite right. The cathedral is about a thousand years old, but Harold could tell you the exact date I'm sure. He is our historian and can always be relied on to supply any facts we are unsure of."

"I don't know about that." Harold smiled. "I have only scratched the surface. There is so much to discover about Salisbury. For instance, the present cathedral was started in 1220 and not fully completed until the 1330s. That is when the spire was added. Before that the Normans built a cathedral at Old Sarum, just outside the city, on a hill. There is not much left of it today as most of the stones were carried down to the water meadow to build the new cathedral. Still, it is worth having a look just to see the outline of the original cathedral."

"What I find amazing is that they took so long to build it. From 1220 to 1330 is over a hundred years," I said.

"Well, you see they were building for the third millennium. They expected Christ to return after one thousand AD, but when that didn't happen they built a cathedral that would last at least another thousand years."

"I didn't know that, Harold," broke in Elsie. "You certainly are knowledgeable." The note of admiration in her voice was unmistakable, but Harold seemed unaware of it and continued to direct his remarks to me, as I leaned forward, listening intently.

"I don't think time mattered much to those early cathedral builders," he continued. "What was important to them was to construct a building that would be to the glory of God, however long it took. For instance, a stone mason might spend his entire life working on the cathedral. If you look around the Chapter House you can see where the individual masons obviously copied the faces of people they knew and made caricatures of them. Anyway, you mustn't let me run on. I am a positive bore on the subject of the cathedral."

"Not at all," I murmured. "It's fascinating and I would love to explore it."

"Well, just say the word and I will be more than happy to take you on a historical tour of Salisbury."

"And you couldn't have a better guide than Harold," drawled Elsie. Something in her tone made me look at her quickly. *Was this something she had shared with Harold and now he was offering to show it to a newcomer? Oh, dear, this could be difficult. The last thing I wanted was to encroach on somebody else's territory.*

"Oh, I wouldn't want to take up your precious time, Harold," I said quickly. "You must have been around all these places hundreds of times."

"No, really, it would be a pleasure." Harold spoke sincerely and seemed quite unaware of a stiffening in Elsie's manner, but I saw it and it made me uneasy. *What was the connection beween her and Harold?*

I was relieved when Mr. Forster turned to Jim and asked him how his motorbike was performing. From being silent all the time Harold had been speaking, Jim was now full of animation as he held forth on the subject dearest to his heart. I watched the faces around the table and noticed the faraway look in Harold's eyes. He clearly had no interest in motorbikes, nor had Elsie, for though she gazed politely at Jim, it was obvious that her thoughts were elsewhere.

At last Mrs. Forster began clearing away the plates. Elsie and I jumped up to help her.

"No, you go into the sitting room and I will bring you in a cup of tea."

"Then I really think we should be getting along," I said, glancing at my watch. "It's three o'clock already."

Half an hour later Jim and I were once more back on the road heading for Laverstock. As I dismounted from the bike I began thanking him, but he cut me short.

"Look, Rhoda, it's early yet, why don't we take a turn in the gardens? I can show you around."

Looking at his eager face I did not like to say that I was already familiar with the grounds.

"That sounds a good idea. It does seem a shame to go indoors when the sun is shining," I said.

At the end of our walk we stood on the rise gazing at the delicate spire of the cathedral outlined against a pale blue sky.

Suddenly it seemed to me like a finger pointing upwards to God.

"It is so beautiful, I can hardly believe it was built such a long time ago. After listening to Harold I feel I know so much more about it now."

"Oh, old Blakey! All he's interested in is history and such-like. Gosh, he even rides around on a rusty old bicycle. I don't think he'd know one motorbike from another."

I looked at Jim in surprise. He sounded so contemptuous.

"I suppose he is a bit unusual."

"Downright odd. He spends most of his time studying birds, going around with a pair of field glasses and a sketchbook."

"So he's an artist then?"

"I don't know about that. I've never seen anything he's painted."

"I should love to see some of his work."

"Oh, he keeps it hidden away in an old hut he calls his studio, at the back of Elsie's place."

I was intrigued.

"Well, he must at least have shown his paintings to her."

"Possibly. It's a funny thing about those two. She's keen as mustard on him and he doesn't even seem to notice."

"What does she do for a living?"

"Oh, she doesn't work. No need. Her family has money and her mother is a bit of an invalid and Elsie stays home to look after her."

So that explained her sophisticated dress sense and expensive clothes. Jim was obviously bored with this talk of Harold and Elsie.

"Look, Rhoda, what about coming skating next Saturday night? A group of us is off to Bournemouth on our motorbikes. Now that you've sampled mine you know you'll be safe." He gave me a lopsided grin and I found myself agreeing to go with him, but as we walked back to the house I was thinking of Harold cycling on his own along a quiet lane, and I had a twinge of sadness that he would not be one of the crowd roaring down to Bournemouth next Saturday night.

CHAPTER FIVE

On Monday morning I woke early, a good twenty minutes before my alarm was due to go off, so I lay and reviewed the events of yesterday. Foremost, was the meeting with Harold. At the thought of him my heart began to thump. The only other man who had affected me like this was Bob and it was more than six months since I had broken off our engagement. I felt a pang as I pictured his laughing blue eyes and teasing smile. Bob would have fitted in well with the motorbike crowd. How often I had been on the back of his bike as he roared down country lanes then stopped outside some quaint old pub in the middle of nowhere. Bob was certainly fun to be with and I sighed, lying there in the darkness. It had been hard breaking off with him, but I knew I could never marry a man who was an agnostic. It would be a betrayal of all that I believed. All the same, it had been a tough decision to make and I was glad that I was right away from him or I might have weakened.

My mind switched back to Harold. Instinctively, I knew that any beliefs he held would be the same as mine. As the son of missionaries he would have absorbed his Christian faith from early childhood, as I had. How similar our backgrounds were, and it was amazing that we should meet in Salisbury, of all places. Perhaps it was meant to be.

Even as I toyed with this idea, a picture of Elsie flashed before me. Beneath that cool exterior, I sensed there was a determined woman and it was plain that she regarded Harold as her property.

The alarm rang suddenly and I was jerked back to the present. This was my first day on the wards as a mental nurse and I must be alert and single-minded. As I buttoned on my uniform I thought of the coming interview after breakfast with Matron and Dr. Branson .

Tiptoeing from the room I looked back at Joan's bed where all I could see was a huddle of bedclothes. Probably she was like Iris, one of those girls who didn't bother about breakfast. Well, that was her affair, but I knew it would never do for me; I must have something substantial to start the day with, or I would flag halfway through the morning.

I was surprised to find the dining room nearly empty, so I helped myself to bacon and eggs from the sideboard and sat down at a table on my own. When I had finished I still had another forty minutes before my interview, so I pushed open the French doors and walked into the garden.

It was one of those still autumn mornings with a slight mist hovering above the trees. I wandered across the lawn to the rise to get a view of the cathedral spire. This morning it appeared more ethereal than ever, hovering above the mist, and the words "a faery land forlorn" sprang to my mind. It was true, there was something magical about Salisbury. It conjured up pictures of knights and ladies and castles, all the colour of medieval England. Looking across at the spire, my imagination was stirred. With an effort, I recalled myself to the present and hurried across to the house.

On entering the foyer I saw the morning bustle had started. A couple of maids walked past, their arms full of linen and groups of people were leaving the dining room. Amongst them was Maisie.

"Hello, Rhoda, I was looking out for you at breakfast, but you were nowhere to be seen. I wanted to hear all about your adventures yesterday."

"I'll see you at lunch perhaps. I have to report to Matron's office in five minutes."

"Good luck. She's quite a dear really." Maisie gave me a quick smile and was gone.

It was now nine o'clock. I tapped at Matron's door and she called out briskly to come in. The small room seemed crowded as I entered, but there were only three people present: Matron, Dr. Branson and Dr. Hall.

"Sit down, Nurse," said Matron kindly, indicating a chair in front of her desk. "You look surprised at seeing us all here, but Dr. Branson and Dr. Hall have a particular reason for being present at this interview. Your case is rather different from most of our trainee nurses, as you appreciate, since you have already passed your first State Prelim. examination. You also have experience in a general hospital. What you need to realise is that mental nursing requires different skills from general nursing, although the same devotion to duty applies to both. I will ask Dr. Branson to explain in more detail the way we view the patients under our care, here at Laverton House."

She turned her head to indicate the man at her side. I looked across at him. He had a smooth bland face but the eyes behind the thick-lensed glasses were shrewd, as well as kindly.

He studied me for a moment without speaking.

"I do not know what you have heard about mental hospitals, Nurse Pritchard, but they are not the madhouses of popular fiction. When we have patients with severe mental disorders they are controlled by medication, not straitjackets, which is why we have to be very careful about the way we administer drugs. Your general training should be useful here.

Most of our patients are not severe cases. Some suffer from depression or mild neuroses which makes it difficult for them to cope in the outside world. We provide a kind of sanctuary for them, where they are not required to make many decisions and so are freed from the stresses of everyday life. This freedom from responsibility allows them space to recover a certain amount of equilibrium.

You have probably heard the term 'Nervous breakdown.' This occurs when someone is placed under more stress than they can cope with, at any one time. Some hospitals treat this by administering electric shock treatment. Now here at Laverton House we do not believe in this. As far as I am personally concerned, electric shock treatment is like flogging a tired horse. A person under severe stress simply needs time to recover and should be given recreation, good food and exercise, but above all, freedom from responsibility."

He stopped and gazed searchingly at me.

"Have you any questions at this point, Nurse?"

"No, Sir."

"Good, then I will leave the field open now for Dr. Hall."

He sat back in his chair and pressed his fingers together. I looked across at Dr. Hall whose sharp eyes were fixed on mine. I felt uncomfortable under that piercing gaze but nerved myself not to look away.

"Well, Nurse, I have very little to add to what Dr. Branson has said. I, myself, am a doctor of medicine not psychiatry, so I deal with the physical ailments of our patients. I also attend the staff, so if you feel unwell at any time you can call on me, after first reporting to Matron, of course."

He paused and looked down at a pile of papers on the desk in front of him.

"I am also the business manager of this home and it is in that capacity I am here this morning. You are here as a probationer and after six months, if we are satisfied with you, we will sign you up to a permanent nursing contract. In the meantime, I will need you to sign these papers agreeing to our terms." He pushed a document across the table to me.

"Now, please take a few minutes to read these through before you sign."

At first the words made no sense but as I focussed on the document I saw it was as he had described. Dr. Hall handed me a pen. Quickly I signed and gave the paper back to him, sensing his impatience to be gone. Abruptly, he stood up and with a curt nod to me and to the other two he left the room. After he had gone there was a palpable release of tension. Dr. Branson lit himself a cigarette and offered one to Matron, then to me.

"Now this afternoon, Matron, would you bring Nurse Pritchard to my office and I will run through the course of study she will be following. In the meantime, I expect you have other plans for her."

"Yes, I have. I would like Nurse to become familiar with our usual routines, so I have arranged for her to be attached to one of our senior nurses and to accompany her on her rounds this morning."

"In that case I will leave you. Goodbye, Nurse Pritchard, I will see you this afternoon."

With that he stood up slowly and stretched. I could not help comparing his calm demeanour with Dr. Hall who was like a coiled spring.

When he had gone Matron gazed at me thoughtfully for a moment or two.

"I think we could both do with a cup of tea after all that," she said smiling and reached for the bell pull. Almost immediately Millie appeared.

"Bring us tea and biscuits, there's a good girl, and make sure you warm the teapot." She then looked across to me. "Now while we are waiting I will explain some practical matters to you, Nurse."

She went through a long list of items while I listened carefully and this continued as we sipped our tea, so that my head began to whirl. At last she stopped and lit a cigarette.

"When you have finished your tea I will take you to meet Nurse Rimmington whom you will accompany on her rounds this morning—or rather what's left of it," she added, glancing at her watch. She stood up and automatically I stood too and followed her sturdy form out of the room.

Nurse Rimmington turned out to be a tall young woman with glasses and a firm and efficient manner. I felt at home with her immediately. I knew the type from my days in general nursing. She did not waste words but kept her instructions to a minimum.

"The maids do the general cleaning here, but we are expected to see that the patients are properly washed and dressed and given help if they need it. At this time of the morning some have pills to take and I will be overseeing that," and she opened a door.

I recognised the female patient who had been in the dining room when I had lunch on my first day. The woman was painfully thin and stood in front of her dressing table mirror clad only in her petticoat. She was gazing mournfully at her reflection.

"I'm so fat," she wailed, turning sideways and touching her hip. I stared at her in amazement.

"I can't wear any of my clothes, I look so dreadfully fat."

"Now, now, Tuffy," said Nurse Rimmington soothingly. "I'll find something you will be able to get into today," and going to the wardrobe she took out a blue woollen dress.

"I think you will find this comfortable."

I watched, tempted to giggle, but I saw that Nurse Rimmington maintained a perfectly straight face as she helped the tiny woman into a dress which was at least one size too big for her.

Nurse Rimmington then handed her a pill with a glass of water and she took it docilely.

A few minutes later as we left the room Nurse Rimmington remarked, "Tuffy has had an obsession about her weight for years and it doesn't matter what anybody says to her, nothing will convince her that she is not fat. The best thing is to go along with her."

I nodded and followed my mentor into the next room. If this was mental nursing then I certainly had a lot to learn.

CHAPTER SIX

The next day I was having breakfast when Jim came to my table. "I'm awfully sorry, Rhoda, but something has come up and I won't be able to take you skating on Saturday after all—and I was looking forward to it," he added regretfully.

"I hope it's nothing serious."

"I don't know. My mother has been unwell for some time and Dad telephoned to say I should go home this weekend." Jim was frowning.

"It sounds as if your family needs you. I will pray for your mother, Jim."

"Will you really, Rhoda?" He looked at me gratefully. "Do you know, prayer is the furthest thing from my mind and yet I suppose if we really believe everything we hear on Sundays it should be the first thing we turn to."

"It's just when I was seriously ill a few months ago I found that all I could do was pray, and I did recover, so I know prayer works," I said.

"You'll have to tell me all about it. I'm interested, but now I have to rush."

I looked after him thoughtfully. I was not really sorry to miss the skating on Saturday night, because it would bring back too many memories of Bob, and I wanted to forget him.

That afternoon when I came off duty Joan came into the room and flung herself onto the bed.

"You look tired," I commented, noting the dark circles under her eyes.

"Oh, no more than usual," she said shrugging. "I was talking to Maisie a few minutes ago. She wants us to go and join her for a drink at the Duck and Swan this evening."

"Good idea, it looks a quaint old pub."

At 7 o'clock we joined Maisie in the foyer and walked down the road to the inn. We each ordered a cider and sat in a quiet alcove. I looked at the faces of my companions, Maisie's open and untroubled, Joan's shadowed. Maisie chattered happily but Joan said little.

"Tell us about some of the interesting patients at Laverton, Maisie. From what I gather there are a few," I said.

Maisie leaned forward and lowered her voice. "Some of them are quite notable. For instance, Daphne, the quiet lady who sits in the corner of the dining room and is always on her own. She is the wife of Mr. Riley, the inventor of the Riley car. He comes down each weekend to take her out for a drive. Look out for him next Saturday. He has a brand new Riley, naturally."

"Yes and Hor., I mean Dr. Hall," Joan covered her slip quickly, "has just bought the latest Riley."

"That must have cost him a bit," I commented.

"Almost as much as a Rolls," said Joan.

"At the prices he charges his patients he can well afford it," laughed Maisie. "It would be nice if a bit more came our way. Anyhow, it's about time we toddled back. It'll soon be closing time."

As we left the tavern I noticed several male glances cast in our direction.

Back at the house Joan and I said goodnight to Maisie at the foot of the stairs before going back to our room. While we were preparing for bed Joan looked up while brushing her hair and said, "Rhoda, I'm going home next weekend and I wondered whether you would like to come with me."

"But surely your parents would prefer to have you all to themselves."

"No, I'm sure Mum and Dad would love to meet you. Actually, it would make it easier, Rhoda. I often don't know what to talk to them about and they would be interested in you, especially as you come from New Zealand. Do say yes," and she looked at me pleadingly.

I had a quick pang of regret. That would mean no Sunday morning service and no glimpse of Harold, but I didn't like to refuse Joan as it seemed important to her.

Sometime later, after I had switched off my bedside light, I lay thinking about Joan. What secret was she carrying that made her appear troubled and why did she find it difficult to communicate with her parents? As I drifted off to sleep I seemed to see Dr. Hall standing beside a smart new Riley motor car beckoning to Joan to climb into the passenger seat, while an elderly couple were clutching at her arm trying to pull her back.

The week passed swiftly and on Friday evening Joan and I took a bus to the central station in Salisbury from where we would transfer to the Bournemouth bus.

I found it exciting, to be free for the weekend and going somewhere new. As we approached the city, I gazed around, intrigued by the quaint shop fronts with their bow windows and leaded panes. It was like entering a medieval world, except that the people strolling along the streets were in modern dress.

"It's all so interesting!" I exclaimed. "I love Salisbury."

"Do you? It all looks perfectly ordinary to me," said Joan languidly.

"That's because you're used to it, but I still can't get over how old everything is."

Joan didn't reply but settled back in her seat and closed her eyes. I glanced at her. She still looked pale and there were dark shadows under her eyes. Suddenly her eyelids flickered as though she were aware that I had been scrutinising her.

"You don't look awfully well, Joan. Are you sure you are all right?"

"Oh perfectly, but Mum will be quizzing me, I know. It becomes quite tiresome answering her questions."

I couldn't help a twinge of envy. *What must it be like to have a mother to worry about you*? There was no-one really to care that much for me, not since Mum had died when I was eleven. Joan was really very lucky but she did not seem to realise it.

For the remainder of the journey we were wrapped up in our own thoughts and spoke very little. It was dark when the bus slowed down, outside a well-lit public house.

"Oh, there's Dad!" exclaimed Joan, pointing to a man standing under the inn sign. It was too dark to see his features, but he appeared short and stocky and was leaning on a stick.

As soon as the bus stopped we hurried to the door. Joan was the first to leap down on to the pavement. She ran to her father and flung her arms around his neck.

"Dad, it's so good to see you. Oh, and this is Rhoda," she added, waving me forward.

"Glad to meet you, my dear. Any friend of Joanie's is a friend of mine," and he looked fondly at his daughter.

Joan tucked her arm under his.

"It's a bit of a step to our house, but you're a good walker, Rhoda," and she put her free arm into mine.

Mr. Russell had a torch which was just as well because there were no street lights in the narrow winding road we were now on. Joan chattered gaily as we walked and I was amazed at the transformation in her. She was quite different from the quiet preoccupied girl of the last few days.

We crossed a hump-backed bridge where water rushed noisily beneath us, as it poured through the arches of a mill. Then we were climbing a hill, past large houses on one side and sloping fields on the other. At last, we stopped outside a wooden gate and Joan announced, "Home at last. Welcome to Hilltop, Rhoda."

Mr. Russell lifted the latch and stood back to let us through. Joan rushed eagerly forward and I followed. Even in the darkness I could sense that the garden was lovingly tended and full of flowers.

A light over the porch gave a friendly welcome and even before we had reached it, the door was opened and a white-haired lady stood framed against the light. Joan threw herself into her mother's arms and watching them together, a lump came into my throat.

"Come on in, girls," said Mrs. Russell. She spoke with a warm country burr.

"You must be frozen, walking all that way from the bus stop. I've lit a fire in the sitting room."

She turned to me. "So you are Joan's friend," and she took my hands in hers. "My, you are cold, my dear. Come on through to the fire and warm up," and she led me into a large comfortable room where a fire was blazing. On either side of the hearth were two baskets. In one a cat was curled up fast asleep, but a little black spaniel leaped out of the other and, barking excitedly, jumped up at Joan.

"Jack is so pleased to see you. I think he knew you were coming because he's been scratching at the door to go out all afternoon," said Mrs. Russell.

By now Joan had lifted the little dog and he was trying to lick her face while she held him away from her laughing.

I stroked the silky hair on his back and he turned his head from Joan to lick my face.

Just at that moment Mr. Russell entered the room. "Well, Jack has made a friend of you, Rhoda," he said smilingly. "Now, boy, give the girls a chance to take their coats off," and he lifted the dog out of Joan's arms while Mrs. Russell helped us off with our coats.

"Now I'll make you a cup of tea and you can toast crumpets over the fire. I've put a plate of them on the table. They're Joan's favourites," she added.

Mr. Russell drew up some chairs to the fire and told us to sit down and make ourselves comfortable. Then he took a long toasting fork and skewered a crumpet on it, bending down to the blaze.

"Here, Dad, let me do that!" exclaimed Joan taking the fork from him.

He sat back in his chair with a sigh of relief. "I'm not as young as I was and I must confess, after that walk I'm glad to sit down."

A few minutes later Mrs. Russell came in with a tray of tea things and busily began pouring tea and buttering crumpets. As I sat in the circle by the fire I gazed around at the rosy faces in the firelight. Once again I envied Joan her loving parents.

"How is your leg, Dad?" asked Joan, looking up at him. "The last time I was home you seemed to be in a bit of pain."

"Oh, I get the odd twinge of rheumatism now and again. It's worse in the damp weather, but there, at least I've got a leg, not like some of those poor devils I was in the trenches with."

"Were you in the Great War, Mr. Russell?" I asked.

"Yes, on the Somme. I was one of the lucky ones. Hundreds of poor blighters lost their lives. I had a bullet in my thigh so I was invalided out quite early on. Men beside me lost their legs or worse, so I've a lot to be thankful for. Some of the poor devils never got over it. Their nerves were shot to pieces and they ended up in mental institutions for the rest of their lives," said Mr. Russell quietly.

"I was reading in the paper the other day that Germany is getting strong again, now that Hitler and his Brown Shirts have got into government. It said there could be another war one day." I watched Mr. Russell as I spoke.

He shook his head vigorously. "Never! It will never happen again. Stands to reason there couldn't be another war. Not after what happened last time. It would be sheer madness. No, don't you take any notice of warmongers, my dear. Your generation won't have to go through what we did."

I was reassured and sitting in the warm glow of the fire that evening I felt very safe and secure.

It was the same when I was lying tucked up in bed in the cosy little spare room with its sloping roof and tiny windows. The floral curtains were tightly closed as though to keep out the dangers of the outside world. There was so much warmth and love in this house I felt nothing harmful could ever enter it.

The next day being Saturday, Joan and I were left to sleep in and it was late in the morning when we went downstairs. Mrs. Russell was bustling round preparing dinner.

"I'll make you a cup of tea and there is some breakfast laid up for you in the dining room. Then why don't you go for a walk through the forest and take Jack with you?" she suggested, as the little dog jumped up at Joan. "Dinner won't be ready until one o'clock and it would do you good, Joan, to have a walk and get back the roses in your cheeks. You are looking far too peaky."

Joan gave me a sideways glance and quickly said, "That sounds a good idea, Mum."

Half an hour later we set out from the house with Jack straining at his lead. As we walked across the green half a dozen geese waddled towards us stretching out their necks and hissing at Jack. Joan let him off his lead and he ran barking at them so that they scattered in all directions, squawking indignantly.

We stood and laughed until at last Jack came back to us, panting from his exertions.

"You are getting too fat for chasing geese," said Joan bending down and stroking the little dog while he looked up at her adoringly.

"I do miss Jack at Laverton House. Dr. Hall can't bear dogs," she said inconsequentially.

I glanced at her. At the mention of his name it seemed a shadow came across us.

"You are so lucky to have a home like yours, Joan, with such loving parents. I wish …" and I left the sentence unfinished.

"I suppose I am," said Joan. "Especially as they are my adoptive parents."

I stared at her.

"That surprises you doesn't it? It did me, when I found out a couple of years ago. It was when I was filling out my nursing application and had to produce my birth certificate. Then I saw that my name was not Russell. I couldn't believe it at first and I was angry with Mum and Dad for keeping it from me."

"I suppose they thought it would upset you to know."

"Possibly, but it was far worse when I found out at seventeen. Naturally, I wanted to know all about my mother but they weren't able to tell me much, only that she had wealthy parents and when they knew she was pregnant they made arrangements for me to be adopted."

"So what did you do then?"

"Well, what would you do? Of course, I moved heaven and earth to try and find her."

"And did you?"

"Yes, and I discovered that she was married and had three sons. She had married a solicitor and they were very well off." The bitter note in her voice was unmistakable.

"Did you try to get in touch with her?"

"No, she had given me away and now she had a family of her own. I wanted nothing to do with her."

I was silent. Joan was obviously deeply hurt by this mother who had given her up.

"I suppose if you look at it from her point of view …" I said at last.

"I'm not interested in her point of view. All I know is that she didn't want me." By now we had stopped walking and Joan turned to me with tears in her eyes. "If you only knew, Rhoda, what it feels like to learn you are adopted when you have thought all your life you were the child of your parents. You think you are someone and then you find you are someone else."

"But there is another way of looking at it," I said trying to comfort her. "The people who adopted you really wanted you. And really, Joan, you couldn't have more loving parents than yours. In fact, ever since I met them I have been envying you. I lost my mother when I was eleven and the aunt who brought us up after that, never really had time for me."

It was Joan's turn to stare.

"I had no idea. You seem so well-balanced, Rhoda. I can't imagine you having a difficult childhood."

I shrugged. "Well, you just have to get on and make the best of things, don't you? Anyway, let's turn back. It will soon be dinner time and your mother did say one, didn't she?"

Joan whistled to Jack and the three of us returned the way we had come. A light shower made us break into a run so that by the time we reached Hilltop we were flushed and panting when we burst into the house.

Mrs. Russell smiled when she saw us.

"Well, I must say you both look better for being out in the fresh air. Now go and get ready for dinner. It will be on the table in five minutes."

During the meal I could not help thinking of what Joan had told me and found myself observing her and her parents closely. It was obvious that Mr. and Mrs. Russell adored their adopted daughter. It might have been very different if she had remained with her natural mother.

CHAPTER SEVEN

Sunday passed all too quickly. We walked to the little village church with Mr. Russell while Mrs. Russell stayed home to prepare a hearty Sunday lunch for us all. At three o'clock Joan and I were ready to leave, so that we would have plenty of time to catch our bus. Mr. Russell was going to accompany us to the bus stop. As Mrs. Russell stood at the door to see us off she put her arms around me and hugged me as if I were her own daughter.

"Come back and see us soon, Rhoda dear. Look upon this as your home now, since your father is so far away in New Zealand."

Then she turned to Joan with tears in her eyes. "Take care of yourself, Joanie. You are looking far too pale and thin. I worry about you in that place. Please come home and see us more often."

Joan's lips were trembling and she looked away, unable to meet her mother's eyes. Then she moved forward in a rush and threw her arms around her.

"I promise, Mum, I will come home more often," she said, her voice muffled against her mother's shoulder.

Mrs. Russell patted her back as though she were a small child. "Time to go," she said at last, "or you will be missing that bus."

Jack was sitting quietly beside us, his tail and ears drooping.

"Goodbye, old boy, I won't be long," and Joan bent down fondling his ears. Then she picked up her bag, brushed at her eyes and took the arm that her father offered her, while I stood by watching.

As we set off down the path both of us looked back for a last glimpse of Mrs. Russell who stood waving on the doorstep.

When we reached the bus stop the bus drew up almost immediately.

"Bye, girls, come home soon," were Mr. Russell's parting words and I felt warmed that he had included me.

The bus was nearly full but we managed to find a seat near the back. Once we were seated Joan turned to me. "Well, you certainly made a hit with Mum and Dad, Rhoda," and she gave a little laugh. "I think they have adopted you too."

"I do hope so. Oddly enough, I feel more at home at your place than I do at Aunty's. She's a good housekeeper and does her best for us, but the house never feels homely."

For the remainder of the journey neither of us had much to say and I noticed that the closer we got to Salisbury the more Joan seemed to withdraw into herself. It was the same when we changed to the Laverstock bus. Silence hung heavily between us until at last I said, "Joan, are you feeling alright, you've hardly said a word since we left Woodgreen?"

"There's a lot on my mind, Rhoda. Please take no notice. It's leaving home and coming back to this place. I do hate it!" she said passionately. "It's not really the place or the job, it's the people; well one person in particular."

I thought it best not to question her, so I kept quiet.

"When we are back in our room I'll tell you the whole story. I simply have to tell someone or I'll go mad."

I reached across and patted her hand. It felt icy and I felt a surge of pity for her.

Fortunately there was nobody in the foyer when we entered the house and there was a Sunday stillness over everything. Once we were in our room Joan dropped her bag inside the door and flung herself on the bed, shading her face with her hand. Late afternoon sun was streaming into the room and it felt warm and peaceful. I opened my bag and began unpacking.

"Oh leave all that for now, Rhoda, please. I need to talk to you. Draw up a chair and come and sit beside me." Joan's voice was tremulous.

I did as she asked and waited for her to speak.

"I suppose you've guessed by now, Rhoda," Joan said, pulling herself to a sitting position. "The person who is making life intolerable for me here is Dr. Hall. Oh, it was alright at the beginning, he was very kind to me and so was his wife. I thought he was only taking a fatherly interest in me, but after a while I discovered it was more than that. One day when Mrs. Hall was out shopping and I was in the house alone with him, things got out of hand. He began kissing me and well, you can guess what happened then. I was determined it wouldn't happen again but he had a kind of hold over me and I couldn't resist him. He is very persuasive and of course he is experienced with women."

As she talked I tried to imagine being in thrall to a man like Dr. Hall, but my imagination failed. I gazed at Joan with mounting indignation. *What right had a man in his position to take advantage of a vulnerable girl!*

Joan glanced at me. "You're shocked. I can see you are."

"No, I'm angry at Dr. Hall."

"You can't blame him alone. After the first time I should have made sure it didn't happen again."

"But it is all over now, isn't it?"

Joan looked down. "I'm afraid not," she faltered.

"But surely you can tell him you don't want to continue," I said.

"Oh, it's not as simple as that. You don't know him."

"Well, if it were me, I'd tell him straight I wanted nothing to do with him."

"That is what most people would say, but you don't know the hold he has over me."

"I'm beginning to realise, but, Joan, for your own sake you have to keep away from him." I thought for a moment. "You could start by going home more often, and you could spend time with people your own age; join in with the activities that the nurses are always planning."

"I suppose so," and she looked down at her hands, twisting her handkerchief in them.

I felt a spurt of impatience. Here was a girl in the hands of an unscrupulous man and yet she seemed reluctant to give him up, but in Joan's position would I really be any different? I thought of Bob and the way I had needed to distance myself from him, otherwise I knew I would give in to him. Love was a strong emotion and its pull could be irresistible.

I could think of nothing more to say to Joan. I sent up a silent prayer for wisdom.

"Look, Joan, can I tell you about something that happened to me?"

"Yes, please do." She looked up eagerly.

"Well, I was in love with a young student called Bob. He was at Oxford and while he was there he began to mix with other students who were atheists. He started reading books they lent him and the long and the short of it was, he lost his Christian faith. I had just gone off to Birmingham to nurse and he sent me long letters trying to prove that the Bible was not true and had only been written by men. His arguments were so convincing I was beginning to believe them, until I fell desperately ill with pleurisy and pneumonia. It was touch and go whether I would pull through. When I was unconscious I had a vision of Jesus as the Good Shepherd. He reached out and took my hand and said He would lead me through this valley, meaning the Valley of the Shadow of Death, and at that moment the crisis came and I began to recover."

I paused, knowing I had Joan's complete attention.

"It was after that I knew I had to break off my engagement to Bob, because it was more important for me to follow Jesus than to get married to someone who didn't believe in Him, but it hasn't been easy. I still have strong feelings for Bob, but now I am right away from him it is easier to keep my faith strong. Whenever I feel like giving up, I turn to the twenty-third Psalm and it comforts me."

I saw there were tears in Joan's eyes.

"Do you think you could read it to me, Rhoda? I haven't got a Bible," she said quietly.

"Of course," and I went across to my dressing table and opened the top drawer. I took out my worn little Bible and it fell open at Psalm twenty-three. I read aloud the familiar words, but my voice broke when I came to the final verse.

There was stillness in the room.

"Please pray for me," whispered Joan, so I bent my head and prayed. I did not consciously form the words; they seemed to come from somewhere deep inside me. When I finished there was a look of peace on Joan's face I had never seen before.

CHAPTER EIGHT

I was relieved to hear on Monday morning that Dr. Hall had gone to a conference in Vienna with his wife and would be away for a couple of weeks. Joan seemed almost light-hearted at the news. Later in the day I had a chance to speak to Maisie.

"I think Joan needs taking out of herself. Next time we all have a day off together let's go to Salisbury market in the morning and then a matinee in the afternoon."

"I'm all for that," said Maisie enthusiastically.

I put the idea to Joan that evening and she looked at me shrewdly.

"You're trying to wean me off Dr. Hall, Rhoda."

"Well, while he's out of the country you could get used to spending a little time with us girls."

"I'm willing to try."

By the time Dr. Hall returned from Vienna, Joan was almost independent of him. I say almost, because once I caught her looking wistfully through the window at his Riley when it was parked in the drive.

One lunch hour, about a fortnight later, Jim came over to me in the dining room. I asked him how his mother was.

"She's made a remarkable recovery," he said thoughtfully, "because the doctor told me he had given up on her and for some unknown reason she suddenly got better. So prayer does work, Rhoda."

"I know it does."

"Anyway, now Mum's all right I can go out and enjoy myself. Next Saturday night a group of us are going to Bournemouth ice-skating. Would you care to come, Rhoda, that is, if you have nothing better to do—and if you don't mind riding on the back of my motorbike?"

"I'd love to. Would you mind if Joan came as well?" I asked tentatively.

Jim looked startled.

"Joan? She never does anything with us. We have asked her once or twice, but she is always 'otherwise engaged'. She never lets on, but we have seen her driving off in the Bentley or the Riley. It would be a first if she went out with us."

"Well, I'll put it to her and I think you'll be surprised."

That evening I told Joan of the arrangements for Saturday night and her face lit up.

"I'd love to go. I've always wanted to try ice-skating and it sounds fun to all be going on motorbikes."

Next morning as I was passing through the foyer I glanced at the notice board and saw that the duty roster for the coming week had been pinned up. My name was listed for Saturday evening, which meant I would not be able to go to Bournemouth after all.

Slowly I walked up the stairs thinking about next Saturday. Would Joan want to go on her own with a group of people she hardly knew?

When I pushed open the door she was sitting on her bed reading. She looked up with a smile.

"I've just seen the duty roster for next week and I'm down for the whole weekend, so I won't be able to go to Bournemouth on Saturday night, after all." I studied Joan anxiously.

Her face fell. "Oh, that's a shame. It won't be the same without you."

"But it needn't make any difference. You'll be able to go with Jim."

"I suppose so, but I'm sure he'd rather have you on the back of his bike."

"I expect he'll see it as a great honour if you are his pillion passenger. I think they all feel you are a cut above them."

"I suppose that's because of Dr. Hall."

"Yes, and this is one way of proving them wrong."

"All right, I see your point. I will go, I promise."

When I woke up on Saturday morning the sun was already high. It was luxury not to have to get up to an alarm ringing in my ear. I crossed to the window and drew back the curtains. Sun streamed into the room and I found myself humming as I began to prepare for the day. Even though I couldn't go skating that evening I was not going to let that spoil anything.

The hours passed quickly and I saw Joan only briefly on the stairs before she went out.

"Enjoy your evening and don't have too many falls on the ice."

"I don't intend to fall over at all," she retorted.

We laughed and as I watched her running up the stairs I felt glad that tonight at least, she would be with people her own age.

Saturday was always quiet for the duty nurses as many of the patients were taken out by friends or family. The afternoon was uneventful and I was glad to come off duty at ten o'clock. As I relaxed in a hot bath I thought of Joan and the others probably leaving Bournemouth now. I pictured her on the back of Jim's motorbike and smiled to myself. Riding pillion was rather different from sitting in the passenger seat of the Riley.

When I finally went to bed I fell into a deep sleep and did not wake until the sun was slanting across the room through the gaps in the curtains. Lazily I turned over, savouring the fact that this was Sunday and I was free all morning. I glanced across at Joan's bed, expecting to see the usual hump under the bedclothes. Then I sat up in surprise. The bed was fully made and had obviously not been slept in. *Where was Joan*? I felt a quiver of alarm and sprang out of bed. *I must go and find Jim. He would know where she was. Perhaps they had called in at her parents and Joan had decided to stay the night. Yes, that was the only logical explanation.*

As I went into the dining room I saw some nurses sitting around a table talking animatedly. They looked up as I came in and one called out, "Hey, Rhoda, have you heard the news?"

"What news?"

"About Joan. She had an accident last night in Bournemouth."

I felt a cold shiver go right through me.

"What happened?"

"Nobody knows, except that she's in hospital in Bournemouth."

"Thank you," I said automatically and left the room quickly. My heart was beating fast and for some seconds I stood irresolute, wondering what to do. I thought of Matron. She would have definite information about Joan.

When I entered her office, Matron was sitting at her desk busy with papers. She looked up enquiringly.

"Yes, Nurse Pritchard."

"I am concerned about Nurse Russell. She didn't come in last night and I heard talk in the dining room that she had met with an accident."

"I'm afraid that is true. As you probably know, she went ice skating last night in Bournemouth. Apparently she fell and broke her leg on the ice. It is quite a serious break and they are keeping her in hospital for a while. It will take time to mend and of course she won't be able to work for some weeks."

I felt strength draining from me.

Matron said, "I think you had better sit down, Nurse, you don't look well."

She came out from behind her desk and laid a hand on my shoulder.

"I'll ring Millie to bring you a cup of tea," and reaching behind her, she tugged sharply at the bellpull.

When the girl appeared she told her to be quick.

I was sitting slumped in a chair. "It's all my fault, Matron. I urged her to go skating and she had never been before. I should have been there with her."

"Nonsense, my dear, Nurse Russell is quite able to look after herself. What happened is an accident, pure and simple and you are not in any way responsible."

Millie came in with a tray and Matron proceeded to pour out the tea.

"Now drink this. I have put plenty of sugar in it because you've had a shock."

As I sipped the hot sweet tea I began to feel better.

"Now you go back quietly to your room and lie down for an hour and when you feel more yourself come back to my office and we'll discuss what can be done for Joan."

I felt grateful for Matron's solid common sense and shortly afterwards went back upstairs and lay on my bed. Although I couldn't sleep I began to feel calmer and by the time I went back to Matron's office I felt almost normal.

Matron immediately got down to practicalities.

"I have spoken with Dr. Branson and he will drive you to the hospital this afternoon, Nurse. Be waiting for him in the foyer at one thirty. I will leave it to you to collect up all the items you think Nurse Russell will need, and pack them in a suitcase."

She smiled. "Now go and get yourself something to eat because I'm sure you've had no breakfast."

I did as she suggested and though I was not hungry, I managed a slice of toast with my tea. Back in the bedroom I went methodically through Joan's drawers, taking out underclothes and nightwear and any other items she might need, all the time fighting back the feeling that I was invading her privacy.

I hesitated before opening the top drawer of the dressing table. Here were her most intimate possessions: makeup, toiletries and photographs. In a corner of the drawer was a book bound in red leather. I recognised it immediately as Joan's diary because she wrote in it each evening. What secrets did it contain? It should not be allowed to get into the wrong hands, so I wrapped it in brown paper, tied it with string and addressed it to Joan.

I packed everything into the small suitcase that she used for her visits home, including the current Daphne du Maurier novel that she had been reading, and her volume of Walter de la Mare's poems.

Promptly at one thirty I was in the foyer. Dr. Branson arrived five minutes later. After apologising briefly, he picked up the suitcase and suggested that we leave immediately. I walked with him to his car which was parked in the drive. It was an older model Riley and outwardly unpretentious, but inside it was lined with soft leather. As we set off down the drive I settled back into my seat enjoying the luxurious upholstery. After one or two pleasantries the doctor made no further attempt at conversation, yet the silence did not feel awkward. The soothing hum of the engine was making me feel pleasantly drowsy when suddenly Dr. Branson spoke. "I have been thinking about Nurse Russell's parents. They should be informed of her accident. I looked up her records and saw that their address is Woodgreen which is not far from here. Have you visited her home, Nurse Pritchard?"

"Yes, not very long ago."

"In that case, I think you would be the best one to break the news to them."

My heart began to pound. *How would these dear people feel when they heard their beloved Joan was in hospital*? I dreaded being the bearer of bad news.

All too soon we branched off from the main road at Woodgreen village and were driving slowly up the hill.

"There's the house," I said pointing. "It's called Hilltop."

The doctor stopped outside the gate and reached across me to open the door.

"I'm sure you will find the right words to say," he said, patting my arm reassuringly.

I sent up a silent prayer as I walked to the front door. I knocked and waited but there was no response. I knocked again but there was still no answer. It could be that they were working in the garden, but when I went to the back of the house everything was shut up. Then I remembered. Mr. and Mrs. Russell had gone to stay with friends in Cornwall. Joan had mentioned it a few days ago.

I returned to the car and told Dr. Branson.

"Oh well, at least we tried," was all he said, as he turned on the ignition. It did not seem long before we reached Bournemouth and were driving through suburban streets lined with pine trees. Between the branches I caught a glimpse of the sea shimmering in the distance. Even the light here seemed brighter somehow. The houses we passed had an air of solid permanence as though this were a resort for the comfortable middle class.

The hospital was in keeping with the buildings on either side and looked as though it had once been a large home which had been added to, with wings at either side. In the spacious grounds were several out buildings.

Dr. Branson parked in front of the house in the spaces reserved for staff, and when we entered the foyer he strode up to the reception desk and was greeted with a smile by the nurse on duty.

"We have come to visit Miss Joan Russell who was admitted last night with a broken leg," he said briefly.

The nurse glanced down at the register.

"Yes, she is in Ward G. I can get someone to take you there, Dr. Branson." I was surprised that she knew his name.

"No need, I know my way."

He beckoned to me and together we walked along the white walled corridor. There was the usual hospital smell and sniffing it, I felt a sudden nostalgia for the life I had known in a general hospital. I looked with envy at the nurses passing us in the corridor.

At last we came to Ward G. A senior nurse sitting at a desk looked up at us enquiringly.

"I'm Dr. Branson from Laverton House in Salisbury and this is Nurse Pritchard. We've come to visit Miss Russell."

"Certainly, Doctor, said the nurse deferentially. "I'll just see if she is awake," and she left us, returning a few minutes later.

"Miss Russell is ready to see you. Please go in," and she pushed open a door further down the corridor.

Dr. Branson strode into the room and because I was behind him I did not at first see Joan. When I caught sight of her I gasped. This white-faced girl could not be Joan. She looked so young and childlike, with the dark hair clinging damply to her head and her eyes large and shadowed.

She smiled weakly. "I'm so glad to see you, Rhoda. I've had a terrible time. I've never known such pain."

I reached across and took her hand in mine. Hers felt small and weak.

"I'm so sorry I wasn't with you, Joan. I should never have let you go on your own."

I had forgotten Dr. Branson was beside me and was surprised when he spoke.

"You mustn't blame yourself, Nurse Pritchard. Your being there wouldn't have made the slightest bit of difference." He glanced at his watch. "Now I will leave you two together, while I go and speak to the doctor in charge of Nurse Russell."

When he had gone I pulled up a chair to the bedside. "What happened exactly, Joan?"

"It's all a bit of a blur, but I think I had just let go of the bar and the next moment I collided with someone and went over. I suppose it was the way I fell, but I heard a crack and then felt a terrible pain in my leg. I think I fainted. When I came to, there were people standing all around me and an ambulance man lifted me on to a stretcher. Then I think I fainted again and the next thing I knew I was in the ambulance and they must have given me some pain relief because I felt no more pain. After that they brought me into casualty here and set my leg. I don't remember any of that because I was under anaesthetic. And now here I am as helpless as a baby," and she smiled wanly.

"Well, you are in the best place, at the moment anyway. When I saw Matron this morning she said it may be some time before you can return to work—so relax and enjoy being waited on."

"I could think of better places to have a holiday," said Joan, wryly.

"That reminds me, we called at your parents' place on the way here, but there was no-one home. I think you said they were going to Cornwall to stay with friends?"

"That's right. I'm glad they don't know about this, not yet anyway. I will write to them and explain everything."

"Perhaps they might even take you to Cornwall for a couple of weeks."

Joan's face lit up.

"What a good idea. I've been lying here dreading what will happen when Dr. Hall knows. He is bound to ask me to go and stay with him and his wife and that is the last thing I want."

She looked thoughtful for a moment.

"You know, Rhoda, until I had the fall I was really enjoying myself with Jim and the others. They were such fun and I enjoyed riding on the back of Jim's motorbike. He is really nice and I think he might like me a little. He even suggested we do this again."

A wistful look came into her eyes.

"I realise now what I've been missing, spending all my time with the Halls and their friends. They are sophisticated people and educated, but not really any fun. With Jim and the others there was something so …" she searched for the right word.

"Wholesome," I supplied.

"That's right, and they're also uncomplicated."

I leaned forward and patted her hand.

"I'm so glad you have discovered that, Joan."

"But I'm scared of Dr. Hall. He has a kind of magnetism that makes it impossible to resist him. Do you know, when he was in the navy they had a nickname for him, Mephistopheles."

"That means Satan." I paused, thinking. "Perhaps we are being a little melodramatic. He is after all only a human being."

"You don't know him like I do, and I can tell you he does have some sort of powerful hold over people."

I thought of those piercing dark eyes that seemed to see right through me and I shivered.

"Let's talk of something else, shall we? When I get back this afternoon I will tell Jim we visited you in hospital. I expect he will want to know all I can tell him about you."

I was watching Joan closely and at the mention of Jim's name an eager look came into her eyes. Just at that moment the door opened and in walked a man, whose authoritive manner immediately marked him out as a consultant. Dr. Branson was behind him.

"Well, how is the patient today?" said the surgeon heartily. "Looking much more cheerful I see. You have been through quite an ordeal, my dear, but we managed to do a neat job on your leg and you should be running around in a few months' time. In the meantime, the best thing you can do is rest and let that leg heal."

He gave Joan a kindly smile then turned to Dr. Branson, "I enjoyed our chat, Doug. Look forward to seeing you at the next dinner." Then he was gone.

Dr. Branson looked down at Joan thoughtfully.

"Well, you heard what Mr. Donaldson said. He was the surgeon who set your leg. It was quite a tricky procedure but he is pleased with the outcome. He says you will be here for another week, and then he recommends you return home and keep off that leg for at least six weeks. It will be a bit tedious for you, but I expect you will have a few visitors to keep you occupied," and his eyes twinkled. "Now I think we had better be on our way. Your suitcase is with the nurse at the desk outside and I'm sure if you require anything else Nurse Pritchard will get it for you."

"Of course," I said promptly, feeling a surge of pity for Joan. She looked so small and vulnerable lying there and I hated leaving her. I reached over and took her hand in mine. Joan clung to it for a moment.

"Don't forget what we were saying," I said.

"No, I won't."

"And I'll write most days and tell you the news."

"Oh, I shall look forward to that," she said eagerly.

At the door I turned and waved. My last glimpse of her was a small lonely figure lying in a narrow hospital bed.

As soon as we arrived back at Laverton House I sought out Jim and it was evident from the way he questioned me on everything to do with Joan that his interest was greater than merely that of a concerned friend.

"How did she look to you?" he asked anxiously.

I hesitated before answering. "A little pale which is not surprising after what she had been through in the past twenty-four hours."

"Do you think she is strong enough to have visitors, or should it be only family?"

"I think she would love to see you, Jim, and anyway her family are away on holiday at the moment and they don't know about her accident yet."

"In that case, I will go down tomorrow as soon as I am off duty."

I smiled to myself. *How delighted Joan would be to see Jim walk into the ward. It would be the best tonic she could have.*

I sat down that evening after my duties were over and wrote an amusing account of the day to Joan then posted the letter in the box in the lobby, knowing that it would arrive the following morning at the hospital.

By the middle of the week I had an enthusiastic reply from her, full of Jim's unexpected visit.

The rest of the week went quickly and once again Saturday came around. I was on a morning shift, but had nothing planned for the evening. After I came off duty I went to the dining room and sat down with a cup of tea. Jim strolled over to my table.

"Hello, Rhoda, mind if I join you?"

"Do, I was just thinking it is a whole week since Joan's accident."

"That's what I wanted to speak to you about. I'm planning to take a run this afternoon to visit her. Would you like to come?"

"Well, yes I would, otherwise it may be a long time before I get a chance to see her."

"Good, I'll meet you in the foyer at two thirty."

Half an hour later I was climbing onto the back of the motor-bike. Fleetingly, I thought of that other occasion some weeks ago when I had ridden pillion to the gospel hall. Longingly I thought of the simple service and the Forsters.

"Now, we'll bc off, hold on," and Jim kicked the motor into life.

It was an exhilarating ride and I gave myself up to the pleasure of speeding through the countryside with the wind in my hair. At last, we came to the outskirts of Bournemouth and Jim slowed down as we approached the hospital. For some reason I felt a twinge of nervousness as I dismounted from the motorbike.

Jim marched confidently up to the desk. After a brief word with the receptionist he returned to me.

"We can go right through to Joan's ward," he said.

Together we walked along the now familiar corridor. When we reached the ward the nurse on duty gave us a warm smile.

"We've come to visit Miss Russell," said Jim.

"She's got someone with her at the moment, but I'll go through and tell her you are here."

My heart was thudding. I had a sick premonition about that person.

The nurse returned.

"The other visitor is leaving in a few minutes and then Miss Russell would like to see you." She returned to her desk while we waited.

After some minutes the door opened and a man walked out. My heart did a somersault. It was Dr. Hall. He gave us a brief nod of acknowledgement, but his eyes were cold.

Eagerly Jim pushed open the door. "Jim, Rhoda!" Joan exclaimed. "How wonderful to see you! I never imagined you'd be coming today."

"Wild horses wouldn't keep us away, would they Rhoda?" said Jim smiling broadly down at her.

"Certainly not," I replied. "We saw Dr. Hall leaving just now. Did he cut his visit short because of us?"

Joan's expression changed. "No, he was about to go anyway. He said that I will be able to leave here in a week's time. He had it from the surgeon who did the operation. Apparently, I am making a quicker recovery than they expected. Dr. Hall tried to persuade me to convalesce at his home, but I told him my parents had arranged for me to go to Cornwall and stay with my aunt and uncle."

"Thank goodness for that!" I exclaimed, relief surging through me.

Jim looked puzzled. "I would have thought you'd be pleased to take up Dr. Hall's offer, Joan."

"I might have once, but all that is changed."

Jim grinned at her boyishly. "So that means you have time for us now."

"Yes, I realised that night in Bournemouth how much fun I was having with you all—until the accident of course," and she wrinkled her nose.

"Then as soon as you are up and about, you'll come out with us again? Perhaps you might even agree to go out with me and Rhoda, just the three of us," Jim said laughing.

He went across the room and fetched a couple of chairs to put by the bed and soon we were chatting away happily.

Half an hour later the nurse appeared at the door."Visiting time is over, I'm afraid," she said.

"Oh, so soon!" and Joan's face fell. "Now both of you, don't forget to write. I do enjoy your letters, Rhoda."

"I promise to write as well," said Jim promptly.

"And I will keep you both posted on everything that happens in Cornwall."

As I bent to kiss Joan goodbye I noticed that her eyes were bright with unshed tears.

"It's been lovely to see you both today," she murmured. "More than you could ever know."

I squeezed her hand then turned quickly and left the room, leaving Jim alone with her.

A short time later Jim and I were walking along the corridor saying nothing, both busy with our own thoughts.

Uppermost in my mind was the knowledge that Joan was going to be removed from Dr. Hall's orbit. It was also clear that she and Jim were interested in each other. It could be said that this was a fortunate accident.

CHAPTER NINE

The following weekend I was free on Sunday. I knew Jim was on duty because I had checked the roster, but I wasn't going to let that stand in my way. I was going to the gospel hall. Someone would surely lend me a bicycle. I went to ask Jim's advice.

"That's no trouble, Rhoda. Leave it to me."

Sure enough on Sunday morning he wheeled a bicycle around to the front of the house.

"It's not the smartest model you've ever seen," he said, pointing to the scratches on the mudguard, "but I think it will get you there. I've pumped up the tyres."

"Thank you, Jim; I'll take care of it. I'm glad it's got a basket," I added, placing my handbag in it.

A few minutes later I was cycling down the drive feeling gloriously free. It was so silent on the bicycle, quite different from the motorbike, except for the rush of wind in my ears when I sped downhill. Very soon I left Laverstock and was out on country roads with high hedges on each side that I could barely see over. It would be tempting to stop and hunt for mushrooms in some of the fields, but not this morning. At last I came to a row of houses on the outskirts of a village and remembered that the gospel hall was at the end of them.

It was very quiet. A few cars were parked outside the building but there was nobody about. Was I late? I glanced down at my watch—five to eleven. Perhaps the service started at a quarter to eleven. Feeling a little self-conscious, I tiptoed to the door and peeped round the corner. Heads were bowed so people were obviously praying. I could easily slip in to the back row without being observed.

Moments later I was in the same seat as the last time, except that now I was on my own. Curiously, I studied the backs of heads and yes, there was Harold a few rows in front, his head bent in prayer or meditation. I was filled with an overwhelming sense of happiness and closed my eyes, uttering a silent prayer of thanks that I was able to be here this morning.

Peace filled the little building and as I sat in that quiet atmosphere all my anxieties ebbed away. The closing prayer came all too soon.

Immediately, there was a hubbub as friends greeted each other, and I was about to slip out when Harold turned and smiled at me. He edged his way past the knots of people chatting in the aisle and at last was standing in front of me.

"Rhoda, this is fortuitous. I was hoping I'd have an opportunity to see you again and show you some of the sights of Salisbury. Are you doing anything for lunch?"

"Well, no."

"Good, then let me take you to a place I know, where we can talk. How did you get here, not on Jim's motorbike obviously?"

"I came by bicycle."

"Good, that makes two of us. Couldn't be better." Harold's eyes were alight with enthusiasm. I felt excitement bubble up inside me. Lunch alone with Harold! I would never have imagined it possible.

"Let's go then, shall we?" he said, heading towards the door.

Outside we mounted our cycles with Harold leading the way. He kept looking over his shoulder to check that I was keeping up with him. After about three miles he slowed down and pointed to the right where an ancient inn, shaded by a large chestnut, overlooked a wide courtyard where people sat drinking at tables.

We put our cycles on a stand at the side of the courtyard and Harold led the way to a vacant table. He pulled out a chair for me and seated himself opposite. The autumn sun was pleasantly warm on the back of my neck, and the only sounds were the murmur of voices from the other tables and the quacking of half a dozen ducks waddling across the yard in single file. It was an idyllic scene, but for me the best part was being here alone with Harold.

He passed the menu across to me.

"I usually have a Cornish pasty," he remarked. "They make their own here and they are quite delicious. I wash mine down with a glass of cider."

"Then I will have the same," I said promptly.

The waitress, a rosy-cheeked country girl, took our order and returned soon after with the drinks.

We sat sipping cider in the sunshine without speaking for some moments.

"Jim was telling me that you are an artist, Harold."

"Oh, just an amateur. I couldn't afford to turn professional. Materials can be quite expensive and then there is the hire of a studio. If it weren't for Elsie I would have nowhere to paint. She has helped me a lot."

I felt a stab of envy for this girl who was able to provide Harold with what he needed.

"My dream has always been to have a studio of my own. I saw the ideal place at Ford, near Old Sarum. I could take you there today if you like. It is only a few miles from here and then we could walk up the hill and look at the site of the old cathedral."

"I would love that."

Just then our pasties arrived, warm from the oven, and smelling delicious. We stopped talking and ate with relish, but as soon as we had finished Harold suggested we get straight on our way. He paid the bill and we mounted our bicycles. This time we rode at a leisurely pace, side by side along the quiet country roads. Suddenly a cock pheasant ran across in front of us, followed by a couple of hens.

"Look at that plumage!" exclaimed Harold. "Isn't it brilliant?"

"Rather different from the nondescript little females."

"Quite the reverse of the human species," and Harold grinned at me. His eyes were very clear against his lightly tanned skin and my heart skipped a beat.

"Birds are a challenge to paint," he said. "Every feather has so many shades."

"How do you manage to paint them at all?"

"There's no secret, really. You have to use your eyes and notice the subtleties of shading. For instance, what colour are those trees over there?"

"Green, surely."

"Yes, but if you look closely you will see there are many shades of green amongst them. The trick is to capture them. In nature the variety of shading is infinite. Even the best artist can't rival nature."

As Harold talked I felt my eyes being opened to a whole new world, in which colour and shapes formed beautiful and complex patterns. I was so taken up with what he was saying I did not notice the hill on our left.

"Well, here it is, Old Sarum," said Harold waving his arm towards the mound that rose abruptly beside us. "Archeologists say that there were people living here three thousand years before Christ."

"I can't imagine anything so old," I said, amazed.

"Then after that it was an Iron Age hill fort, one thousand years BC."

"I wonder what life was like at that time."

"Well, think of the Bible," said Harold slowly. "This hill was a fort at the same time King David was ruling Israel."

"And we still read the psalms that he wrote," I said, thinking of the twenty-third Psalm which meant so much to me. "And I suppose people then were not so unlike us today."

"No, still fighting, but also writing beautiful poetry and constructing elaborate buildings."

I looked up at the hill which was covered with tussock and patches of wildflowers and I couldn't imagine it being any different from the way it was today. Suddenly a skylark began singing above us, pouring out a joyous cascade of sound as it mounted higher and higher.

"It's so peaceful here," I murmured.

"It is now, but once this hill would have rung with the clash of steel, as soldiers fought to the death."

We continued our climb then, saying very little to each other because there was no need.

When we reached the top Harold pointed to the ditch which encircled the hill.

"That was already here when the Romans came to Britain in 53 AD. They merely strengthened the ramparts and used the hill as a garrison."

"What happened after they left?"

"The Saxons took it over, so that they could protect themselves against the Vikings who sailed across from Denmark in the summer months to steal and plunder. Then after the Saxons came the Normans, when William conquered Harold."

"Your namesake," I said smiling up at him.

"Yes and not a very lucky fellow. Did you know he was killed when someone fired an arrow at random which shot him in the eye? That was how the Saxons lost the battle of Hastings. If it hadn't been for one arrow, English history might have been very different. We wouldn't have had stone castles for instance," and he pointed to the ruin which towered above us. It still retained a certain grandeur, despite the broken walls and gaps in the stonework. Here and there sheep were grazing on the grass that grew inside the walls of what had once been rooms in the castle.

"It is so quiet and deserted!" I exclaimed.

"It makes you think, doesn't it?" said Harold. "Kingdoms rise and fall over the centuries and all they leave behind are a few ruins."

I glanced at him. "Surely some poet has written about this."

"Yes, Shelley did when he wrote Ozymandias, after visiting Egypt and seeing the sphinx in the desert."

Slowly and thoughtfully Harold quoted the lines at the end of the poem:

"My name is Ozymandias; King of Kings:
Look on my works, ye mighty, and despair!"
Nothing beside remains. Round the decay
Of that colossal wreck, boundless and bare,
The lone and level sands stretch far away."

"Those words express exactly what I feel when I look at all this," and I waved my hand towards the castle and the hill.

"Do you like poetry, Rhoda?"

"Only the sort I can understand. I like poems that rhyme and have a definite rhythm," I said, feeling not in the least embarrassed.

"You would like Tennyson then."

"The Lady of Shalott?"

"That, among others. I particularly like his Idylls of the King."

"I've never read them."

"Then I'll lend you my copy. I'm sure you will love it."

Harold's voice was warm with enthusiasm and I glanced at him, noting the glow in his eyes. How different he was from most young men I knew. His knowledge of history and his interest in poetry struck a chord in me. I felt I could spend hours in his company and never be bored.

"But what is really interesting is that flat area, over there beside the castle," said Harold pointing.

"What is special about it? All I can see is grass."

"That is where the original cathedral stood, which the Normans built at the end of the 11th century. The reason there is nothing left of it, is because they used the stones to build the walls of the new cathedral."

"If they already had a cathedral up here why did they want to build a new one?" I asked.

"Oh, there were a number of reasons. The church authorities said that it was cold up here and that the sound of the wind interrupted services and shook the church; also that the castle officials harassed the churchmen. I think it suited the king anyway, who was Henry III, because without the cathedral there would be more space for the castle. Anyway, whatever the reason, the bishop and the members of the chapter decided to build a new cathedral down on the water meadows."

"You seem to know a lot about it, Harold."

"I suppose that is because I live in Salisbury where the cathedral is so prominent. I never get tired of learning about it. For instance, did you know that Salisbury cathedral spire is the tallest in the United Kingdom, yet it was never part of the original building plan? It was probably added about one hundred years later, in the 13th century—and it is still here today. Remarkable isn't it?"

"Yes, it is so delicate looking, yet it must be very strong to have survived all these years," I said wonderingly.

"Those medieval craftsmen certainly knew a thing or two. There is much more I could tell you about the cathedral, but I don't want to bore you," and Harold glanced at his watch.

"Four o'clock already. I still haven't shown you where my dream studio is. Perhaps we should leave it for another day and make our way down the hill to collect our bicycles, that is, if some gypsy hasn't purloined them. Then it would be a long walk home wouldn't it?"

I laughed. Harold's mood of thoughtful reverie had disappeared in a matter of seconds. He was now cheerfully practical.

He rode with me all the way back to Laverton House, but refused when I invited him to come inside.

"I am on duty this evening at the school where I teach," he said regretfully, "but I would like to show you around the cathedral another time. May I write to you so that we can arrange a day?"

My heart leapt.

"Yes, I would like that. I have so enjoyed today."

"It has been a pleasure for me as well," said Harold quietly and I detected a tremor in his voice.

As he mounted his bicycle and rode down the drive I stood and watched him out of sight. I felt that some special bond had been forged between us that day.

A week later a package was delivered to me. My heart was thumping as I studied the address neatly written in an unfamiliar hand. This must be the book of poetry that Harold had promised me. I tore off the wrapping and found an envelope tucked inside the front cover. With trembling hands I opened it and read:

Dear Rhoda,

Here is the book of Tennyson's poems I promised you when we walked to the top of Old Sarum last Sunday. I want you to accept it as a gift in memory of that special day. Rarely have I enjoyed a walk so much and I look forward to other such occasions in your company, if that is agreeable to you. Unfortunately, I am unable to suggest a date earlier than the end of November, because I am on duty at the school for the next two weekends between 2pm and 7pm. Please let me know if you are able to take time off on a Saturday or a Sunday at the end of the month.

I remain yours very sincerely,
Harold

I read the note several times, lingering over the phrase, "rarely have I enjoyed a walk so much." Behind the formal expression I sensed that Harold had deeper feelings for me than he was willing to articulate, or was I reading too much into those few words? At any rate, he did want to see me again and that was what mattered, even if it were not for another month. My spirits rose, and as I turned the pages of the little leather volume of poems I imagined myself and Harold discussing them together.

Then I sat down straight away and wrote a reply, thanking him for the book and saying that I would let him know the days I would be free in November.

CHAPTER TEN

The months passed quickly and it was now August 1932. I had been at Laverton House almost a year. I suppose my outings with Harold marked the passage of time because we only managed to meet at monthly intervals. We went for long walks or cycle rides and that is how I became familiar with the countryside around Salisbury. Harold knew the history of every little village and hamlet and, being a naturalist and bird watcher, he was full of all kinds of out-of-the-way information. I drank in everything he could tell me and I suppose he was flattered to find a girl who had the same interests as himself.

He let drop one day, a little remark about Elsie that was very revealing. "I suggested to Elsie one evening that we take a walk to Stonehenge while the moon was coming up, but she said she wanted to listen to the light programme on the wireless. I never asked her again."

I made no comment at the time, but I turned this over in my mind. I knew that Harold enjoyed my company, yet I wondered what his real feelings for me might be. Did he regard me merely as a friend and companion, or did he find me attractive as a woman? I knew the effect he had on me; whenever he looked into my eyes or touched me lightly on the arm to point out some place of interest; it was like an electric shock shooting through my arm, but what did he feel for me? It was very baffling and I would lie awake at night going over every detail of our times together.

I said nothing of this to Joan who had made a good recovery from her broken leg and was now very serious about Jim. She commented one day when I returned from a walk with Harold, "When is that chap going to take you out somewhere decent? All you ever do is go walking together." Then she laughed. "If

I didn't know you better, Rhoda, I'd wonder what you got up to in those lonely places."

Although I laughed with her, the light remark rankled. She had put into words what I had been feeling for a long time.

Shortly after this something came up that took my mind off Harold. I was called into Dr. Branson's office. He looked at me fixedly for some moments.

"I have been watching your progress since you came to us, Nurse Pritchard, and I find you a competent nurse and a level-headed young woman. You may recall that when you first arrived here I told you that our attitude to patients who suffer from what is popularly called 'a nervous breakdown,' is rather different from some mental institutions. We believe that such people should not be subjected to shock treatment, but what they need most to help them recover is good food and exercise, rest and recreation but above all, freedom from responsibility.

Now we have just admitted a Major Grantly who has been in the army for some time, but was promoted to a position requiring much responsibility. The demands of the job caused him considerable stress and reawakened symptoms of shell-shock which he suffered during the Great War. His is a mild form of nervous disorder and I am confident that after some months of our kind of treatment he should regain his equilibrium and be able to return to his military duties once more. Apparently he has an aversion to Irish people and so it would not be suitable for any of our Irish nurses to care for him. We learned that he has spent some time in New Zealand.

After discussion with Matron, I have decided that you would be a suitable person to special Major Grantly. Your main duties would be to accompany him on walks, read to him and provide him with companionship. When dealing with someone like this it is better to be a good listener, rather than a talker. Whatever he might tell you in confidence, you must not discuss with other nurses. You are in a position of trust and anything he tells you must go no further."

I nodded. "I quite understand, Doctor."

"Would you be willing to undertake responsibility for this patient, Nurse Pritchard? It would be a good test of your mental nursing skills."

I thought for a moment before giving an answer.

"I would certainly like the opportunity, Sir, but is there not somebody else on the staff with more experience than I have?"

"Yes indeed, but I think you are well able to cope with the challenge, Nurse Pritchard. Please report to my office tomorrow afternoon at 1.30 pm and I will introduce you to Major Grantly."

He smiled and stood up. It was my dismissal so I thanked him and left the room.

I felt a mixture of excitement and trepidation the next afternoon as I stood outside Dr. Branson's office. What would the Major be like? Would he be one of those brusque army types, with a bristling moustache and an equally bristling manner? If so, how would I cope? Tentatively I knocked at the door and at the curt, "Come in," entered the room.

It was all I could do to hide my surprise. The Major was smoking a pipe and seemed to be swallowed up in the deep armchair in which he was sitting. He sprang to his feet as soon as I came in and although he stood very straight I could see he was scarcely taller than I was.

"This is Nurse Pritchard," said Dr. Branson inclining his head towards me. "She is from New Zealand, Major. You spent some time out there I believe."

"Five years actually, when I was posted there after the Great War. It was the best time of my life because that is where I met my wife. She was a New Zealand girl. The prettiest girls are to be found in New Zealand," he added and winked at me. "Yes, I'm sure Miss Pritchard and I will get on famously."

"I have told Nurse Pritchard that she is to be your special nurse while you are here and she will accompany you on walks and generally be a companion to you," said Dr. Branson.

"Are you familiar with many card games?" queried the Major, turning to me.

"Hardly any, I'm afraid."

"Never mind, I will teach you. I'm sure you're a quick learner. What about chess?"

"Oh yes," I said eagerly. "I'm not very good, but I do enjoy it."

"Splendid, we'll have a game later this afternoon, but perhaps we could go for a walk first and get to know one another."

Dr. Branson leaned back in his chair, pressing his fingers together and looking pleased.

"I suggest, Nurse, you take the Major for a walk through the grounds of Laverton House before venturing further afield."

"In that case, my dear, let us be gone," said the Major opening the door for me.

We went through the main doors and into the garden. It was a golden afternoon and the sun shone down with the gentle warmth of autumn, illuminating the bright red and gold leaves.

"From up here you can see the cathedral spire quite clearly," I said, leading the Major to the rise.

"What a marvellous view! Quite magical, isn't it?"

I looked at him in surprise. His reaction so matched my own, the first time I had seen the spire.

"Now, I suggest that tomorrow we familiarise ourselves with the countryside around here and then we can spread out, eventually exploring the cathedral itself. But perhaps this is all known territory to you?"

"I'm getting to know it, but always discovering something new. I've only been here a year."

The Major sounded surprised. "Where were you before?"

"I was doing my State Prelim at Birmingham Infirmary."

"So why did you switch to mental nursing?"

"It's rather a long story."

"And I would like to hear it, so tell on."

Rather hesitantly I embarked on an explanation of my illness and what had led me to apply for the job at Laverton House. The Major listened attentively.

"You must have been very disappointed having to give up general nursing." He looked at me sympathetically. "Life can be hard sometimes. Don't I know it, but I'm sure you don't want me to burden you with my worries."

"But I do," I replied. "I want to know whatever you would like to tell me."

He drew on his pipe without speaking. "Some other time, perhaps. Let's just enjoy the beauty and peace of these surroundings."

As we continued our walk the Major amazed me with his knowledge of trees and plants and I began to wonder why on earth he was in a mental hospital. He seemed saner and more balanced than most people I knew.

All of a sudden an aeroplane roared overhead. The Major flung himself on the ground clutching his hands to his ears. For a moment I hesitated, wondering what I should do. Then I knelt down beside him.

"It's only an aeroplane," I said gently, "and it's gone now."

He took his hands away from his ears and stood up awkwardly, brushing leaves from his suit.

"Sorry, my dear, just can't help it. Every time I hear a plane it takes me like that. A hangover from the last war I suppose."

"Perhaps we should go back indoors now. It must be nearly tea time," and I glanced at my watch.

As we walked back to the house I was thinking*, so this is what it means to be shell-shocked*. The only other person I had known who was said to be shell-shocked was my book-keeping tutor at the secretarial college, and that was only hearsay from the other students. As soon as there was a chance, I would report the Major's behaviour to Dr. Branson.

However, there were no opportunities to speak to the doctor that afternoon. After tea, which I took in the dining room with the Major, I went into an adjoining room where card tables were set up. I fetched a chessboard and chessmen from a cupboard while the Major settled himself comfortably in a chair and took a pull at his pipe. For the next hour very little was said as we silently did battle. After the Major had checkmated me he leaned back in his chair and looked at me appreciatively.

"You play a good game, my dear. I see I will have to be on my mettle when next we meet over chess." He glanced at his watch. "Six thirty. It must be time you were released from duty. I'll look forward to seeing you tomorrow. Perhaps we can go for a proper walk then, weather permitting."

"I do hope so," I said, collecting up the chess pieces. A few minutes later as I was leaving the room I glanced back at the Major and saw that he was sitting back in his chair puffing at his pipe, totally relaxed.

In the corridor I came face to face with Maisie.

"Well, you have created a stir, Rhoda. The whole of Laverton House is buzzing about you. You've only been here a year and Dr. Branson has given you a plum job, specialling the Major. Watch out, Rhoda, or they'll be calling you the Doctor's pet."

I felt embarrassed.

"It's only because he's been to NZ," and I lowered my voice, glancing around uneasily. "Also the Major has an aversion to the Irish, and you know how many of them there are on this staff."

"Yes, and you are general trained. Oh, you don't have to convince me, Rhoda. I can see perfectly well why Dr. Branson selected you for the job, but there are people around here who don't look at it that way. It's a bit unfortunate that you and Joan are sharing a room, as it's common knowledge that she is the favourite of Dr. Hall and his wife."

"Oh, goodness, I seem to be caught up in a web of intrigue."

"That's what it's like in a small place. I suppose you never met this before, coming from a large general hospital."

"Oh, gossip is pretty lively there too, but I suppose you can get away from it more easily."

"Well, make up your mind that if you want to keep any privacy here, say nothing to anyone about your personal affairs," and Masie tapped her nose meaningfully with her forefinger."

"Now, to change the subject, what are you doing this evening? Perhaps you would wander down to the Duck and Swan with me and we could have a quiet drink together."

"I'd like that, Masie, it seems ages since we had a good chat."

"I'll see you in half an hour then, in the foyer."

That evening when we were sitting in our usual alcove Maisie brought up the subject of the Major again.

"The whole place is talking about Branson giving you the job, specialling the Major. The Irish nurses are furious."

"Well, I can't help that," and I shrugged. "It appears the Major has a thing about the Irish, so it would hardly be tactful to push one under his nose. Anyway, I discovered today he is shell shocked," and I described what had happened that afternoon.

Maisie listened carefully. "You dealt with that very sensibly, Rhoda. I suppose your general nursing helps you keep a cool head in an emergency." She looked at me thoughtfully. "Yes, I can see why Branson chose you for the job. He's no fool and he only wants the best for an important patient. You did know the Major advises the government on military matters, didn't you, and he has a lot to do with the secret service?"

"How do you know that, Maisie?"

"Oh, one hears a thing or two," and she gave a light little laugh. "Anyway, it's about time we toddled back. It'll soon be closing time."

Back at the house I said goodnight to her at the foot of the stairs and went thoughtfully to my room. It had been an eventful day.

CHAPTER ELEVEN

I woke up feeling that something special was going to happen today. Then I remembered, I was to go walking with the Major in the afternoon. I hummed as I buttoned up my uniform. This was going to be a good day.

In the dining room I helped myself to bacon and eggs and made my way to the end of the room. I was just passing a group of Irish nurses sitting at one of the tables near the servery when O'Mally stood up suddenly and lurched against me. My tray tipped and all the plates slid to the floor.

"Oh, how clumsy of me, to be sure," she said with mock horror and a titter went round the group.

I bent down to pick up the pieces of broken crockery while one of the maids hurried forward with a dustpan and brush.

I would have stalked out of the dining room, but to do so would have given these Irish nurses the satisfaction of knowing I was upset. No, I must carry on as if nothing untoward had happened, so I went back to the slide and helped myself to another plate of bacon and eggs. This time as I passed their table I gave it a wide berth.

I was hardly seated when Ruth, the Irish nurse I had spoken to on my first Sunday morning, came over to my table.

"I saw all that happen and it was no accident!" she said indignantly. "O'Mally knocked against you deliberately. Look, Rhoda, I just want you to know that the Irish are not all like those cats. Do you mind if I sit down with you for a moment or two?"

"Please do."

"They are peeved because they think Dr. Branson is favouring you, but he is a clever man and knows what he's doing. If he's given you the Major to special it's because he knows you're

DEWALT 18V.
DCB 182 BATT
DRILL DCD 985
TYP 11

ROMAN A QUAIL 0207
2640725

- PP # 504166635 - JEAN - ESTA. J500973205. EXP. 18/5/2021. GRANTED 19/5/2016
- 518015306 · MG · J500968975. EXP. " "

5 YRS 09/06/2026

US ESTA = 24/7/15? ESTA 24/7/15.
+ 2 YRS

GROUP ID 7342068875. 14/8/2013.

2 YEARS. AUTH. EXPIRED

TUE 6/6.
1300 - 1400.
NEW COMMISSIONING.

WK 10 W/C 5/6?

THUR 29/6.
C/LTS F1 2Hr 15
F/A TEST 1Hr
F/EXT 35m
BASEMENT PLANT 30 45
W/C ALARMS 40
ROOF PLANT 45 25
EXT BUILDING CHKS 30-45.

MON
- FIRE EXT.
- AUTO DOORS.
- BASEMENT PLANT
- ROOF LOFT PLANT
- O/S LTS? (M)

TUE
- EXT BUILDING CHKS 30
W/C ALARMS 40
MEETINGS.
1300 - 1500?

THUR
F/A TEST
EXT BUILDING CHKS
CAL #1 (3M)

ESSENTIAL PPM SCHED
ESSENTIAL TIMESHEET
PPM COMPLETION
RG TIMESHEET.

FIRE EXT - 40m
BASEMENT PLANT - 1Hr
W/C ALARMS - 40m 20
ROOF LOFT PLANT. 45m
CAL #2 3M. 1Hr
EV CHKS. 1Hr 30

AUTO DOORS? - TUE? 30
SHOWER DESCALE? - 2Hr 15m
EXT BUILDING CK.? - 1Hr
6M TMV - 5Hrs/FLOOR

40
40 20
45
1:30
1:00
1:00
2:15
:30
1:00

9 x TASKS?

6 Hrs |||| 20

6 Hrs |||| 20m

9 Hrs 20m

||||| 45
6 Hrs
|||| 35.

the right one for the job. So take no notice of them, Rhoda. Nothing like this will happen again, not if I have anything to do with it."

"That is kind of you, Ruth, but I can take care of myself, you know. Please don't report O'Mally."

"Don't you worry, I won't. There are other ways to stop bullying." She glanced at her watch. "I'm afraid I must be off.'

"And I must too," I said, getting up quickly and leaving the rest of my breakfast untouched.

Life at Laverton House was hardly a bed of roses I thought ruefully*, but I mustn't let this incident get me down. If I am to be a successful mental nurse then I must stay calm and unruffled at all times, or what good will I be to the patients?* No doubt many of them carried around their own private hell with them. Even the Major, who had seemed so balanced, had turned into a terrified child at the mere sound of an aeroplane.

The rest of the morning passed quickly. Promptly at one o'clock I went to the lounge and found the Major waiting for me. He sprang from his chair as I entered the room.

"Well done, Nurse, punctual to the minute. Now shall we set off right away?" He patted his pocket. "I've got an Ordnance Survey map with me so we shan't get lost."

As we walked along the drive he talked eagerly about the route and the sights we would see. It was another still and sunny afternoon and with each step I felt my spirits lift. Conversation flowed easily between us and I felt very relaxed with this man, whose age and experience were far removed from mine.

"And why did you leave your home in New Zealand?" he asked.

"My father wanted my brothers and sisters and myself, to go back to England to visit our family here. He had promised that to my mother when she was dying."

"So he brought you all over?"

"Well, no, he wasn't able to come. He had to stay back in New Zealand to support us. Our aunt accompanied us."

"How many of you were there?"

"Five and I was the eldest."

"That was rather a tall order for your aunt."

"Yes, it wasn't easy for her, especially as my youngest sister was only five."

"So where are the children now, back in NZ?"

"No, they are living with my aunt in Somerset."

"And your father?"

"He is still in New Zealand. He married again."

"Hm, and you are on your own here in Salisbury. Do you miss your family?"

"I miss the children."

"But not really your aunt." The Major smiled down at me. "I think I get the picture. You wanted to get away from home."

"Well, yes, I suppose that's right."

I wondered whether it was in order for me to put questions to him, or should I leave the Major to volunteer information about himself?

As though tuning into my thoughts he said, "I suppose you are wondering about my family. As I think I mentioned yesterday, I married a New Zealand girl and we had twenty very happy years together. Unfortunately, she died in a motor accident leaving me with one son. By that time he had come to the end of his schooling, so he was not really dependent on me and now he is grown up and busy leading his own life."

He stopped and pulled the map out of his pocket. "I think it is time we consulted the oracle. We are here," and he stabbed at the map. "If we continue along this lane we will eventually come to a stream and after that a steep hill." He folded up the paper.

We continued along the narrow lane between banks of straggling grass, neither of us speaking for some time. The peace and silence were soothing, the only sounds being the faint murmur of running water nearby. We turned a bend in the lane and there in front of us was a stream crossed by a small wooden bridge. On the far side of the bridge a young man was leaning over the wooden railing gazing intently at the water. In his hand was a sketchbook and while we watched, he glanced down at it and made one or two jottings. He seemed oblivious of us, but then glancing over his shoulder he laid his finger against his lips then looked down at his book again.

With a shock I saw that it was Harold. He had obviously not recognised me, so I said nothing to the Major but waited until Harold beckoned us forward. He was still intent on the water and took no notice of us as we quietly crossed the narrow bridge, keeping well behind him. Once we were on the other side we continued walking, but my heart was beating fast and I hardly trusted myself to speak.

"Did you see what that young man was sketching?" the Major asked me.

"Not really." The truth was I had been so taken up with watching Harold I had been aware of nothing else.

"I think he was studying some ducks. I would have liked to ask him, but he didn't seem to invite questions. Unusual young man," finished the Major thoughtfully. I glanced at him wondering whether to mention I knew the artist, but on balance decided not to. After all, it might look strange that Harold had not acknowledged me. For the remainder of the walk I forced myself to concentrate on what the Major was saying. His observations on the countryside were always interesting and informative.

At the end of our walk, as we were turning into the drive, the Major stopped suddenly and laid a hand on my arm. With his other arm he made a sweeping gesture from right to left. I followed the direction of his hand noting the backdrop of hills with fluffy little clouds sailing above them in a pale blue sky.

"This is the England we fought to preserve in 1914," he said slowly, "but it looks as though we might have to do it all over again."

I stared at him.

"But we were told the Great War was ..."

"The war to end all wars. If only that were true, but already there are rumblings across the Channel. For instance, there is the rise of the Nazi party in Germany under Adolf Hitler. That is bad, very bad." Noting my shocked expression he patted my arm, "But don't you worry, my dear. I may be wrong, I sincerely hope so. Now shall we go inside and have some tea?"

Some time later as we sat in the crowded dining room the Major kept up a flow of lively talk, but a shadow had been cast over my mind by his reference to war and I felt a sense of foreboding.

Following tea, the Major and I sat over our chessboard scarcely speaking and after a hard fought battle I managed to checkmate him. As he lit his pipe the Major said admiringly, "I don't know when I enjoyed a game of chess more. Playing with you takes my mind off everything."

....

Over the following months my life fell into a pattern. I worked with the other patients in the morning and spent the afternoons with the Major. As winter gave way to the spring of 1933, steadily and imperceptibly the Major began to get better.

One day we were out walking as usual and a silence fell between us. Then the Major turned to me, "Since coming here and spending time with you, my dear, I feel rejuvenated. In fact, Dr. Branson says that I should be able to leave quite soon."

I felt a stab of dismay. "I am glad for you, Major, but I shall miss you." My walks with him were the highlight of my days, and I enjoyed our conversations, where his experience and maturity opened up a new world to me. We carried on walking, saying very little for some minutes.

"My son is coming to visit me tomorrow," said the Major unexpectedly, "and I would like you to meet him. He proposes to take me into Salisbury to have tea at the Red Lion. Would you like to join us, Nurse? I'm sure I can get Dr. Branson to agree to your having the afternoon off—as it is all in the line of duty," and he winked at me.

"Are you sure that I would not be in the way?" I asked tentatively. "After all, it must be some time since you saw your son."

"When he sees you it will be his old father who will be in the way," said the Major gallantly. I found myself blushing. "No, it will be a pleasure for both of us to have your company."

We continued walking down a quiet lane and came across half a dozen hares or rabbits dozing in the sunshine. Hearing footsteps they woke and scampered off. An aeroplane droned lazily overhead and I glanced anxiously at the Major, but he merely remarked, "What a peaceful afternoon."

How different this was from our first walk, when he had thrown himself to the ground on hearing a plane.

Later in the day the Major spoke to Dr. Branson who readily agreed that I could accompany him and his son to Salisbury, and as I was to be their guest I need not be in uniform.

That evening I tried to come to a decision over what to wear. I did not want to appear over-dressed, yet at the same time I wanted to look my best. I consulted Maisie who had a good eye for clothes.

"I think you should wear the yellow blouse with your brown skirt. Yellow seems to do things for you and the two go well together."

"I think you're right, Maisie. Very well, the yellow and brown ensemble it will be." Then I added thoughtfully, "I wonder what the Major's son is like."

"Bound to be short like his father. Probably smokes a pipe and wears awful tweeds," Maisie said mischievously.

I gave her a little push.

"You might be surprised. He could be tall, dark and handsome. Anyway, I'm having afternoon tea in Salisbury and that's all that matters."

It had been arranged that I should meet the Major and his son in the sitting room at two thirty. I checked my appearance in the mirror before going downstairs. The yellow and brown outfit certainly looked smart and I smiled at myself in the glass.

It was unusually quiet that afternoon and there was nobody about as I went downstairs to the vestibule. I paused, feeling suddenly nervous, before pushing open the sitting room door. Two men were standing in front of the window with their backs to me. One was the Major and next to him was a tall man in a smartly cut suit. They were busy talking and did not hear me enter, but as I walked across the room they both turned around. The Major stared.

"Well, Nurse, I never would have known you. How smart you look. We were just admiring the view, and I was telling my son about those lovely walks we take together. Let me introduce you. Nurse Pritchard, this is Lawrence, my son."

The tall young man stepped forward and took my hand in a firm grasp.

"Am I to call you Nurse Pritchard all afternoon or can I take the liberty of using your Christian name?" He leaned forward and smiled, his dark blue eyes glinting with amusement.

He is like a matinee idol, I thought, *with his smooth black hair and neat moustache, and he is as unlike his father as it is possible to be.* I thought fleetingly of Maisie's remarks and smiled.

"I'm Rhoda, now that I'm off duty."

"And I'm Larry. Now that's settled, shall we be on our way? Our table is booked for 3.15."

At the door he let his father go first and stood back politely for me, but I sensed his impatience to be off. It was the same when we were outside. Even the Major had to quicken his pace to keep up with his son. Lawrence's car was in the drive, a low-slung sports model and though I knew very little about cars I recognised that this one was expensive.

He opened the passenger door for his father then assisted me into the back seat.

"There's not much room, I'm afraid, and it will be a pretty snug fit even for a petite little thing like you," he said, closing the door.

It was as well I was not any bigger because it certainly was a tight squeeze.

Larry drove slowly, but I had the impression he was holding the car back and given the chance he would have put his foot down and let it go. I could not follow the conversation between the two in the front, so I settled back in my seat and enjoyed the changing scene outside the window.

I glimpsed the cathedral spire as it rose needle-like above the city and felt as I always did, that there was something mystical in its beauty.

At last we entered Salisbury itself and as Lawrence drove along those narrow intersecting streets I noticed that he did not hesitate but seemed to know exactly where to go. Finally, he turned a corner and there in front of us was a courtyard with the life-sized figure of a lion beside the entrance, proclaiming that this was indeed the Red Lion Hotel.

Larry parked the car and the three of us walked across the courtyard, past tubs of bright red geraniums, to the reception area. We entered a small dark lobby where the only light came from a tiny leaded window and a single electric bulb over the front desk, yet for all that the dimness seemed in keeping with the heavy oak beams and panelled walls. This was a place that had stood for centuries and no doubt would go on for many more. Against the opposite wall stood a heavy oaken clock and suddenly it started to strike with a tinkling sound and a row of medieval figures marched in a circle at the top. I gazed at it fascinated.

"How old is that clock?" I asked the clerk who had looked up when it began to strike.

"Oh, about six hundred years or thereabouts," he said casually.

I was about to ask another question but just then a waiter came forward and conducted us into a room with a low beamed ceiling. He led us to one of the alcoves where the table was laid for three, with a starched white cloth and bone china teacups.

Lawrence pulled back a chair for me before sitting down between his father and myself.

After a few minutes the waiter returned pushing a trolley on which were cakes and dainty sandwiches. He placed these ceremoniously on the table and last of all set down, in the middle, an enormous china teapot.

"Would you do the honours?" the Major asked me.

I felt self-conscious as I lifted the heavy teapot and my hand wobbled.

When at last the tea was poured I was able to take in the details of the room. The small leaded window next to us allowed in very little daylight but the fire blazing on a huge hearth gave the room a warm glow. There were other little alcoves like ours where diners were quite private.

"Rather different from New Zealand isn't it, my dear?" said the Major, noticing the direction of my eyes. "Odd to think that this place was here long before the days of Captain Cook."

Larry looked across at me. "Dad told me that you came from New Zealand when you were a child. Did you know that my mother was a New Zealander, which makes me half one as well?"

He was studying me intently and I couldn't help noticing how handsome he was, with his smooth black hair, clipped moustache and dark blue eyes. It was strange that I could admire him, yet be unaffected by his good looks.

"I think I am beginning to forget New Zealand," I said quietly. "It all seems like a distant dream now. In the mining village where I grew up, old Maori women with tattoos on their chins used to crouch at the side of the main street smoking their clay pipes and behind the shops were bush-covered hills. It is so different from England it's like another world."

"Do you think you will go back?" asked Larry.

"I hope to one day, because my father is still there. But what about you, Lawrence; I don't even know where you live?"

"I would like to know more about you before we start on me," and Larry grinned, looking suddenly boyish. "For instance, have you any strong attachments here?"

"I was almost engaged but that is over now."

Larry seemed to relax. "So you are free as air?"

"Yes, and happy to remain that way, for the present anyway," I replied with a light little laugh.

"Come, come, I think you are being rather personal, Lawrence," said the Major looking reprovingly at his son.

"I probably am. Forgive me, Rhoda, but an attractive young lady like you prompts that kind of question." His tone was no longer teasing.

"So it is my turn now to ask questions?"

"Very well, go ahead. I think you wanted to know where I live."

"Yes."

"I have an apartment in Wimbledon overlooking the Common, in a large house which used to belong to one family, with servants of course. My apartment comprises a bedroom, living room, kitchen and bathroom so it is quite spacious. As the station is at the bottom of the hill I have a brisk fifteen minute walk each day to catch my train. It is a pleasant location and I can almost fancy myself in the country, yet it is only half an hour from Wimbledon to Waterloo Station."

"I suppose you work in the city then."

"Yes, like all those other poor devils, who have to earn their living sitting behind a desk all day."

"Where is your office?"

"Right in the heart of London. I work for Lloyds, the insurance company."

"They insure ships, don't they?"

"That is what they are famous for. Have you been to London lately, Rhoda?"

"As a matter of fact I've never been there at all," I said feeling young and inexperienced.

"Well, we must remedy that," and Lawrence's voice was warm and eager.

"Look, Rhoda, are you interested in art because if you are, there is a special exhibition of Monet's works at the National Gallery? Trains leave Salisbury every hour and I think it is only a three hour journey to London. If you were to leave at nine you would be at Waterloo by twelve. Then we could go to lunch first before seeing the exhibition. What do you say?"

"It sounds very exciting," and as I looked across the table at Larry's shining eyes I felt myself being swept along by his enthusiasm, yet something made me hesitate.

The Major evidently noticed this because he said to his son, "Don't rush the girl, Larry. If she's never been to London before it is a bit much to expect her to arrive at a busy station like Waterloo and find her way into the city."

"But I would meet you, Rhoda, of course, and you would not get lost in the crowds."

"Thank you, but there are other things to think of as well, my off duty times for a start."

"Yes, I was forgetting, you are a nurse and duty comes first." This was said with a shade of irony and I was just about to reply when the Major interrupted.

"Speaking of art exhibitions, I wonder if that young man we met on the bridge exhibits his work. He interested me because I'm sure he was studying birds when we came upon him that day."

"I happen to know him," I said quickly, "although he didn't recognise me that day; he was so absorbed in watching the ducks and yes, he mostly paints birds but he also does a bit of landscape painting I think. Actually, I've never seen any of his work and as far as I know he does not exhibit it."

As I spoke I wondered, not for the first time, at Harold's reticence to show me his paintings. Perhaps he did not feel free to invite me to his studio because it belonged to Elsie's family. The Major's voice broke into my thoughts.

"Well, I would be grateful if you could find out more about what he paints because if he does bird studies, I might be interested in buying one."

"Dad goes in for paintings of birds and he has some rather fine ones, but most of them are by well-known artists," explained Lawrence.

"All the same, there was something about that young man," said the Major thoughtfully. "I think it was his total absorption in what he was doing. Seemed to suggest a true artist."

So much so, he never even noticed me, I thought wryly, but all I said was, "I'll find out for you, Major, and let you know."

Conversation became general after this and I enjoyed being with two men of such wide interests and experience. I was sorry when it was time to return to Laverton House.

As he helped me from the car, Lawrence said quietly, "I will be in touch with you, Rhoda. I want to get to know you better—and to show you London as well." Then he took my hand, quickly raised it to his lips and kissed it. His words and this oddly European gesture caught me off guard and all I could mumble was, "That would be nice, Larry."

CHAPTER TWELVE

That evening I went in search of Jim. His motorbike was parked in its usual place so I knew he had not gone out. I stopped one of the male nurses and asked him where I might be able to find him.

"I saw Jim a few minutes ago heading towards the recreation room. He's bound to be there."

I thanked the attendant and made my way to the annex at the rear of the house, which was a popular meeting place for the nurses. I could hear voices and the occasional burst of laughter even before I reached the door, and as I went in it was difficult at first to distinguish anyone through the wreaths of smoke. Then a voice behind me said, "Rhoda, what are you doing here?" and turning around I saw Jim regarding me with a quizzical expression.

"I could ask the same of you."

"I am here to play indoor bowls. Would you like to join us?"

"No, thanks, I don't know how you can even see to play, in all this fug," I said, dabbing at my eyes which were stinging from the smoke. "Actually, I came to ask if you knew Elsie's address. The Major is interested in seeing Harold's pictures and I understand he uses a shed at the back of Elsie's place as a studio, so I thought it would be best to contact her."

"As it happens, I do have her address, right here," and he whipped from his pocket a small notebook with a pencil attached, made a quick jotting and handed me the torn off sheet. I thanked him then went quickly towards the door, longing to escape from the smell of smoke.

Back in my room I took out the note and for some time sat gazing at the address: The Paddocks, Nutgrove Lane, Ford. It sounded rather exclusive.

Pulling out my writing pad I wrote a short letter to Elsie, explaining that the Major would like to see some of Harold's pictures with a view to buying one, and whether a convenient time could be arranged for us to visit his studio. I also wrote a brief note to Harold. Then I went downstairs and posted both letters in the box in the lobby. Maisie happened to be passing. She looked at me mischievously. "Well, you were right about the Major's son and I was wrong. He was tall, dark and handsome."

You were spying on us."

"Pure coincidence. I happened to be standing at the window when you were going out to the car."

"So now I suppose, you want to know everything that happened."

"Of course."

I hesitated, before launching into an account of the afternoon tea party. When I came to the end I found Maisie looking at me, her eyebrows raised.

"You're holding something back, Rhoda. The handsome stranger wants to see you again, doesn't he?"

"Well, yes, but I'm not sure whether I really want to get involved with him."

"What! You can't mean that."

"It's hard to explain," and I looked down at my hands.

"You are a strange one. I know half the female staff here would jump at the chance to go out with him."

"Is that a fact?" I said laughing and ran up the stairs.

Two days later a couple of letters arrived for me. I recognised Harold's writing instantly and tore open the envelope, my heart pounding. It was only a brief note to say that the Major and I would be welcome to visit him in his studio at two o'clock on Friday afternoon. Then I read Elsie's letter which was written on headed paper and was a confirmation of the date and time.

I immediately went in search of the Major to tell him the good news and found him in the sitting room reading the paper.

He looked up with a pleased smile when I came in.

"Have you come to play chess with me?"

"Yes, and to tell you that Harold has invited us to visit his studio this coming Friday, at two o'clock."

"Good, I will order a taxi. Now let us get on with a game."

I gave careful thought to what I would wear on Friday, something not too dressy, but casually smart, and I finally decided on a white sweater with my plaid skirt. As a last little touch I added a red scarf.

When I went downstairs to join the Major in the vestibule he looked at me appreciatively.

"You do look nice, Rhoda. That red scarf really does something for you. I like to see you out of uniform," he added.

I smiled at him, warmed by the compliment.

The taxi took us by the usual route towards Salisbury then branched off to Ford. Now we were in the depths of the country and after about half a mile of bumping along an unmade road we turned into a drive. The wrought iron gates were open and carefully the taxi nosed its way along the gravelled surface between the oaks and sycamores that bordered the drive on both sides. Then I had my first glimpse of Elsie's home, a sprawling Elizabethan manor house with walls of warm red brick and exposed timber beams. Above the tiled roof chimneys rose, twisted in fantastic patterns.

"A fine place," commented the Major.

"Yes," I murmured, and my heart sank. If Elsie's family lived here then they must be very wealthy and that would make her even more desirable to a struggling young artist.

The Major handed me out of the taxi and we walked across the gravelled drive to the heavy oaken front door. The Major gave the bellpull a sharp tug. Almost immediately the door was opened by a smart maid who invited us to step inside.

"I will get Miss Elsie for you," she said and disappeared.

This gave us an opportunity to take in our surroundings. The lobby was panelled in typical Tudor fashion, yet the furnishings were surprisingly modern and comfortable. A picture on the opposite wall was illuminated by a shaded lamp. It was of pheasants feeding in a hoar frost, their plumage vivid against the white ground. The Major wandered over to look at it.

"Hm, by H. Blake, I see. If this is an example of his work then he is a fine artist. I look forward to seeing his other paintings."

Just then Elsie appeared. Even in the dim light I could see that she was elegantly dressed in a simple blouse and skirt.

"I'm sorry I kept you waiting," she said politely, looking at the Major. "Can I offer you a cup of tea before we go out to the studio?"

"That is very kind, but I think we would both prefer to see the paintings first. Isn't that so, Rhoda?" said the Major to me.

"Oh yes."

"Well, in that case, follow me and I will take you there. The studio is some distance from the house," Elsie explained, leading us along a narrow passage which ended with a low door. She pushed it open and we found ourselves at the back of the house in a courtyard with a cluster of buildings on the opposite side.

"The studio was once a potting shed," she said, indicating a long low building. "I have had a skylight added as it was far too dark before."

By now we were at the door of the building and Elsie gave a light tap before opening it. She beckoned to us to follow her.

We stepped directly into a room which was so light that I blinked. At the opposite end Harold was standing before an easel, his back to us. He appeared not to have heard us come in.

"Harold," said Elsie, "I've got some visitors for you."

He swung around, and then came towards us, a brush in his hand. He looked from the Major to me with a puzzled expression. Then his face cleared.

"Oh yes, you wrote to me, didn't you, Rhoda and I suggested you come on Friday afternoon. Goodness, is it that already?"

"Harold forgets what day it is when he is busy on a painting," smiled Elsie.

"You are a true artist then," said the Major. "Do you mind if I have a look at some of your work?"

"No, of course not, but I'm afraid a lot of it is unfinished."

In one corner a number of boards were leaning against the wall. The Major lifted them up one by one and studied them.

"I see you work in oils and water colours."

"Yes, I find oils suitable for scenes, but I prefer water colours for birds so that I can reproduce the subtle colours of the wings."

"You certainly achieve that. Look here, Rhoda," said the Major. "Observe the feathers on this duck; they look so real you feel you could touch them."

He lifted another picture and stood gazing at it for a long time. It was an eagle perched on a crag in a lonely landscape of heather-clad hills.

"Where did you paint this, Scotland?"

"Yes, I cycled up there last holiday and was fortunate enough to see an eagle and paint him. He was so majestic and powerful I felt overawed."

"You have certainly captured that quality in your painting." The Major paused before speaking again. "Harold, I am very impressed by what I have seen this afternoon. I would like to buy the eagle painting if you are prepared to part with it—at any price you like to name. I would also like the one of the ducks. When I get back to London I am going to take them to an art dealer friend of mine and I'm sure he will agree that you have great talent. I feel that you should be exhibiting your work and letting the art world see what you can do."

There was silence when he had finished. Elsie and I looked at Harold expectantly. He was gazing at the Major, stunned.

"But I'm only an amateur," he said at last.

"This is not the work of an amateur," said the Major firmly. "No, you deserve to be recognised. Now what do you want for the paintings?"

"I have no idea."

"Very well then, I will pay you twenty-five guineas for each," and the Major took out his cheque book. Quickly he wrote a cheque and handed it to Harold who was still looking bemused. Then the Major picked up the paintings and tucked them under his arm.

"Now, my dear," he said to me, "we had better be getting along. I asked the taxi driver to wait for an hour." He glanced at his watch, "and that is nearly up."

"I will be in touch with you, Harold, very soon and thank you, Miss Sumner, for making us welcome," and the Major bowed slightly to Elsie.

"I'll show you a quick way to the front of the house," she said and led us outside and across the courtyard to a door set in the wall. She opened it and once more we were in front of the house where the taxi was waiting.

"What a gifted young man! He will go far, I know it," was the Major's comment to me as he helped me into the back seat.

My thoughts were in a whirl. If Harold was destined for fame in the art world he would no doubt leave Salisbury behind and that would be the last I would see of him, but on the other hand, so would Elsie.

CHAPTER THIRTEEN

There were only two days to go before the Major was to leave and I felt heavy-hearted as we played chess together for the last time.

"You will come and visit me won't you, Nurse?" said the Major, looking up at the end of the game. "I live in Surrey and I have a very good housekeeper who loves it when people come to stay because then she can show off her hospitality skills. Do say you promise to come."

"I would love to," I replied and meant it. I had become very fond of the Major during the past months and it would make it easier saying goodbye to him if I knew I would see him again.

"And the young artist, Harold; as soon as I am home I will contact some of my friends in the art world. That young man has promise and I look forward to hanging his pictures on my wall. I have already planned where I will put the eagle." As he spoke my heart began to thump. *Why did the mention of Harold's name have this effect on me? Stop being silly,* I told myself crossly.

After I left the Major, I was crossing the vestibule when I came face to face with Dr. Hall. I felt myself grow pale as I encountered those piercing eyes.

"May I have a word with you, Nurse, in my office, if you please?"

My stomach seemed to drop away as I followed him into the room. He did not ask me to sit down, but went to the window where he stood looking out for a few moments. When he turned around he gazed steadily at me in silence, his eyes probing mine.

"Whatever is said in this room I do not want repeated to anyone. You understand that, don't you, Nurse Pritchard?" There was a note of menace in his voice.

"Yes."

I steeled myself to meet his eyes.

"I don't know what Joan has said to you, but knowing her as I do, I can well believe that she has confided in you intimate details of her association with me. I also detect your hand in that foolish jaunt to Bournemouth a year ago. Misguidedly, you attempted to get her mixing with a group of young people who are far beneath her."

I felt indignation rising in me.

Keeping my voice low and controlled I said, "I think that is hardly fair, Dr. Hall. All of the young people Joan was with that night are members of the staff here and she is one of them. And yes, I did encourage her to go to Bournemouth, to get her out of herself because she seemed unhappy."

I looked at him steadily and he continued to meet my eyes, but there was a flicker in them that told me he understood what I was implying.

"Right, we will say no more of this," he said finally. "I think we understand each other. Joan has to make important decisions for herself without pressure from friends, however well-meaning. I ask you to remember this, Nurse Pritchard, during the rest of your time here, however short or long it might be."

I could not miss the unspoken threat behind these words. As my employer he had the upper hand and could easily find a reason to dismiss me.

"Now, let me wish you good afternoon," he said icily and held the door open for me.

I went straight to my room and sat on the edge of the bed. My mind was in turmoil and for some time all I could do was wait until my heart stopped pounding. Eventually, I slid to the floor and knelt by the bed, my head in my hands. I prayed, "Please help me, God."

That was all I could say, yet almost immediately I felt calmer and was able to think clearly. Should I resign my post here and go back to Bath? Surely there were many private mental hospitals in the vicinity and I would have no difficulty finding a nursing position with my background. It would mean I could be near the family as well and how delighted the children would be. The prospect was attractive.

Yet, if I were to leave now, wouldn't I be playing into Dr. Hall's hands? I thought of those hypnotic eyes and what Joan had told me of the hold that man had on her. No, I could not abandon her. Furthermore, I enjoyed working with the patients at Laverton House and it had been a joy to see the Major recover from his breakdown; perhaps there would be others like him that I could help. My time here had shown me that I had a gift for working with mental patients and when they were with me they were soothed and quieted. Also, I had grown to love Salisbury and the countryside near Laverstock. Then there was Harold. My heart twisted in my breast. No, I could not run away from all this.

When I got off my knees I was resolved. I would stay on at Laverton House and face whatever difficulties came my way.

I went down to the lobby at two o'clock and saw that Dr. Branson was with the Major. The two men were chatting, but stopped as I approached.

"This is the young lady whom I have to thank for my recovery," said the Major warmly.

"Yes, we are very fortunate to have Nurse Pritchard on our staff. In a short time she has shown she is a capable nurse."

"With exceptional abilities," added the Major, smiling at me. "Now, here is my son, right on the dot," as Larry strode into the foyer. Dr. Branson stepped forward and shook his hand, then excused himself.

"It's good to see you again, Rhoda, I mean Nurse Pritchard," said Larry, his eyes twinkling. Then he turned to his father. "If you are not in too much of a hurry, Dad, perhaps we could stop for a cup of tea before we start on our journey. Would you join us Nurse Pritchard?"

"Well, yes, thank you, I'll arrange for a tray to be sent to the sitting room," and I slipped away.

When I returned, father and son were talking animatedly.

"I've just been telling Larry about my suggestion for you to visit us in Surrey."

"Then I could be there too and show you some of the sights in our part of the world. Perhaps we could even take in a show in London," said Larry enthusiastically.

"And I could take you to an art exhibition," put in the Major.

"It all sounds perfect, but what about my duties? It's rare for us to have two days off together."

"I don't think you need worry about that. I will have a word with Dr. Branson." The Major gave Larry a significant nod. "And now I'm afraid we must be setting off. Thank you for all you have done for me," he said warmly, taking my hand.

"And that goes for me too. Thank you for all you have done for Dad," Larry added. "I shall be in touch with you."

For a few moments both men hesitated, then the Major turned briskly on his heel and Larry followed. At the door he looked back and gave me a slight wave. I sighed. With their going I felt suddenly empty. How I would miss the Major and our times together, the games of chess and our walks. Heavy-hearted I left the room and began climbing the stairs.

"Hey, Rhoda!" called a voice behind me. It was Maisie. "I've been looking for you everywhere. I'm free this afternoon. Shall we go down to the Duck and Swan and have a drink? It's a lovely afternoon."

Looking at her bright face I felt the gloom lift from me.

"I'd love to," I said.

CHAPTER FOURTEEN

Christmas was fast approaching and I heard from Maisie that the staff were planning to put on a concert for the patients. Several of the nurses had recently got together to discuss it and interest was running high. Maisie herself was one of the prime movers.

She came to our room one evening when Joan and I happened to be off duty at the same time.

"I think we should put our heads together and work out a sketch based on some funny incident at Laverton House this year," she said enthusiastically.

"Let me see, there was that time the cooks put salt instead of sugar in the dessert," I said, remembering.

"That would be perfect," Maisie exclaimed. "Let's do it!"

Joan screwed up her face. "Count me out. I'm no good at acting and anyway it would take up a lot of time, with rehearsals and everything."

"Time better spent with Jim," said Maisie, winking at me. "Yes, we understand, Joan, you have your priorities."

So Maisie and I set to work with much hilarity and planned our skit. After that we met regularly to practise.

One evening Maisie came to my room and said, "You do realise don't you, Rhoda, that the concert is only the Saturday after next. I've been talking to Jim and he says he has invited Harold."

I felt suddenly nervous, imagining Harold in the audience that night.

"Is something the matter, Rhoda?" Maisie was looking at me curiously.

"It's just that I hadn't realised how close the concert is. And the thought of acting in front of a real live audience makes me shake."

"I can't imagine you getting stage fright. It's more likely I'll freeze up and forget everything," she said airily. "Anyway, I'd better be off now and get ready for duty."

When she had gone I collapsed into the nearest chair, my mind in a whirl.

The next few evenings we practised our sketch feverishly, to be ready for the dress rehearsal on Friday night.

Our item was at the end of the programme. As we came off stage there was a spontaneous outburst of clapping from the other performers and I knew that we need have no fears for Saturday night.

All the same, the morning of the concert I woke with a feeling of dread. What would Harold think when he saw me acting in a frivolous little sketch? He always seemed so serious and intellectual. Well, it was too late to change anything now.

Throughout the day, every time I thought of the concert my stomach lurched. After coming off duty in the afternoon I still had a couple of hours to spare, so I tried to read a book to quieten my nerves.

All the performers had been told to be ready an hour beforehand and wait in a back room behind the stage; there was to be no mingling with the audience until after the show. Maisie and I sat together and chatted quietly while some of the others played cards.

The first item was a quartet playing some popular tunes. At the end there was loud and enthusiastic clapping.

"There must be quite a big audience out there," whispered Maisie.

"I feel quite scared," I said.

"So do I, but they say if you're not nervous you don't perform well."

"In that case we should be a roaring success."

Maisie giggled. "I just wish our item wasn't at the end of the programme. It's such a long time to wait. I suppose the idea was to send the audience off with a smile on its face."

At last the moment came. Our names were called so we went on stage and took our positions for the first scene which was set in the kitchen. Maisie had stuffed a pillow under her smock in imitation of Cook's generous figure. I was her feather-brained assistant and wore an overall.

When the curtain went up Maisie was studying a recipe book and I was standing at an open cupboard. As the skit was in mime one of the male attendants came forward holding up a board, with the words: *Cook is busy preparing a pudding for dinner*. Behind Cook's back I was jigging to an imaginary dance tune and not listening to instructions, so that instead of measuring out the sugar I dipped my spoon in a jar of salt and added it to the other ingredients in the bowl.

When Cook lifted the pie out of the oven a few minutes later she surveyed it with pride and self-congratulation. The audience was laughing heartily by now and I forgot to be nervous and began to enjoy myself. In the second scene we changed roles. Maisie was now the maid while I was the guest of honour at the dinner. I licked my lips as I gazed with anticipation at the delicious looking pie which Maisie set in front of me. I took a generous bite and then my mouth contorted and I coughed and spluttered into my handkerchief. From then on, I quietly got rid of the evil mixture by feeding it to a dog under the table which was promptly sick. By now the audience was rocking and after the curtain came down the applause was deafening.

When Maisie and I went backstage the others gathered around us.

"Well, you certainly brought the house down," commented O'Mally, much to my surprise. After the incident with the tray she had kept out of my way. "I wouldn't have guessed you were such a comedian, Rhoda. You should be on the stage."

I smiled. This was high praise indeed.

"Quick Rhoda, we have to change and meet the others for supper," said Maisie impatiently, pulling at my arm.

A few minutes later, when I was combing my hair, I scarcely recognised the pretty girl in the mirror with the flushed cheeks and sparkling eyes.

Jim met us at the door.

"I've reserved a table for us all," he said hurriedly. "The others are waiting for you two, but look sharp, or we may lose our seats."

We followed him into the dining room and as we went through there was a ripple of applause.

"You two are famous now," Jim said with a grin, but I hardly heard him; I had spotted Harold sitting at a table with Joan. The heat rose to my cheeks and my heart began to pound.

As we moved towards their table Harold sprang to his feet. "I don't think I've ever laughed so much!" he exclaimed. "Your act certainly stole the show. I think you could make your living on the stage, Rhoda."

"No danger of that; I'll stick to nursing," I said laughing. "Anyway, it's good to see you here, Harold."

Jim had seated himself next to Joan and was whispering something to her and she was laughing up at him. Looking at them sitting close together I wondered what Dr. Hall would think if he could see them now. I remembered his veiled threats to me and feared for Jim. I turned to Harold.

"How is your painting going?"

"It seems to have ground to a halt recently," he said slowly.

"Oh, why is that?"

"Well, you see I am making arrangements to go to Penang to be with my parents. My father recently had a stroke, only a slight one, but my mother is concerned about him. She would like me to go and assist them with their work out there. She is afraid that my father will try to do too much and bring on another stroke."

I felt a shock of dismay.

"How long would you be away, Harold?"

"I can't be sure; it might be a while. It all depends on Father's health."

"What about your painting?"

"I will still try to do a bit, but I think most of my time will be taken up with the work. Father has been translating some of the Bible into a local dialect and I will probably help with that."

Maisie had been listening to us and interjected. "Have you any paintings to sell, Harold? My father owns a small hotel and he is always on the look-out for works by local artists."

"I have a few. I was keeping them to exhibit sometime, but I suppose the more I can sell the better, so they don't have to go into storage."

"Where are you going to store them?" I asked, dreading the answer.

"Elsie has offered. She says my studio won't be used while I'm away and she will be quite happy to have my paintings there for as long as necessary."

My heart sank. Again Elsie was making herself indispensable. Suddenly all the pleasure went out of the evening. The excitement of performing on stage and seeing Harold afterwards was spoiled by the news that he was going away.

I hardly knew how I got through the rest of the evening. I chatted and laughed but my heart was not in any of it. Every time I looked at Harold, a feeling of desolation swept over me.

Eventually, he glanced at his watch. "Well, I must be getting along." Then he turned to me. "I do hope I will see you before I leave, Rhoda. I would like you to have one of my paintings. Do you think you could visit my studio next week—if you are free?"

"I would love to," I said quietly. "I'll let you know my off-duty times."

"Good, that's fixed then," and standing up he shook hands with everyone, leaving me until last. He held my hand for a long moment and said softly, "Until next week, Rhoda."

When he had gone Maisie said to me. "I think that young man is keen on you."

"What makes you think that?"

"Oh various small signs." She added slyly, "and I think the feeling is reciprocated."

I felt myself blushing. "You are just an incurable romantic, Maisie."

"And I'm never far wrong," she replied with a laugh.

CHAPTER FIFTEEN

One grey day in early March 1934, I stood gazing out of the bedroom window, a letter from Harold in my hand. It was now three months since he had left England. He had written a few times from Penang describing his life in the Mission compound and the daily routine: translation work in the morning; in the afternoon, either teaching or visiting the sick in nearby villages, which often meant cycling long distances. He always wrote cheerfully, but reading between the lines, I knew that with such a busy schedule he would have little time for painting. My heart ached as I glanced across at the picture of the ducks he had given me. I had chosen this particular painting because it reminded me of the day the Major and I had come across him on the bridge, watching the ducks in the stream.

Just then the door opened and Joan came in. She walked with not a trace of a limp and it was difficult to remember that she had ever been on crutches. There was a new soft look about her face and her eyes glowed. Looking at her I thought how different she was from the miserable, lack-lustre girl I had met when I first came to Laverton House.

Seeing the envelope in my hand her eyes widened. "Have you had a letter?"

"Yes, from Harold in Penang."

"Oh, I thought it might have been from the handsome Larry."

I felt vaguely annoyed and said rather sharply, "Since the Major left I have only heard once from Larry, so I doubt whether I'll ever see him again."

Oddly enough, the following week I had a letter from him. He wrote amusingly about nothing in particular and it wasn't until the last few lines that he came to his real reason for writing. He would like me to spend a day with him in London. He said that he would meet me at Waterloo station, and then, after we had done a bit of sightseeing, we would go to a special exhibition of paintings at the National Gallery.

It all sounded very exciting and I immediately went down to the lobby to study the duty roster which was posted there for the month of March. I saw that I was free on Thursday and Friday of the following week, and so I decided to write immediately to Larry.

His answer came back promptly. Thursday was perfect for him and he would meet my train, which left Salisbury at 8am and arrived at Waterloo station at 11.30. To give myself plenty of time I ordered a taxi to pick me up at 7am.

I thought very carefully about the clothes I would wear that day and finally chose a dark maroon suit because I had heard that London was a grimy place and even white underclothes became grey after one day's wearing.

On Thursday morning everything went according to plan. The taxi arrived punctually and after a short drive to the station I had time to pick up a paper and buy myself a bun and a cup of tea at the station café.

As I waited on the platform I was filled with excitement. *I, Rhoda Pritchard, was going to London, one of the greatest cities in the world.* The thought was overwhelming. *But just suppose something happened so that Lawrence was not there to meet me? What would I do and where would I go?* I seemed to hear Aunty Edith saying with asperity, "You have a tongue in your head don't you?" Then I remembered the text that hung on the wall in the kitchen at home, "I will never leave thee nor forsake thee," and there, on that windy platform as the train drew in with a hiss of steam, my fears fell away.

I found an empty compartment and watched, through the misted window, the familiar landscape of Salisbury slip away. Then I opened the paper and was soon immersed in the front page story of the theft of a famous painting from a London gallery. So far Scotland Yard had been unable to trace it. The thief must have had access to the gallery because there was no sign of a break-in. The painting had been cut out of the frame which meant it could be carried very easily out of the gallery without being noticed. It was part of a special collection and for the time being, that section of the gallery was to be closed to the public.

I folded the paper and sat back in my seat thinking. This was like an Agatha Christie mystery, although there was no suggestion of a murder. I let my imagination play with the elements of the story and after some time fell into a doze. I woke with a jolt when the door to the compartment was pushed open. A man entered and sat down in the corner farthest from me. He put his briefcase on the seat beside him and I noticed that, threaded through the handle, was a long tubular shaped package. The man's hat was pulled well over his eyes and so only the lower part of his face was visible. My paper was lying next to me with the front page story open to view. The man glanced at it, then sank further back into his seat.

By now I was fully awake and sat tensely gazing out of the window, although now and again I couldn't resist glancing across at the man who appeared to be asleep, though I was sure he was watching me. It was unnerving and I wished I could find some reason to leave the compartment, although if I did it could look as though I were suspicious of him; so I stayed where I was.

At last the train entered the outskirts of London. Names flashed past: Wimbledon, Earls Court and finally Waterloo.

When the train stopped the man stood up and opened the door to the compartment, courteously standing aside for me. He smiled and I saw that his teeth were very stained. He was emaciated and there were bright spots on his cheeks. I registered all this subconsciously. It was obvious to me that the man was seriously ill and could have pneumonia. A draught of cold air came through the open door and he began to cough, great racking coughs that shook his slight frame. The briefcase jerked in his hand and the long cardboard tube fell on to the floor with the edge of a painting protruding from one end of it. That confirmed my suspicions; he was indeed the art thief, but as he continued to cough I lost all fear of him and laid my hand on his arm.

"You're not well," I said. "You should be in hospital."

"What makes you say that? Are you a nurse?"

"Yes, I've worked in a fever ward and nursed patients like you. It looks to me as though you have advanced pneumonia. You need medical treatment urgently."

I noticed then that the sleeves of his jacket were frayed and his trousers worn and baggy, yet his voice sounded educated.

"And who's going to look after my wife and child while I'm in hospital? I've been out of regular work for months and the casual work I pick up barely feeds us. That's why I stole the painting." He pointed at the cardboard tube lying at his feet. "You guessed, didn't you? I saw you watching me and you had that newspaper beside you. Well, go ahead and report me to the police, but if you do you'll be depriving my wife and child of a way out of poverty."

I thought carefully before replying. "I won't report you, but I think you should hand the painting over to the police and hope that they will take the case no further. You'll never get away with it anyway; all of Scotland Yard is looking for that painting. I'm sure if you explained why you took it and that you are desperately ill, they'd be lenient and they might even help you and your family."

My eyes were brimming with tears. I felt overwhelming pity for this poor wreck of a man standing before me and wished I could do something for him. A sudden thought came to me. "Look, I'm meeting someone at Waterloo Station. He's a businessman in the city and will know what to do, I'm sure. I think you could trust his advice, that's if you're willing to try. Would you mind telling me your name? Mine is Rhoda Pritchard." I laid my hand on his arm feeling the frail bones under the sleeve.

He hesitated then lifted his head, looking me full in the eye.

"My name is Richard Naylor, and yes, Miss Pritchard, I'll do as you say. There's something about you that makes me trust you."

"Good, then let us go now, shall we?"

When we left the train he came with me trustingly, like a child, and as we walked side by side along the platform nobody took any notice of us. I scanned the people coming towards us. *What would I do if Lawrence did not appear*? Just at that moment I caught sight of him, a worried frown creasing his handsome features. For a split second he looked at me without recognition, then smiled, relief lighting up his face.

"Rhoda, I was just beginning to think you were not on this train and what I would do if you weren't, and here you are, after all."

Then he noticed the man beside me and raised his eyebrows.

"I didn't know you were going to have a companion for the journey."

"This is Richard Naylor," I explained. "He shared my compartment, Lawrence. He is very sick and I think he should go to hospital, but first we have to report to Scotland Yard, that he has the missing painting and is prepared to return it."

Lawrence said quickly, "Right, we'll pick up a taxi outside the station. Follow me," and he strode towards the exit. I tucked my arm into Richard's, half afraid that he might bolt, but he went with me docilely enough and together we hurried to keep up with Lawrence.

Outside the station a row of taxi cabs was waiting and after a brief word with the driver of the first Lawrence signalled to me to get into the back. He waited for Richard to get in next and then climbed in after him. Nothing was said on the short journey to Scotland Yard and I stared fascinated at the famous landmarks we were passing: the Houses of Parliament, Westminster Abbey and Big Ben. It was hard to realise I was in the heart of London, the legendary city that went back hundreds of years. I looked up at the face of Big Ben and saw that there were only ten minutes to go until twelve o'clock. Then I noticed that the taxi was slowing down.

"Here we are," announced Lawrence. "This is Scotland Yard."

While he was paying the driver I gazed up at the Victorian building so famed in literature, when suddenly the man beside me began to cough, great hacking coughs that seemed to tear him in two. I put my arm around his shoulders until the spasm had passed, while Lawrence waited.

"The quicker we can get through all this the better. This man is seriously ill," I said urgently.

"So I see," replied Lawrence. He pushed open the heavy door in front of us and I followed him into the entrance hall, Richard stumbling at my side. Lawrence went to the desk and spoke briefly to the young constable on duty who picked up a phone and talked rapidly into it. Almost instantly a police officer appeared at the desk.

"Please accompany me," he said briefly and led us along a panelled corridor. Then he pushed open a door and ushered us into a large bare room where another officer who was obviously of senior rank was seated behind a desk. A row of chairs was ranged in front of it.

"I'm Inspector Barnes. Please be seated," and he waved towards the chairs. We sat down, but the sergeant who had conducted us there remained standing.

"Now before we begin, would you please give me your full names and addresses?" he said, turning first to Lawrence. After he had taken down each of our details he leaned forward and gave his full attention to Richard.

"Now Mr. Naylor, I understand that you wish to return the painting that you took from a private gallery in London yesterday. Is that correct?"

"Yes, sir," said Richard quietly.

"Would you please give me a full account of the robbery, beginning from the time you entered the gallery until you left it." His voice was warm and even friendly. *He would have made a good psychiatrist* I thought, watching him.

Richard calmly described step by step his theft of the painting.

He had waited until the gallery was empty of people, just before closing time and then had quickly cut the canvas out of its frame using a razor blade. Immediately afterwards he had wrapped the blade in a handkerchief and dropped it into the nearest rubbish basket. Then he had rolled up the painting, tucked it under his mackintosh and left the gallery unobserved.

After that he took a train home to Basingstoke. Listening to him I thought it all sounded amazingly simple.

The inspector showed no reaction but merely asked, "What did you do the next day?"

"I put the painting into a cardboard tube and took it with me to the station at Basingstoke. Then I caught the 9.30 train to London. I intended to take the painting to an art dealer I know who would have paid me a good price for it. I looked for an empty compartment but couldn't find one. When at last I came on a compartment with only one young woman in it I decided to take my chance. Then when I was sitting down I noticed she had a newspaper on the seat beside her and on the front page was the story of the robbery. I saw her looking at the cardboard tube and I knew she guessed I was the thief. As soon as we got to Waterloo I intended to make a dash from the compartment but I had a fit of coughing. She was very concerned and said she was a nurse and that I should be in hospital. Then I broke down and confessed that I had stolen the painting. She said I should turn myself in and return the painting, so here I am."

The Inspector looked thoughtful and turning to me said, "Do you corroborate this story?"

"Yes, Sir, but I would like to add that this man is seriously ill and should be admitted to a hospital straight away. Just before we came into the building he had a severe coughing fit and he's obviously feverish." I glanced across at Richard who was unnaturally flushed.

The inspector nodded to me. "I will order an ambulance as soon as this interview is over."

Then turning to Richard he said, "I regret I have to charge you with theft, but in view of the fact that you have returned the painting I am sure the court will take a lenient view of your case."

"I just have one thing to add, Sir," said Richard. "I committed this robbery for the sake of my wife and child. I have been out of work for weeks and there is no money to pay the rent. The landlord is turning us out next week."

A look of sympathy crossed the inspector's face. "It is a pity you didn't apply to one of the charities that help out families in need. Theft is never the answer. However, we will do all we can to assist your wife and child and in the meantime we will get you into hospital."

Richard looked up at him, his eyes brimming. "Thank you, Sir, I don't care what happens to me, so long as my family are taken care of," and his voice broke.

The inspector cleared his throat. "I promise you everything possible will be done for them and I will arrange for a police officer visit your wife today."

"Excuse me, Sir, would it be possible for me to accompany the police officer, so that I can speak to Mrs. Naylor personally?" I asked.

The inspector looked thoughtful. "I see no reason why not, Miss Pritchard. As a psychiatric nurse you would be ideally suited to deal with a situation like this. I will make arrangements for you to accompany the officer."

Richard turned to me and placed his hand on mine. "You don't know how much this means to me, Miss Pritchard. I know you will have just the right words to say to Molly. Tell her that I did it all for her sake, but I realise now it was a mistake to look for an easy way out of our troubles. Tell her too, that I am determined to get better and come home to take care of her and little Amy."

Looking at the sick man's face I felt great pity for him. I smiled and patted his hand reassuringly. "I promise I will give her all the comfort I can."

The inspector coughed and it was clear the interview was at an end.

"Goodbye, Richard," I said quietly and stood up. "Don't worry; I know with God's help everything will work out for the best."

He smiled and there was hope in his eyes. "Thank you, I believe it will."

Lawrence and I followed the sergeant back the way we had come. At the reception desk he asked us to wait and then left us.

When we were alone Lawrence turned to me."Well, it seems this is the end of our planned outing in London. Are you prone to these adventures, Rhoda? Perhaps next time we agree to spend a day together I should come and fetch you. Train journeys are obviously too hazardous."

"I'm sorry, Lawrence, but you understand I couldn't turn my back on that poor man and his family."

"I understand—and I also realise that behind that lovely face of yours is a kind heart. It is selfish of me not to want to share you, but I can't help feeling sorry that this happened today of all days. Perhaps next time I will have you all to myself." Behind his light words I sensed his regret.

"I am sorry not to be spending the day with you after all, Larry, and I hope there will be another occasion," I said quietly.

Just then the sergeant reappeared. "If you are ready, Miss Pritchard, would you accompany me please?"

"Time to go, Rhoda," said Larry. "Take care of yourself and I will be in touch with you very soon."

He turned away from me and I felt a pang as I watched him walk towards the door. The sergeant said gently to me, "If you are ready, Miss, we should be on our way." I squared my shoulders and followed him, telling myself I was doing the right thing and there were bound to be other occasions to meet Lawrence in London, but all the same I couldn't help wishing that things had turned out differently today.

CHAPTER SIXTEEN

That night it was a long time before I was able to sleep; the events of the day kept running through my mind. Most vivid of all was the visit to Mrs. Naylor. The poor woman's face had gone deathly white when she saw a policeman standing on her doorstep.

"It's Richard, isn't it?" she said faintly and swayed. I leaned forward and took her arm to steady her.

The sergeant said quickly, "It's alright, Mrs. Naylor. Your husband is being taken care of in hospital. I'm Sergeant White and this is Miss Pritchard. We've come to talk to you about your husband. Would you mind if we came in?"

The woman nodded and led us along a narrow passageway into a mean little sitting room where the floor was covered with faded linoleum. In the centre was a threadbare rug with several hard-backed chairs surrounding it. Although the room was clean it looked cold and cheerless. Mrs. Naylor gestured towards the chairs.

"Do sit down. I'm afraid they're not very comfortable," she said apologetically.

I noticed that she was still very pale.

"You look a little faint. Would you like a cup of tea? I would be happy to make it, if you don't mind me using your kitchen," I said hesitantly.

"That's very kind. I would do it myself, but I feel a bit unsteady. The kitchen is at the end of the passage. You'll find everything to hand."

I got up immediately and went to the kitchen. Like the sitting room, it was spotlessly clean, but bare. At least there was some warmth coming from the stove where a kettle was boiling on the hob. A teapot and cannister of tea were on the bench beside it.

Milk and sugar were in a pantry, but very little else. I quickly made the tea and put everything on a tray. When I returned to the sitting room Mrs. Naylor was leaning back in her chair, her eyes closed and the sergeant was busy writing in a notebook. As I entered they both looked up and smiled.

"You weren't long!" exclaimed Mrs. Naylor.

"No, everything was so well organised in your kitchen, I found all I needed. Milk and sugar?"

"Yes please."

"And you, Sir?"

"The same, thank you."

The bustle of pouring out the tea and passing it round seemed to restore a sense of normality to this rather unreal situation and I was pleased to see colour returning to Mrs. Naylor's cheeks. After she had taken a few sips of her tea she looked at me curiously.

"You said you were nothing to do with the police, so how is it you know about my husband?"

"Well, I happened to be in the same compartment as Mr. Naylor when he got on the train at Basingstoke. I had just been reading the report in the paper about the theft of the painting and when I saw the cardboard tube your husband was carrying I put two and two together."

"So you reported him?"

"No, he began coughing and as a nurse I knew instantly that he was seriously ill and probably had pneumonia and I told him he should be in hospital. That's when he confessed that he had stolen the painting. I advised him to turn himself in, because he had no chance of getting away with the theft. It so happened that I was meeting a friend at Waterloo Station and he organised a taxi to take us all to Scotland Yard. After your husband had been interviewed the inspector called for an ambulance to take him to hospital and that is where he is now. Oh, and Richard said to tell you he intends to get better and come home to look after you and little Amy."

The woman's face softened. "Dear Richard, that sounds just like him."

"He also said he regrets trying to find an easy way out of his financial difficulties."

The woman put her head in her hands. "Oh, if you only knew how I pleaded and pleaded with him not to steal the painting, but he said it was the only way."

I laid my hand gently on the woman's shoulder; it felt thin and bony under her cardigan.

"There is another way, you know. There are charities that are very willing to help people like you who are having a struggle financially, especially when the husband is out of work."

"I tried to tell Richard that, but he wouldn't listen."

"Well, now he sees things differently and I'm sure the sergeant here will tell you what can be done," and I nodded towards the officer.

He cleared his throat. "I have a list of charities in this area and I will be arranging with them to visit you, Mrs. Naylor. In the meantime, if you will let me have the name of your landlord I will contact him so that you will not be forced out of your home."

"Oh, thank God for that," and the woman's voice cracked with relief.

"Now we must be on our way," said the sergeant.

As I stood up, Mrs. Naylor took both my hands and clasped them between her own.

"Thank you so much, Miss Pritchard, for all you've done. You don't know how much it means to me to know Richard is being looked after and that we won't lose our home."

Soon afterwards I left the house with the sergeant. As we got into the police car I looked back at the house, which was just one of many in the Victorian brick terrace, and I wondered how many similar tales of hardship were to be found behind those doors.

The next morning I woke feeling unrested and often during the day I had lapses of concentration. I felt relieved when the time came to go off duty. As soon as I was in the bedroom I threw myself into an easy chair.I felt the need to put my thoughts into some kind of order. First, there was Lawrence. My initial impression of him was as a suave and sophisticated young man who liked driving fast cars, yet yesterday he had shown himself to be compassionate and down to earth. How capably he had taken charge of the whole situation when he met me, accompanied by a strange man at the station. Even though it meant giving up his plans for the day, he had immediately assumed responsibility for Richard and the return of the painting. It was only when he was saying goodbye to me that he gave any hint of what it had cost him. I knew I could no longer dismiss him lightly from my thinking as I once had; he deserved better than that.

All of this was going through my mind when there was a light tap at the door and Maisie's blonde head appeared around it.

"Are you busy?"

"Not really, just thinking."

"What on earth about?"

"Yesterday and everything that happened."

"Don't tell me you met a handsome stranger and went off with him when you were supposed to be spending the day with Lawrence?"

"Well, I met a stranger anyway," and I told her about meeting Richard on the train. Maisie listened wide-eyed.

"Gosh, it sounds like something out of a detective novel. Lawrence sounds very capable and kind."

"He is."

"What a shame you didn't get the chance to spend the day with him. Do you think he'll ask you again?"

"I hope so," I said slowly, surprised at my own response. Once I wouldn't have cared whether or not I saw Lawrence again, but since yesterday everything had changed.

CHAPTER SEVENTEEN

A couple of months went by. It was now May and as the spring flowers appeared and the trees burst into fresh green leaf I began to feel restless. I had heard nothing from Lawrence since that fateful trip to London and I had almost made up my mind that I would not hear from him again. Then one day a letter arrived.

Dear Rhoda,

I expect you had given me up by now, but I have been out of the country on business for a month. Anyway, please forgive my lack of communication. I would very much like to see you again. How would you like to spend a weekend at my father's house in Godalming? I have spoken to him and he said he would be delighted to entertain you. I would come down to Salisbury by car and stay a night at the Red Lion then drive us both to Surrey. Do let me know if this is feasible and fits in with your off duty times, then I can go ahead and make arrangements.

Love Larry

I was just reading it for the second time when Joan came into the room.

"Is that another letter from Harold?"

"Well, no, it's from Lawrence."

"The Major's handsome son. You know what they say, 'Better a bird in the hand than two in the bush' and Harold is a long way away and you don't know when he'll come back. Larry is here and available so don't eat your heart out over Harold."

I laughed. This sounded like common sense, yet I could not stop my heart turning over at the mention of Harold.

There was something about Joan's voice, a kind of suppressed excitement and I looked curiously at her.

"What's up with you, Joan? You look different somehow."

She laid her finger to her lips and glanced around conspiratorially.

"Promise you won't say anything to anyone."

"Of course not, but what is the big secret?"

"Jim and I are going to get married."

"But you have only known him a short time."

"No, I haven't; it's at least eighteen months. Anyway, is that all you can say? Aren't you going to congratulate me?"

"Well, yes, but what about your parents? Have you told them?"

"Not yet, but they will be happy for me, I know."

"How will Dr. Hall take it? You've managed so far to keep your friendship with Jim a secret, but once he knows about your engagement it might be a different story. I'm just afraid for Jim."

Joan looked thoughtful. "I've thought about that too, so that is why Jim and I will keep it quiet. You are the only one to know."

I stood up and gave her a hug.

"Sorry to be a wet blanket, Joan. I really am happy for you. Jim is a good man, but at the moment, if you don't mind me saying, he is not earning enough to support a wife."

Joan's face fell. "I know you're right, Rhoda, but if we both save hard we could marry in a couple of years' time."

I said nothing. I had heard about the difficulties of long engagements and the strain they put on couples, but I didn't want to sound negative when Joan was obviously so happy.

Later that evening I sat down and wrote to Lawrence, thanking him for his invitation. As it happened, I was due for a weekend's leave at the end of May, which meant I could finish my duty on Friday afternoon and be free until Monday afternoon.

Lawrence's reply came back promptly. He would stay overnight at the Red Lion on Thursday and fetch me at four thirty on Friday afternoon.

I packed carefully. As the weather was still cool I would need some warm clothes, but there might also be a trip to the theatre or an evening out somewhere, so I included my smartest outfit, a red jersey dress. Joan insisted on vetting each item and after much discussion she gave her approval of my clothes.

"Now that dress is very soignée but it does need something to lift it, so I am going to lend you my marcasite necklace, Rhoda."

"Oh, no, Joan, suppose something happened to it. I know it's special because your parents gave it to you on your seventeenth birthday, didn't they?"

"Yes, but I still want you to wear it, Rhoda. You're the next best thing to a sister to me and sisters borrow each other's things, don't they?"

I hugged her and felt a lump in my throat. "All right, if you insist, and I promise I will take great care of it."

When Friday came I was quite nervous at the thought of seeing Lawrence again. I waited in the lobby for him and he arrived promptly at four thirty. As he came striding through the open door I was struck once again by his film-star looks; the dark wavy hair swept back from his forehead, the square jaw line and deep blue eyes. He was wearing a well-cut jacket that was obviously expensive and looked the last word in sophistication. I wondered fleetingly what he saw in me, a simple girl from New Zealand. Perhaps it was just that I was different from the girls he usually took out.

His eyes swept over me appreciatively and I was glad I had taken Joan's advice and worn my new tweed costume. It was smart, yet casual and suited me well.

Lawrence picked up my suitcase and together we walked to the car. As he opened the passenger door I couldn't resist glancing back at the house where I knew we were being watched by several pairs of eyes, amongst them Maisie's, who had said mischievously she would be spying on us from the dining room window.

Lawrence drove carefully down the drive, but once we were through the gates he put the car into a higher gear and I could feel the engine surge forward. Soon we were on the open road and the car picked up speed. Lawrence did not try to make conversation but concentrated on his driving, so I settled back to enjoy being driven in comfort through ever-changing countryside. After a while I began to feel drowsy and must have fallen asleep because I was jolted awake when Lawrence stopped outside an inn.

"Wake up, sleeping beauty. It's time for a break."

I rubbed my eyes. "How long have we been on the road?"

"At least two hours. We're about half way."

As we went in I noticed how smartly the little waitress stepped forward to take our order and couldn't seem to keep her eyes off Lawrence.

We didn't linger over the meal but were soon on our way again. By now it was dark and Lawrence drove carefully, keeping his speed down within the range of the headlights. This second half of the journey seemed much longer than the first, but finally we turned off the main road and entered a winding road lined with tall trees where the houses were set well back.

"Welcome to Surrey," said Lawrence. "It isn't far to Godalming now."

Some miles further on he slowed down and turned into a wide drive. The headlights picked up the front of the house which was red brick and half covered with ivy. A light in the porch over the door gave it a warm and welcoming look.

"Here we are, home at last. Welcome to Rest-a-While," said Lawrence lightly.

"Oh, what a lovely name!"

"And I trust it lives up to it." Lawrence stretched and yawned. "I certainly could do with a good rest. How do you feel, Rhoda?"

"Oh, fine, but as you know, I slept half the way."

"Now come on, Miss Pritchard, Dad will be impatient to see you," and Lawrence opened the car door for me.

We climbed a short flight of steps to the porch which was flanked by stone pillars. On each side of the door were tubs of flowers which gave a homely touch to the rather imposing entrance.

Lawrence rapped on the door and almost instantly it was opened by a comfortable looking woman with grey hair drawn back from a smooth round face. As soon as she saw Lawrence she smiled with pleasure.

"Mr. Lawrence, how good to see you! You've had a long drive haven't you? You must be tired."

The Major appeared behind her.

"Now don't stand on the doorstep but come right on in," he said. "Is that Rhoda I see in the shadows? Welcome my dear," and reaching forward he took my hand between his own. "I expect you will want to freshen up after your journey, so Gladys, please take Miss Pritchard to her room."

"I'll bring your suitcase," said Lawrence promptly.

I walked behind Gladys up the wide staircase while Lawrence followed. I noticed that even though it was night the house gave an impression of spaciousness and light. When we reached the landing I happened to glance up at the wall and my heart missed a beat, for there in front of us was Harold's painting of the eagle. Lawrence made some remark about the house but I didn't take it in.

"So what do you think of that, Rhoda?" he asked and I mumbled mechanically, "Very interesting."

Gladys opened a door off the landing and stood to one side while Lawrence waved me forward into a room which was reminiscent of the one I shared with Joan, except that this room was far more luxurious. Everything was white and gold, from the bedspread to the dressing table.

"Oh, what a lovely room!" I exclaimed.

"It was my mother's. At the end, when she was an invalid and could no longer share with my father she lived in here. She furnished the room herself in her favourite colours, white and gold. It's a very feminine room, don't you think?"

"Yes, and it has a happy feel to it."

"I think people leave something of themselves in a room," said Lawrence thoughtfully, "and I always feel close to my mother when I come in here." Then he became practical. "Now as soon as you've freshened up, come downstairs and we'll have supper. I'm sure Gladys has prepared a special one for us," he added, turning round and smiling at her.

"Your favourite, Mr. Lawrence."

"That means roast beef and Yorkshire pud, followed by apple pie."

"You've hit the nail on the head," said Gladys.

After they had gone I wandered around the room, stopping to examine the dressing table set which was crystal, edged with gold. In the corner was a washstand where a fluffy white towel and matching flannel hung from the railing. I noticed there was a monogram in the corner of each, and as I ran hot water into the basin I wondered what the initials stood for. I would ask Lawrence.

After I had combed my hair and dabbed some powder on my nose I studied my reflection critically. I did not look too weary and the cream jumper I had worn under my costume coat still looked crisp and fresh.

I went downstairs then and found the sitting room without difficulty because I could hear Lawrence's voice quite clearly through the open door. Before going in I hesitated, feeling suddenly shy, but this went as soon as I entered the room. Lawrence came forward and touched me lightly on the arm.

"I was just telling Dad about our little snack en route and assuring him it wouldn't spoil our appetite for supper. Gladys said to go through to the dining room as soon as you came down."

He took my arm, nodded to his father and together the three of us left the room. The dining room was across the passage and I noticed the table had been set for four. Lawrence pulled out a chair for me then took the place opposite, while his father seated himself at the head of the table.

Just then Gladys walked in, carrying a dish on which was a succulent joint of beef. She placed it in front of the Major who began to carve it into thin slices.

Once we had all been served and helped ourselves to vegetables the Major said a short grace. There was little conversation while we were eating. I looked curiously at Gladys who sat opposite the Major. She seemed quite one of the family, although she was the housekeeper. What was her relationship with the Major, I wondered and then gave up the puzzle and concentrated on the excellent meal in front of me.

When we had been through all the courses, the Major turned to Lawrence.

"What have you got planned for tomorrow, Son?"

"I'm leaving that as a surprise, Dad, and taking Rhoda on a mystery tour."

"That sounds exciting, Larry. Are you going to blindfold me as well?" I enquired, raising my eyebrows.

"Not this time, but I guarantee you will be surprised and happy at the end of it." He glanced at his watch. "Ten o'clock already and as we need to set off early tomorrow we'd better get to bed soon. Thanks for a magnificent meal, Gladys. I hope you've got help with the dishes."

"Yes, my niece Mary is in the kitchen right now," said Gladys glancing at the door.

Everyone stood up then and I said goodnight to the Major and Lawrence who were still finishing their cigarettes.

Back in my room I was glad to get into bed where a hot water bottle had been thoughtfully placed between the scented sheets, and after a few minutes I was sound asleep.

CHAPTER EIGHTEEN

Next morning there was a light tap at the door and Gladys came in with a cup of tea on a tray.

"I hope I didn't startle you, but Mr. Lawrence asked me to see whether you were awake and to ask you to come down to breakfast as soon as you are ready."

"Goodness, eight o'clock already!" I said, glancing at my watch. "I've slept so soundly and I would probably have gone on slumbering if you hadn't come in. Thank you, Gladys."

I gulped down the tea, which was only lukewarm, and then concentrated on getting ready for the day. A quick glance through the window showed me that there was a fine misty rain so it might be a bit chilly. I would wear my jersey with the woollen skirt. Just before leaving the room I checked my appearance in the full length mirror on the inside of the wardrobe door. As my Aunt would say I looked sensibly dressed for the weather.

Downstairs I found Lawrence in the dining room sitting in an easy chair with the paper on his knee. He sprang up as soon as I came in.

"Good morning, Rhoda, you look fresh as a daisy," he said, his eyes sweeping over me appreciatively. "Breakfast is all set up in the dining room," and lightly touching my elbow he led me across the hall.

On the sideboard was an array of dishes. "Help yourself to cereal or porridge. Dad hasn't come down yet but I thought we wouldn't wait for him. Don't hurry though, Rhoda, we've got plenty of time."

When we were both seated I thought what a cosy domestic scene this made, just the two of us having breakfast together. Is this what it would be like to be married to Lawrence? I noticed how impeccably smart he was even at this time of the morning, with his clean-shaven face and wavy hair brushed back smoothly from his brow.

Neither of us lingered over breakfast and shortly after nine we were ready to leave the house. I was wearing my gabardine raincoat and matching hat. Lawrence looked at me with approval.

"I can see you are ready for all weathers, and very smart too, Miss Pritchard."

As he held the passenger door open for me he touched my shoulder lightly and I was conscious of the intimate gesture. Carefully he guided the car down the drive and into the road. I looked with interest at the houses we passed, many of them large and set well back from the road. Clearly this was an affluent neighbourhood.

"This is what is generally known as the stockbroker belt," said Lawrence with a laugh, "although that does not apply to us. All Dad's family have been army men and I am just waiting for the next war to go into the air force."

"Surely you don't think there will be another war, not after the last one," I exclaimed.

"Inevitable, I think. You ask Dad. He has inside information because he works for the government. Of course, it's all hush hush because nobody wants to face it. Churchill is called a warmonger by the pacifists, but he can see the writing on the wall. Hitler and his lot are getting quite a foothold in Germany and his message appeals to the masses."

I said nothing. Lawrence spoke with such confidence and who was I to argue with him? All the same, I couldn't believe our government would let it all happen again.

"In the next show there'll be a lot more fighting in the air," he continued. "I'll wager the Huns are already making their planes under cover. Anyway, I've heard rumours that our government intends expanding the RAF later on this year. "

"Because they are getting ready for war? It doesn't bear thinking about," I said, shuddering.

"All right, let's talk about something else. Tell me about your life on the wards."

I was glad to change the subject and launched into a description of some of our more colourful patients.

By now we were on the outskirts of a large town. "This is our destination," said Lawrence as we entered the city streets. "The ancient town of Guildford."

"But why have we come here?"

"Just you wait and see, Miss Pritchard," and Lawrence threaded his way through the narrow streets until we came to the centre of the town. He stopped outside an ancient building with exposed black beams and small lattice windows. Above the low door was painted in bold lettering, Grantly Gallery.

"That's your name!" I exclaimed.

"Yes, because it's my gallery. But I have another surprise in store for you, my girl. Just you wait until we are inside."

He parked the car and the two of us walked through the low door into the gallery, Lawrence ducking his head. We stepped into a large room which looked as if it had originally been two separate rooms now knocked into one. Paintings were well spaced on the white-washed walls to show them off to advantage. I gazed around me.

"Why, most of these are Harold's!" I exclaimed.

"Yes, he gave us permission to exhibit them and sell as many as we could. We've already sold quite a few."

I was so absorbed I didn't notice the man who came quietly and stood beside me. Thinking it was Lawrence I turned to make a comment and found myself looking into Richard's face. My mouth fell open.

He laughed at my astonishment. "Hello, Miss Pritchard. You didn't expect to find me here, did you?"

"No, I thought you were in hospital."

"I was, for quite some time, and then the doctors tried out a new treatment on me and it worked."

"How wonderful! You look so well, Richard. But how do you come to be here?"

It's all through Mr. Grantly. He visited me in hospital a few times and told me about the art gallery he was buying. When I was ready to be discharged he asked me to come and manage it for him. You see, I had been in charge of a private gallery in Basingstoke but I made a foolish blunder and they sacked me. That was when I had the idea of stealing one of their paintings. It was a foolish thing to do and I regret it." He paused and looked steadily into my eyes. "If it hadn't been for you, Miss Pritchard, I would probably be in prison now—or dead."

My brain was whirling.

"But what about your wife and baby? Where are they?"

"I'll take you up to see them soon. They are in the flat upstairs. We are living above the shop, as it were—all thanks to Mr. Grantly."

I turned to look at Lawrence who was beaming down at me.

"I can hardly take this in," I said faintly.

"In that case I think we should all go upstairs for a cup of tea," said Richard promptly.

"Good idea," said Lawrence touching my arm.

Feeling as if this were some kind of a dream I followed Richard and Lawrence up a narrow winding staircase which was barred at the entrance to the landing by a low gate.

"To keep the baby from falling down the stairs," explained Richard unlatching it.

Mrs. Naylor appeared before us, a toddler holding on to her skirts. I stared at her.

Could this smartly dressed woman be the same one I had visited some months ago?

She smiled at me warmly. "You look as if you've seen a ghost, Miss Pritchard."

"I suppose you could say that. I have certainly had a few shocks this morning. First of all, finding that Lawrence owned an art gallery and then meeting Richard here. It has been a morning of surprises."

"Do you know, Miss Pritchard, the day you came to our house with the police sergeant I was at my lowest point? If it hadn't been for the baby I was tempted to take my life. Then after your visit our luck changed. First, the landlord called and said our rent was paid for the next month. Then after him a lady arrived from the Salvation Army with a bag of groceries for us and clothes for the baby. She said she would come each week and see that we were supplied with all that we needed. Then when I visited Richard in hospital I was told they were trying out a new drug on him and were hopeful that he would soon be completely well."

Richard cut in. "And best of all, was when Mr. Grantly invited me to take up the position of manager in his new art gallery after I was discharged from hospital."

"I think that must have spurred Richard on because even the doctors were surprised at his quick recovery," added his wife.

A short time later when we were sitting drinking tea in the cosy little sitting room, with its floral curtains and carpeted floor, I marvelled at the difference between this and the cheerless flat the Naylors had once lived in. And all of it had been accomplished through Lawrence's kindness. I glanced across at him and found his eyes on me. What was he thinking? One thing was certain; my view of him was changing by the minute.

CHAPTER NINETEEN

By the end of the weekend I felt so much at home with Lawrence and his father it was a wrench to leave them. Lawrence offered to drive me back to Salisbury, but I absolutely refused.

"I can take the train from Guildford and be back in Salisbury in a few hours," I said firmly. "It's kind of you to offer, Larry, but quite unnecessary."

"Well, so long as you promise not to get involved with any more criminals I will agree to your going by train," said Lawrence teasingly.

He and the Major saw me off from the station and as the train pulled away from the platform I watched them until they were only small figures in the distance.

I sank back into my seat in the empty compartment and closing my eyes, reviewed the whole of the weekend. It had been a happy and relaxed time and Lawrence had gone out of his way to amuse and entertain me. On Saturday afternoon he had driven us all, including Richard and his family, into the Surrey countryside and treated us to a meal in a country inn. There had been a lot of laughter as we watched the baby feeding the ducks. She had nearly toppled into a stream but was rescued just in time. During the afternoon when the men went for a walk I had a chance to talk to Mrs. Naylor.

"Please call me Molly," she said after a while. "It sounds much friendlier and I do so want us to be friends. I will never forget how you helped me that awful day, when I felt desperate enough to take my own life. If it hadn't been for the baby I think I would have put my head in the oven."

"It's strange," I said slowly, "but often when things are at their worst that is the very time when God intervenes."

Molly stopped. "Do you know, I have never really thought much about God but after that day my ideas changed. I am sure you were sent to us and look how everything worked out. Mr. Grantly gave Richard a job and provided us with a home. By the way, Mr. Grantly seems very fond of you." She looked at me sideways. "He is a thoroughly good man," she added.

"I agree," I said and quickly changed the subject.

Sitting in the train I turned over this conversation in my mind. It was true; Lawrence was kind, thoughtful and generous, as well as being good-looking and fun to be with. Why was it I held myself back from him? The reason was Harold of course, yet he was far away and likely to be overseas indefinitely. In the meantime, here was Lawrence, obviously keen on me. Perhaps the time had come to put Harold out of my mind, yet he had seemed so right for me, with his New Zealand background and his strong Christian faith.

I sighed. Perhaps I had been mistaken about him all along. My mind shifted to Sunday morning when I had accompanied the Major and Lawrence to the local Church of England where they were members. Lawrence had read the lesson and as I listened to his perfect rendition of the Old Testament passage I was struck by his obvious sincerity.

At lunchtime we discussed the sermon and it was clear that Lawrence had a sound grasp of Biblical truths. *Yes, Lawrence seemed right in so many ways, so why was I hesitating? It was surely time to make up my mind.* I came to a decision there and then. From now on I would no longer watch the post expectantly for Harold's letters, nor would I reply to them immediately. I would make my letters brief and friendly but nothing more.

Having reached this decision I began to feel cheerful and even light-hearted. I took a taxi from the station and as we drove through the city streets I caught a glimpse of the cathedral spire and my spirits lifted.

When at last the taxi turned into the drive of Laverton House I felt a sense of homecoming. It would be fun sharing with Joan and Maisie my adventures over the weekend. When I had paid the driver I walked with a light step into the lobby. I mounted the stairs, puffing slightly because of the weight of the suitcase, and pushed open the door to the bedroom.

The room appeared to be empty. Then I heard a sob and saw that Joan was huddled in the easy chair with her back to me. When she turned around her eyes were red and she was dabbing at them with a handkerchief.

"Joan, whatever is the matter?"

"It's Dr. Hall. He found out about Jim and me and there's been an awful row. He's threatening to sack Jim."

"That's dreadful, but surely he can't do that without a good reason," and I went across the room and put my arms around the distraught girl.

"Oh, you don't know him, he'll find a reason."

"How did he find out?"

"It was after we had been to the service at the gospel hall this morning. You know how I've been going with Jim. Well, afterwards we decided to have lunch at the White Hart. It's a bit expensive but it was Jim's birthday so we thought we'd splash out. Anyway, we were at one of the tables and in walked Dr. Hall and his wife. Jim and I were so busy talking we didn't notice them. Then at the end of the meal we got up and walked right past their table. Horace gave me a filthy look and I knew from that moment there would be trouble."

"So when did he threaten to dismiss Jim?"

"It was after I got back here. He waylaid me at the foot of the stairs and asked me to go to his office. He was quite polite then and I thought he would be reasonable, but when I told him I was serious about Jim he saw red. You've no idea the names he called me. Trollop was the least of them and that was when he threatened to sack Jim."

"Do you think he just said that in anger?"

"No, I'm sure he meant it."

I was thinking hard. "In that case we have to stop him."

"But how?" Joan said helplessly.

"Well, first of all we have to pray," I said firmly.

"Do you really think that will make any difference?"

"Yes I do. I've proved it in my own life." I closed my eyes and asked God very simply to look after Jim so that he would not lose his job and also that Dr. Hall would cease to be angry with Joan and leave her alone in future.

When I looked up I found Joan watching me and there was hope in her eyes.

"Now we have to wait and see what will happen," I said quietly.

"You mean, do nothing?"

"Yes."

"But surely there is something we can do?"

"I don't think so, not at the moment anyway."

Joan shrugged. "Well, if you say so. It's strange but I do feel a lot better since you prayed."

"Good, shall we go downstairs then and have some tea and I will tell you about my weekend?"

That night fire broke out in the west wing of the hospital where the male patients were quartered. The orderlies were separated from them by a corridor. Although patients were not allowed to smoke in their rooms, sometimes they were clever enough to evade the rules.

Later on Jim explained to Joan and me what had happened.

During the night he had woken up with the feeling that something was wrong. He got up and went into the corridor but nothing seemed amiss, so he was on the point of returning to his room when he caught a whiff of smoke. He walked to the end of the corridor to where the patients' quarters began and the smell grew stronger. By now he was sure that fire had started in one of the rooms, though it was impossible to tell which one. There was nothing for it but to raise the alarm so he pressed the fire warning button on the wall and immediately the alarm went off. Doors opened up and down the corridor and patients came out of their rooms. Quickly he shepherded them outside to stand in the places allocated during fire drills. Then he did a quick head count and found one of the patients was missing. By now smoke was filling the corridor, but he made his way through it until he came to a closed door. He tried the handle but it would not turn.

There was nothing for it, so he put his shoulder to the door and pushed with all his strength. It gave way and the door burst open to reveal a man lying unconscious just inside the door. Flames and smoke filled the room and it took all Jim's strength to lift the man and carry him back into the corridor, where he fought his way back through the smoke to the nearest side door. His lungs felt as if they were bursting and as soon as he was outside he took in great gulps of fresh air. He laid the unconscious man on the ground and began to apply artificial respiration until finally the man coughed and he began to breathe. By now others had gathered around and when it seemed the man was fully conscious they helped him to his feet.

Firemen were inside the building and it didn't take long for them to douse the flames which were confined to one room.

Outside on the drive Matron was soothing the women patients, some of whom were hysterical, and she called on the nurses to escort them back to their rooms. Dr. Branson and Dr. Hall gave curt directions to the attendants to take the male patients into the recreation hall where the maids were busy putting up stretchers and laying blankets on them. It was not long before the hall resembled a refugee camp. Once everyone was lying down a few male nurses remained, keeping watch around the hall.

Next morning all of the male patients were allowed to return to their rooms except for the man who had been in the burning room. He was in the sick bay being treated for burns.

Jim was summoned to Dr. Branson's office. Matron and Dr. Hall were there as well.

Dr. Branson came forward and shook his hand. "We want to thank you, Mr. Davis, for your courage yesterday, saving a man's life at the risk of your own. If it hadn't been for your prompt action other lives might have been lost, as well as the whole of the west wing going up in flames. You are a very brave young man and we want you to accept a token of our gratitude."

He handed Jim an envelope. Dr. Hall came forward then and also shook his hand.

Later when Jim was telling Joan and me about the interview, he paused dramatically at this point.

"And do you know what was in the envelope?"

"How can we, until you tell us," said Joan tartly.

"One hundred pounds in crisp bank notes."

We both gasped.

"That can go towards our wedding plans, Joanie."

Her eyes were shining with tears. "I can hardly believe it," she murmured.

That evening when we were alone in our room Joan said to me, "So God did answer your prayer, Rhoda."

"Yes, and instead of losing his job, Jim has it for life, I should think," I said laughing.

Neither of us said anymore just then but I did notice a change in Joan from that day. She seemed somehow softer and more thoughtful.

CHAPTER TWENTY

My annual holiday was in the second half of July. I had planned it carefully, one week at home with the family in Paulton and the second week in Devon with Helen, my friend from the secretarial college. She had replied enthusiastically to my letter and said she would love to go on holiday with me. "My father has a close friend, (actually he was Dad's best man) who has offered us the use of his flat at Sidmouth," she wrote. "It happens to be vacant for the week you suggested. Although I have never been to Sidmouth I hear it is an ideal place for a seaside holiday. Anyway, it won't cost us a bean to stay there."

I was not sure which I looked forward to more, my week in Paulton or the seaside holiday in Sidmouth. It was so long since I had been home that I longed to see the children and feel part of the family again. I even thought affectionately about Aunty Edith.

It was a thrill arriving at Paulton station on the first Saturday of my holiday and I looked eagerly through the grimy window at the people waiting on the platform. Surely the young girl in the stylish hat and coat could not be Hazel, but as she caught sight of me she waved frantically and I almost tumbled down the steps in my haste to reach her. We ran into one another's arms and hugged. Then Hazel took a step backwards and surveyed me critically.

"You look older, Rhoda. I think it's your hair. You didn't tell me you'd had it shingled but it really suits you."

"I'm glad you approve. And you've grown up too. You look really sophisticated and I love that hat."

Laughing we linked arms and set off up the hill from the station. On the way I plied Hazel with questions.

"How's Aunty these days? Has she mellowed at all?"

"I think she has, since you left home, Rhoda. I suppose because we're all working now, except for Camellia, she is treating us like adults."

"But tell me about Aunty Nance. You mentioned in your last letter that she hadn't been well. What has been wrong with her?"

"I don't really know. She just seems very quiet and pale for Aunty Nance. You know how full of life she always was."

"Yes, I don't like the sound of that. I will go and see her tomorrow."

"And I'll come with you. Thank goodness it's the weekend and we can spend all the time together."

"But what about Ivor? What will he think about that?" I asked slyly.

"Oh, he's all right. I told him my sister has come home for a few days and I haven't seen her for a long time," she said airily.

When we arrived at Hope Place the door was flung open before we had even had time to knock and Camellia hurled herself at me.

"Steady on, you've knocked my hat sideways," I exclaimed, extricating myself from her bear hug.

"Come and see the cake I've made for you," she said dragging at my hand and pulling me inside, through the hall into the kitchen. Aunty looked up from the cake she was icing and wiping her hands automatically on her apron, she stepped forward awkwardly as if uncertain whether to embrace me. I solved any embarrassment by putting my arms around her and kissing her cheek.

"Well, you are certainly looking well, Rhoda. Salisbury air must agree with you, although I'm sorry to see you've had all your lovely curls cut off."

"I think Rhoda looks really modern," said Camellia admiringly. "I wish I could have my hair shingled."

"Not while I have any say in the matter, Miss. You will keep your lovely long hair. Your father would have a fit if I let you have it cut."

Camellia shrugged and pointed to the cake. "Please let me finish decorating it now that you've smoothed the icing."

Aunty stood back and Camellia bent to the task and was quickly absorbed.

"You'll want to go upstairs and unpack I suppose," said Aunty to me. "The boys will be home soon."

Hazel followed me upstairs and together we hung up my clothes in the wardrobe while chatting non-stop. Soon afterwards we heard the front door click and male voices.

"I must go down and see my brothers," I said and went downstairs. They seemed to fill the little hallway and with a shock I realised they were no longer boys but young men.

"My, you have shot up during the last year. If I'd met you in the street I wouldn't have known you," I said, looking from one to the other.

"And you've got shorter, Sis," remarked Andrew drawing himself to his full height and looking down at me.

"If I'd met you in the street I wouldn't have recognised you, with that hairdo," added David. "Did one of the patients take the scissors to it?"

"Get away with you!" and I pretended to swipe at him.

All through supper that evening family banter continued and I felt glad to be part of them all once more. It wasn't until Hazel and I had gone to bed that we got down to serious talk and she told me more about Aunty Nance. Finally I heard Hazel's regular breathing and knew she was asleep but I lay for a long time gazing into the darkness.

Next morning was bright and sunny and it was with light hearts the two of us set off to visit Aunty Nance. The streets were quiet and as we reached the foot of Paulto Hill a lark began to sing joyfully above us. We stopped to listen and I was reminded of that far-off day when Harold and I had walked up the hill to Old Sarum. A sigh escaped me.

"Are you feeling sad, Rhoda?" asked Hazel.

"No, it was just something I was remembering. It's nothing."

We continued up the hill until there in front of us was the familiar house, square and solid in the morning sunshine, with its grey stone walls softened by climbing roses. I lifted the latch and almost instantly the door was opened by Aunty Nance. She stretched out her arms and I flew into them, hugging her tightly. But what was this? Instead of her usual soft warmth, Aunty Nance felt tiny and almost brittle.

I stepped back and looked at her. "Aunty, you've lost weight!" I exclaimed.

"And a good thing too. I was getting far too fat. Now come on inside and tell me all about yourself. I want to know everything about your life in Salisbury," and she led us through the hall into the tiny sitting room I knew so well.

"Now, before we get started I am going to make you a cup of tea," she said and disappeared.

I looked around the room. It was comfortingly the same, though instead of a fire there was a bunch of everlasting flowers in the grate; on the mantelpiece were the usual photographs with other little knick-knacks, and on the small table inside the door was a bowl of red roses that scented the air. I relaxed. This room always had a soothing effect on me.

Shortly afterwards Aunty Nance came in with a tray and handed us tea in delicate china. Then she looked across at me. "I must say you are looking well, dear. I do enjoy getting your letters, although I think you only tell me half the story. I'm sure there must be some young man in your life."

I blushed. "Well, there is someone I was interested in, but he has gone overseas, indefinitely."

"And now there is someone else, I hope. Better a bird in the hand, you know."

"That's funny; somebody else said that to me."

"There's a lot of truth in these old sayings. Anyway, tell me more about this other young man," she prompted, and very briefly I described Lawrence and the way I had met him through his father. I also mentioned the incident with Richard.

Aunty Nancy listened closely. "He sounds a fine young man, but I think your heart has been given away," she said shrewdly. "All the same, you should give this Lawrence a chance and perhaps in time your feelings will change."

"Now, Aunty, you have quizzed me enough and I want to know all about you. What has been wrong with you? Why have you lost so much weight?"

"Oh, just one of those colds that linger right through the winter and won't go away. I went to the doctor and he prescribed all kinds of medicines, but nothing seemed to work and I just felt off colour all the time. But I am feeling a lot better now that the sun is shining and I'm sure there is nothing to worry about," she ended lightly. "Now let us go into the garden and I'll show you the marvellous vegetables that your Uncle Stan has been growing. I'm sure Aunty Edith would like a few tomatoes and lettuces."

It was obvious she did not want to talk any more about herself, so we got up and followed her outside where all the colours seemed brighter in the morning sunshine. We sat on the seat under the apple tree and chatted happily. It was so pleasant in the garden we were sorry when it was time to go.

"You will come and see me again, before you go away, Rhoda, won't you?" said Aunty Nance wistfully. "I do miss you, dear. You are so like your mother and not a day goes by that I don't think of her," she added.

"I promise, Aunty Nance. Wild horses wouldn't keep me away."

A little later as we were walking down the lane Hazel remarked, "Aunty Nance seemed her old self when she was talking to you, but she is terribly thin, isn't she Rhoda?"

"Yes, I think she should go to another doctor and get a second opinion. If a cold lingers for too long it can develop into something else, but perhaps she is right; now that summer is here she might pick up."

I spoke positively but that night lying in bed I recalled every detail of Aunty Nance's appearance. Apart from being thin there was a pallor to her skin that I had never seen before and a weary look about her eyes. Perhaps it was age, I reasoned. After all, it was a whole year since I had last seen her and people did change as they got older, but the nagging feeling that something was seriously wrong with Aunty Nance kept me awake for a long time.

CHAPTER TWENTY-ONE

The week in Paulton flew by. I devoted nearly every day to visiting the aunts and uncles and felt almost regretful when the time came to set off on holiday to Sidmouth.

I had arranged to meet Helen at Bristol Temple Meads station, from where we were to take the London to Exeter line. It was a thrill to see my friend again after a year. She looked her usual serene self and more like a Madonna than ever, with her glossy dark hair parted in the middle and coiled around her head. We rushed towards each other.

"Rhoda, you've changed," she exclaimed. "You look older, but just as pretty," she added hastily.

"Well, you haven't changed, Helen, thank goodness. You still look exactly as you did at the secretarial college. Wasn't it fun back in those days?"

"Yes, a lot of water's gone under the bridge since then. Anyway, we'd better hurry. We don't want to miss our train. It's waiting at the platform now."

We found an empty compartment at the rear of the train and once we had arranged our luggage on the overhead racks we sat back and studied each other.

"Now, tell me all about yourself, Rhoda. Your letters are so brief these days and I'm sure there is a lot happening in your life."

"No, before I launch into all that I want to hear about you. How's your father?"

"Oh, he's much better these days. You remember how after his stroke we thought he'd never go back to the office? Well, he actually goes in one day a week now. I don't know how much he does there, but it makes him feel part of things and he keeps an eye on Bob."

At the mention of Bob I felt my cheeks grow hot. Helen noticed and she said quickly, "Don't worry, Rhoda, I know why you felt you couldn't go on with Bob. He understood too, but I must admit I felt disappointed at the time. I hoped you and I would be sisters. Still, that is in the past and we've all moved on since then."

"So what is Bob doing now?"

"He's taking a year off to go to Australia. You remember, that was always his dream. He is leaving next month."

I felt glad for Bob. It was good that he was at last able to go to Australia. I knew that he had given up all his own plans to stay and help his father in the law office after the stroke, but it had always been his dearest wish to visit Australia.

Just then the guard blew his whistle and the train began to move.

"Oh isn't it exciting to be going on holiday, just the two of us!" Happiness bubbled up inside me and I felt young and free all at once.

As the train steamed through the countryside we gazed out of the window exclaiming at all the places we passed. Everything looked new and different outside of Bristol. When we finally entered Devon the landscape changed dramatically. Hills rose up on all sides and every now and again we had glimpses of the sea shimmering in the distance. We began to sound like a couple of excited schoolgirls.

"We'll be able to go for swims each day."

"And have long walks along the cliffs."

"And eat Devonshire cream teas in quaint little teashops."

"And walk by the sea licking ices."

Helen's eyes were dancing and I felt as young as Camellia. I thought, any moment now I'll forget myself and start bouncing on the seat.

Sun streamed into the compartment and the colours outside seemed to take on a deeper and more vivid hue. The sky looked bluer and the grass greener than I had ever seen it and even the air seemed to shimmer with a special brilliance. Devon must surely be the most beautiful county in England.

In no time at all, or so it seemed, we were at Exeter station, where we were to change to a branch line to Sidmouth. A few holiday makers like ourselves stood around the platform, the men and women in light summery clothes, clutching bulging suitcases while their children brandished buckets and spades and squealed excitedly.

Eventually, an ancient train rounded the bend. It looked as though it had seen better times and was doomed to spend its final days on this out of the way branch line. Inside everything was old and worn, the upholstery threadbare and the seat backs disfigured where people had carved their initials. Yet this old girl, puffing and wheezing her way through the quiet countryside, was all of a piece with the thatched cottages and sleepy villages she passed through. Anything new and modern would have been out of place. In some strange way the shabby old locomotive added to the holiday atmosphere.

The station at Sidmouth was in marked contrast to the train. It was as neat and pretty as a model for a train set, with hanging baskets and tubs of bright flowers on the platform. Even the station master looked smart in his uniform and gave us a friendly smile as we went through the gate.

"On holiday, m'dears?"

"Yes, we're new to Sidmouth," I said.

"Where be ye staying if I might ask?"

"In Bedford Flats."

"Oh aye, I knows 'em. Very pleasant too. At the bottom of this road. You're just round the corner from the beach there."

I looked at Helen. Her eyes were sparkling and I knew what she was thinking. We would be able to swim at any time of the day if we were so close to the sea. The station master did not seem to be in a hurry and was quite happy to stand and chat, but like me, Helen was impatient to be off, so we thanked him for his directions and started walking.

"I thought we would never get away from him," said Helen with a giggle. "He seemed to have all the time in the world."

"I suppose that's the way of it in these country places. Time doesn't matter. Perhaps we should take off our watches, Helen."

We came to a bend in the road and there before us was the sea, blue and glittering in the sunshine.

"Oh," we gasped in unison.

Forgetting all about Bedford Flats we hurried on down the hill to the esplanade. Seagulls wheeled through the air, crying plaintively as they landed on fishing smacks bobbing at anchor, and in the distance a yacht skimmed across the waves, its white sail billowing. In our nostrils was the smell of the sea, that indefinable blend of seaweed, fish and salt air. We stood entranced by our first glimpse of Sidmouth Bay.

"It's just perfect," I said in a hushed voice.

"Yes, isn't it, but I suppose we'd better go and find Bedford Flats," and Helen sighed.

"I think the station master said they were at the end of this road."

"So we must have passed them as we came down."

We picked up our suitcases and retraced our steps, passing a hotel on the corner.

Just beyond it was a row of terraced apartments, all identical, the two top floors with balconies and the ground floor flats with small gardens behind concrete walls. Bedford Flats was in green lettering in the centre of the block.

"Look out for number nine, Rhoda,"

"That must be it," I said pointing. "Look, on the front door it has 8, 9 and 10. Number nine must be the one in the middle with the green balcony."

We hurried along the path to the front door. After a bit of a struggle Helen managed to open it with one of the keys she had been given and we found ourselves in a hallway with stairs directly in front of us. Panting a little, we gained the first landing and saw on our right a door with number nine on it.

As we went in I had a feeling of déjà vu. Surely I had been here before. Everything seemed familiar, even the umbrella stand which held a striped beach umbrella, a couple of tennis racquets and two stout walking sticks. In the sitting room gaily coloured cushions were scattered over the cane furniture. Magazines and books lay strewn carelessly on the coffee table, and on the sideboard was a pile of cardboard boxes containing games such as drafts, chess and chequers. The room had a recently occupied air as though the owners had suddenly tired of being indoors and had dropped everything to go outside for a walk or a swim. Immediately, we each flopped into the nearest cane chair and lay back contentedly.

"What a gorgeous place! I feel at home straight away," said Helen looking around.

"And we haven't even seen the bedrooms yet."

"If I stay here much longer I'll never want to move. This chair is so comfy."

But I was already at the door. Would the bedrooms be as homely as the sitting room? I felt a little like Goldilocks as I pushed open the bedroom door. Two single beds covered with patchwork quilts stood side by side with a white chest of drawers between them. On top of it was a lamp in the shape of a dolphin, a travelling clock and a couple of books. It looked as inviting as the sitting room and I would gladly at that moment have lain down and pulled the covers over my head. By now Helen was beside me.

"It makes you want to lie down and go to sleep, doesn't it?" she said.

"Exactly what I was thinking. If we're not careful we'll never leave this apartment, it's so comfortable, unless we're driven by hunger that is."

"Which reminds me, we haven't had anything to eat for hours. Let's go and find a cafe," Helen suggested.

We set off down the road to the corner. It was impossible to hurry. There was so much to see as we walked along the broad esplanade. Ranged at the side of it was an endless row of deck chairs where people sat basking in the sunshine as they watched the colourful parade of human life sauntering along the sea front. I noticed the tall elegant buildings across the road that looked as if they belonged to a different era, probably Georgian I thought, as they reminded me of similar buildings in Bath, but these were now hotels, not private residences.

Sometime later, we returned to Bedford Flats. We had purchased a few grocery items which we put away in the cupboard in the kitchen and then kicking off our shoes curled up in a chair each. I picked up an Agatha Christie novel, but after the first few pages my eyes grew heavy and leaning back against the cushion I gave in to a delicious sense of drowsiness. I had not felt so relaxed for months.

....

The week glided by in a glorious golden haze. Each day we got up early and went for a walk along the esplanade. This was an enchanted time, when nobody was about and the only sounds were the plaintive crying of the gulls and the soft swishing of the shingle as it was dragged back and forth by the ebb and flow of the tide. From the top of Jacob's Ladder we could see the whole of the bay spread below us and in the distance the red cliffs of Salcombe Hill.

Then we would hurry back for breakfast, just as the town was beginning to stir, and over tea and toast make plans for the day. If we felt energetic we would go for an all day hike, following the coastal path in either direction and return in the evening sunburnt and pleasantly exhausted. On other days we stayed by the beach lazing in the sun and taking a leisurely dip when we felt so inclined. Each evening we would try out a different café in the town, but much preferred to sit on the seafront eating fish and chips out of paper and sharing our chips with the gulls who watched us out of their beady eyes, ready to swoop for titbits.

I found a travel guide amongst the miscellany of books heaped in one of the cupboards and thumbed with interest through the pages dealing with Sidmouth.

"Listen to this Helen," I said. "Queen Victoria was brought by her parents to Sidmouth in 1819 when she was a baby. Her father was the Duke of Kent and a month later he died from an illness. The house where they stayed is now the Royal Glen Hotel."

"I've seen that hotel. It's just near here. We could go and have a look at it tomorrow."

"Good idea. The book also says that Sidmouth was a popular seaside resort in regency times."

"Which would account for all those elegant buildings along the front that are now hotels."

I consulted the book again. "It says that before the 18th century Sidmouth was a fishing village and right at the end of the town there is a series of small fishermen's cottages.

"Sidmouth is certainly an interesting place."

"I don't think you could ever get tired of it, not if you returned year after year," I said.

"That would be lovely, but I have the feeling that something is going to happen soon that will change all our lives," said Helen thoughtfully.

"What do you mean?"

"Don't you read the papers, Rhoda? They are always talking about Hitler and his Nazi party. Apparently he is becoming very strong in Germany and is threatening some of the countries on the border."

"But that needn't involve us in a war."

"I wouldn't be so sure. We got involved the last time."

I looked in surprise at Helen. I had never known her talk this way before and it made me think. This was what the Major had said on one of our walks and I hadn't wanted to believe him. Supposing it were true and there were another war. Everything that was part of our lives would be threatened. Even this beautiful place might be destroyed. It didn't bear thinking about and I shivered.

We dropped the subject then and began to make plans for the next day, but I never forgot our conversation that evening.

Finally, our holiday came to an end and it was time to pack up. As we turned the key in the door for the last time I felt regret that we had to leave Sidmouth behind and return to normal life. This had been a magical week and one I would look back on, as being completely happy and carefree.

CHAPTER TWENTY-TWO

Very quickly I settled back into the routine of life at Laverton House and the holiday in Sidmouth became a distant memory. Christmas came and went with all the usual festivities and then it was January when the days were short and dark. The first flakes of snow fell on Boxing Day and snowfalls continued well into the new year of 1935. It was bitterly cold out of doors but indoors fires were kept burning all day long. Laverton House, having been built in Victorian times, was well provided with fireplaces in all of the main rooms.

Since returning from my holiday in July I kept in regular correspondence with those at home in Paulton. Every week I wrote to Hazel but enclosed a separate note to Aunty Edith. When I wrote to Aunty Nance I tried to imagine she was there in the room with me and that we were having a chat about all kinds of things. Her replies were equally chatty and she wrote of the little everyday incidents that filled her days. She never referred to her health and the tone of her letters was always cheerful and positive.

It therefore came as a shock to me when Aunty Nance wrote to say that she had been for a check-up and the doctor had sent her to hospital to undergo tests for cancer. She said a lump had been found in her right breast and it might be necessary to have an operation. I felt stunned. For some minutes I held the letter in my hand, not believing what I had read. *Aunty Nance with cancer!* It seemed impossible. From what I had heard there was no cure for cancer and it was only a matter of time.

Rapidly a plan began to form in my mind. I would give up my position at Laverton House and go back to Paulton to nurse my aunt. I would stay in the house and assist her in every way possible. There was not a moment to be wasted. Her days were probably numbered and I wanted to be with her as soon as it could be arranged. By now my mind was clear. First, I would have to write a letter of resignation explaining my reasons for leaving Laverton House and request that I be excused the usual period of notice. It would probably be best to see Matron first and explain to her in person that this was a matter of urgency to me. I was sure she would understand and do what she could to help.

As soon as I had written my letter of resignation I went downstairs to Matron's office. When I went in she was seated at her desk and looked up with a kindly smile.

"Well, Nurse Pritchard, what can I do for you?"

"I need to go home urgently, Matron. My aunt is ill with cancer and probably has not long to live."

"Oh, I'm very sorry to hear that. I'm sure we can arrange for you to have leave of absence on compassionate grounds."

"I really think I should resign from my position here, because I do not know how long I will need to be with her and the family."

"I see." Matron leaned back in her chair and looked thoughtfully at me. "That is quite a drastic step to take, Nurse. We could not guarantee to keep open a position here for you once you have resigned."

"I realise that, Matron, and I should be very sorry to leave Laverton House, but I have thought about it and this seems the right thing for me to do. I have written out my letter of resignation and have it here."

I passed it across to her. She read it slowly then looked up.

"I seem to recall that you have secretarial training and that before you came here you had been working in an office."

"Yes, that is right."

"Well, it occurs to me that even if we were not able to offer you a nursing position you might be able to assist in the office. In fact, as you know our secretary is nearing retirement and might be very glad to have her place filled. You would be in a unique position, having been on the nursing staff and knowing our routines. Yes, I think this might all fit in."

She smiled. "Leave this with me, Nurse Pritchard; I will have a word with Dr. Branson and Dr. Hall. I am sure they would be very happy with such an arrangement. None of us would like to lose you; you have been an asset to the staff here."

"Thank you, Matron; I would certainly feel happier knowing that I could come back to Laverton House."

"So when would you like to leave, Nurse, as soon as possible I presume?"

"Yes, by the end of the week if that is convenient."

"We will make it so. I know that you will want to be with your aunt immediately. I will arrange for your salary to be paid up until the end of the month. Now, you go away and get packed and if there is any way I can help just let me know." She reached over and patted my hand. "God bless you, my dear," she said warmly.

"Thank you, Matron," I mumbled, tears filling my eyes.

As I left her office and went upstairs I thought, *The die is cast. I am leaving Laverton House. This morning everything was the same as it had been for the last four years and yet in the space of a day everything has changed. After tomorrow this will all be the past.* I gulped. Now I would have to explain to Joan that I was leaving.

She was in our room giving herself a manicure.

"Oh this wretched nail! It keeps on breaking because of that antiseptic they insist we wash our hands with." She looked up and saw my face. "Is something the matter, Rhoda? You look as though you are about to cry."

I rushed over to her.

"I'm leaving here, Joan, for good. I've resigned."

"What!" She looked horrified.

"It's because of Aunty Nance, you know, my favourite aunt, Mum's sister. She has cancer and hasn't long to live."

"Oh, Rhoda, I'm so sorry. I suppose you want to go and look after her, but do you really have to resign? Couldn't you just get leave of absence?"

"I thought of that, but it's not feasible. Anyway, I've talked it over with Matron."

Joan's eyes filled with tears. "Rhoda, I can't bear to think of you not being here. It won't be the same without you. You've been such a good friend to me," and she sobbed.

"You've still got Jim and Maisie."

"But they're not you."

"There is something I must tell you, though," and I told her about Matron's suggestion that I come back on the office staff."

Joan stopped sobbing and listened. "I suppose we won't be losing you completely then, though it will never be the same as nursing together."

"Joan, I'm only twenty-three, but in my life there have been lots of changes and I have learnt that nothing in this life stays the same. When I lost my mother I thought it was the end of the world, but then we had a housekeeper, Mrs. Hopkins, whose husband had been killed in the Great War. She told me that you have to put the past behind you and make the best of today. She taught me that song, "Pack up your troubles in you old kit bag and smile, smile, smile." From that day on I've tried to follow her advice and it has helped me. So Joan, let's do just that. Keep smiling and look on the bright side."

"Rhoda, always the optimist, but I must say it does work for you. You always manage to keep cheerful whatever happens."

"Yes, and so must you, so come on, help me pack will you, you lazy lump?" and laughing through our tears we hugged one another.

Then I dragged my shabby old suitcase from under the bed and began to pack.

On Saturday morning I left Laverton House. I was touched that many of the staff, including Matron, were in the lobby to see me off. Even O'Mally, the Irish nurse, was with them and wished me well with tears in her eyes.

It was hard parting with Maisie and Joan and we all promised to write regularly.

When the taxi arrived everyone crowded around as I climbed into the back and they waved as we went slowly down the drive. My eyes were so misty with tears that the house was a blur as I looked back. It was the same when we drove through Salisbury and passed all the familiar places. When would I see them again? Hardest of all was leaving behind the cathedral. The delicate spire wavered as I looked at it through tear-filled eyes. At last I was in the train and as it pulled out of the station I leaned forward to see as much as possible of dear old Salisbury before leaving it altogether.

The train gathered speed and as we left the city behind I settled back in my seat and began to think about Aunty Nance and how best I could help her. Uncle Stan had written a reply to my letter saying that he would meet me at Paulton station and take me home. Aunty Nance was now very frail but she was looking forward to my arrival. Reading between the lines I could sense his relief that I was coming to assist him in caring for her.

I closed my eyes and prayed silently for wisdom and strength over the next few weeks or months while Aunty Nance lived. I knew that cancer could be very painful in the final stages and I prayed that Aunty Nance would be spared that.

I relaxed then and must have dozed, because when I looked at my watch we were already half way to Bristol. When we arrived at Bristol Temple Meads I changed platforms for the Paulton Radstock train. It was very quiet, being a Saturday afternoon, and as we pulled into Paulton station there were only a few people on the platform. I caught sight of Uncle Stan and Hazel standing together. As soon as she saw me, Hazel came running and threw her arms around me while Uncle Stan stood quietly by.

"I'm glad you're here, Rhoda," she said, a catch in her voice. "Aunty Nance will be so pleased to see you."

"That's right," said Uncle Stan. "As soon as we got your letter she cheered up, but you will see a change in her I'm afraid."

He took my suitcase and led the way to his car which was parked outside the station. Hazel and I climbed into the back and sat close together saying very little. It was comforting to have her there and know that she shared my anxieties about Aunty Nance.

When we arrived at the house Uncle Stan opened the front door and told us to go straight in. It was strange not to be welcomed by Aunty Nance and the house seemed unnaturally quiet. We went into the little sitting room. A fire was blazing in the grate and beside it in an easy chair was a tiny woman huddled under a blanket. I hardly recognised my aunt, her face was so shrunken. Then she smiled and was herself again. I ran across the room and sank on my knees beside her, burying my head in her lap. She stroked my hair.

"Rhoda, you are here at last. I thought I would never see you again and then your letter came. It seemed too good to be true."

"I am going to stay with you, Aunty, for as long as you need me."

"But what about your work, Rhoda?"

"That is all taken care of. I have resigned from my nursing post and when I do go back it will be to work in the office."

"So you will be with me to the end," said Aunty Nance softly.

I did not trust myself to reply.

Uncle Stan coughed. "I'll make a cup of tea for us all. Would you give me a hand, Hazel?"

"Of course," she said jumping up.

We were now on our own and Aunty Nance continued stroking my hair. Finally, she said, "A few nights ago your mother came to me in a dream. She told me not to be frightened of dying because it is just a doorway into a far more beautiful place, and that she would be waiting to greet me and so would my mother and father. When I woke up, Rhoda, I felt so happy and since then all my fears have gone. I know that there is nothing to worry about. And having you here now is the icing on the cake. I feel completely happy."

I looked up at her and it was true. Her face was serene and she was smiling.

During those weeks of nursing Aunty Nance I lost count of the days. As the cancer progressed and the pain worsened Uncle Stan and I took it in turns to sit at Aunty Nance's bedside. We never left her alone. When the pain became unendurable we gave her extra morphine so that she could have some relief. Through it all she never complained, but I knew when she was in pain because she would grip my hand and her eyes would darken. My heart turned over with pity at those times and I longed to be able to bear the pain for her.

Three months passed and winter gave way to spring. Different friends and relatives came to visit briefly, but Aunty Nance had no strength to speak to them and they went away with tears in their eyes. Aunty Edith came regularly; bringing little gifts of homemade cakes or biscuits and bunches of flowers to brighten up the room. She was always gentle and kind and during this time I saw a different side to her. She would insist that I take a break and go for a walk and get fresh air while she sat with Aunty Nance. I was grateful to her and on my walks I breathed in the fresh country air and picked little bunches of wild flowers to take back to the sick room.

Aunty Nance's eyes would brighten when she saw the primroses and wild violets in a vase by her bed.

"I love the spring flowers," she said one day. "They remind me of when I was a girl and Cis and I used to gather them in the lane. Those were such happy days."

One evening after Aunty Edith had been to visit, Aunty Nance asked Uncle Stan and me to come and sit together at her bedside. Her eyes were bright and she seemed more animated than I had seen her for a long time.

She looked lovingly from one to the other of us. "When I am gone I don't want you to be sad for me. I have had a happy life and I know I am going to be even happier where I am going and one day you will both be joining me there. There is an angel in the room waiting to take me home. He is very beautiful," and she looked beyond us. Then her eyes closed and a little sigh escaped from her lips. A deep stillness settled over her.

"I think she has gone," I whispered, but Uncle Stan knew already. His head was in his hands and I could see his shoulders heaving. I got up and tiptoed from the room so that he could be alone with his grief.

CHAPTER TWENTY-THREE

Aunty Nance's funeral brought back poignant memories of my mother's. Once more I was standing with my brothers and sisters beside an open grave, with the smell of white flowers strong in my nostrils. This time it was not my father, but Uncle Stan who was alone and grieving for his wife. I longed to reach out and take his hand but I was not his child and I sensed he wanted to be private in his grief. I looked at each of my brothers and sisters standing composedly in the graveyard and remembered that far-off day when they had been little children and the death of their mother had scarcely touched them.

Aunty Edith took charge of the refreshments back at the house, while Hazel and I assisted by handing around cakes and sandwiches. It was a relief when people went at last.

As we were washing up the dishes Aunty Edith turned to me, "What are you going to do now, Rhoda? Your Uncle Stan will not need your help and it is hardly proper for you to stay with him. I think you should come home with us."

I looked at her startled. I had not thought beyond the funeral, but what she was saying was true. Also Uncle Stan seemed to have withdrawn from me since Aunty Nance's death and I sensed that he wished to be left alone. I quickly made up my mind.

"I will pack up this afternoon, Aunty. I haven't much anyway."

"I'll help you, Rhoda," said Hazel.

Half an hour later my suitcase was in the hall. Uncle Stan was a little surprised to hear I was leaving yet he also seemed relieved.

"I'll drive you all to Hope Place," he offered.

"And I'll come down and see you often," I promised.

"I'd like that," he said simply.

In this way, I found myself back at home sharing a room with Hazel once more. For the first week I was glad to rest and catch up on my sleep. I had not realised what a toll those nights of sitting up and watching by my aunt's bedside had taken. Aunty Edith let me sleep in each morning, providing breakfast long after everyone had left the house.

Then one morning I woke up at my usual time feeling perfectly normal. The tiredness had left me and I began to think: *What am I going to do now? Should I be in touch with Matron and let her know that I was ready to return to work? No, it was too soon. I needed time to recover from Aunty Nance's death. Besides, I was not sure whether I really wanted to return to Laverton House. I had been there four years and perhaps it was time for a change.* As I lay turning these thoughts over in my mind one thing was clear to me, I had to come to some decision about my future.

When I went downstairs to the kitchen Aunty looked up in surprise.

"You're early this morning, Rhoda."

"I couldn't lie in bed any longer. I feel I want to get busy and do something. Is there anything I can do for you, Aunty?"

She gave me a quizzical look. "Well, I could suggest cleaning the silver or perhaps you would prefer ironing. No, Rhoda, what you need is to go for a long walk and give some serious thought to your future."

"How strange! That is exactly what I was thinking when I woke up this morning."

When I left the house half an hour later, I found myself walking in the direction of the station. Perhaps I would take the next train to Radstock for old times' sake, and call in at the Standard Check Book Company and see if Sally was still working there.

My friend, the station master, greeted me with, "Well my love, where have you been all this long time? I thought you must have gone back to New Zealand."

"I've been working in Salisbury for the last few years."

"And now you've come back to Paulton. Well, it does my eyes good to see you once more."

Just then the train to Radstock pulled in with a burst of steam and I climbed on. As I looked out of the window memories came rushing back and I recalled when I travelled each day to work at the Standard Check Book Company. As I looked back, that seemed a very happy and untrammelled time. Of course, I had been much younger then and in love with Bob. I sighed at the memory.

In no time at all we were at Radstock and as I walked down the road from the station I was surprised to see how unchanged everything was. I hesitated for a moment on the doorstep of the Standard Check Book Company. *Was I doing the right thing revisiting the past when I should be thinking of the future? Well, I was here now, so I might as well go in.*

I walked into the foyer and a familiar voice exclaimed, "Rhoda, is it really you?" and Sally jumped up from her desk and bounded across the room to me.

"Oh, Sal, I didn't really think you would still be here." I glanced at her left hand. "And you're married too."

"Yes, a year ago now, and what about you, Rhoda? I see you're not married. What happened to Bob?"

"Oh, that's a long story."

"In that case, I think we should have a cup of tea and catch up on the news. I'm sure Mr. Sutcliff will be delighted to hear you are here. Wait a mo' while I go and tell him," and with that she disappeared through the familiar door behind the reception desk.

A few minutes later she returned. "Mr. Sutcliff would like to see you. He said to ask you to step into his office."

I knocked at the door and when he called brusquely, "Come in," I entered rather timidly.

Immediately Mr. Sutcliff sprang up from his desk and came forward, taking my hand between his. He looked much the same, a little older perhaps and his hair was grey, but otherwise he still had the same brisk manner.

"Miss Pritchard, what a delightful surprise! What brings you here today? I thought you were nursing, or at least married, but I see you are not. Do sit down and tell me all about yourself."

Very briefly I explained how I had left Salisbury to come and nurse Aunty Nance and that she had died and I was uncertain whether to return to Laverton House.

He listened carefully, his chin resting on his hand.

"It is very strange, Miss Pritchard, but the secretary who took over from you is leaving here to be married in a fortnight's time. She only handed in her notice yesterday. It has caught me on the hop rather, as I was not expecting this so soon. In fact, I was going to put an advertisement in the paper today. After what you have told me, would you possibly consider stepping in temporarily? You know the ropes here, and even though you have been out of secretarial work for a little while I'm sure you would quickly pick it up again. Please give it some thought, Miss Pritchard. It might suit both of us—for a short while anyway."

He smiled at me warmly. "I must say you are looking well and not a day older than when you were here. What is it, four or five years? That time has flown. Now do go and have a cup of tea with Sally. Tell her to make the break as long as she likes. I know you will have a lot of catching up to do." With that he stood up and shook my hand again. "Oh, and would you mind letting me know tomorrow, what your answer is?"

"Certainly, Mr. Sutcliff," and I smiled to myself remembering how quickly he liked to get things done.

When I went back to Sally I told her that we could take as long as we liked over our tea break and she led me through into the little side room, where we had sat and shared so many confidences in the past, over a cup of tea.

She threw her arms around me when I told her of Mr. Sutcliff's suggestion.

"Of course you'll come, won't you Rhoda? It will be just like old times."

"I think so, but I'll have to sleep on it."

We chatted together for a while and then I walked back to the station in a completely different frame of mind from when I set out. I now had something tangible to work on and if this was a temporary position I had more time to plan what to do in the future. My heart felt light and my step quickened as I walked along the road.

When I arrived back at Hope Place Aunty was in the little front room with her youngest sister Gladys. I popped my head around the door.

"Hello, Rhoda, I didn't expect you back so soon. That walk must have done you good, you've got some colour in your cheeks," Aunty remarked.

"You look like the cat that stole the cream," said Aunty Glad.

"I suppose it is a bit like that," and I went into the room and sat down, facing the two of them. "The fact is I've been offered my old job back at the Standard Check Book Company," and I told them how this had come about.

"Hm," said Aunty Edith when I had finished. "It still doesn't solve the problem of your future, but I suppose it gives you a little more time to think."

"And I will be earning some money, so I can contribute towards the housekeeping."

"That isn't my first consideration, Rhoda," Aunty retorted.

"But it will help, won't it, Edith?" and Aunty Glad winked at me.

Shortly after that I left them and went upstairs to write some letters. First I wrote to Joan and asked her to share the letter with Maisie. Next, I had the more difficult task of answering Lawrence's latest letter. He wrote quite regularly and although he kept the tone light there was an undercurrent of seriousness behind his words. I knew he wanted to see me again, but I had managed so far to find reasons for not making any definite arrangements. I had the feeling that he wanted me to make a commitment to him and I did not feel ready to do so. Now I was in Paulton and likely to be here for a while I could forestall him. Finally, I wrote to Mr. Sutcliff accepting a temporary secretarial position at the Standard Check Book Company.

For the first time since Aunty Nance's death I felt life was worth living.

It did not take long to settle back into the routine of going to work each day and the months passed swiftly. It was now

August 1936 and it almost felt as though my years of nursing had never existed and that I had been working continuously with the Standard Check Book Company since I was seventeen, except with one difference: Sally was now pregnant and her talk was all of the coming baby. I tried to make myself interested in this momentous event, but I had to confess to myself that babies held little appeal for me.

One day Sally noticed me stifling a yawn and said curiously, "Who are you seeing these days, Rhoda, now that you have broken off with Bob?"

I did not know how to reply. "Oh there is a chap in London called Lawrence. He writes to me regularly, but I've only been out with him a couple of times."

"But you're twenty-four, aren't you, Rhoda? You ought to be thinking of getting married soon or you'll end up an old maid, like your aunt."

I laughed, but her comment set me thinking. I was getting older and most of the girls I knew in the village were either engaged or married. Even Helen told me that she was about to get engaged to one of the young lawyers in her father's firm.

That evening when I went home there was a letter from Lawrence on the hall table. I took it upstairs to read in my bedroom.

I have joined the RAF Volunteer Reserves, he wrote. *It's been my intention for some time as you know, but finally I took the step. I will be at Filton aerodrome the weekend after next and would dearly like to visit you, Rhoda, and meet your family. Please write and tell me when it would be convenient to call."*

As I reread the letter my heart was beating fast. *If Lawrence met the family it would look as though I was serious about him. Perhaps I was being forced to make a decision about him. Anyway, I would have to write and give him an answer, but first I had better sound Aunty out.*

She was in the kitchen preparing dinner.

"Aunty, I have a friend who has joined the RAF Volunteer Reserves and will be staying in Filton in two weeks' time. Would you mind if I invited him here for lunch on Saturday?"

"I don't see why not," she replied, "so long as you help me with the meal preparation. How well do you know this friend, Rhoda, and where did you meet him?"

I told her about the Major and the time I had been to his house. I then added the story about Richard.

She listened carefully. "Well, he sounds a good type of man. I will be interested to meet him."

I smiled to myself. So would the rest of the family, without a doubt. I could imagine David and Andrew wanting to know all about the Air Force and aeroplanes.

That evening when Hazel came in from work I told her about the visit. Her eyes shone with enthusiasm. "How exciting, Rhoda, a real airman! You never told me that Lawrence was in the Air Force."

"He isn't. He's just joined the Reserves. He has a job in an insurance company in London."

"I'm really looking forward to meeting him. Do you think he'll turn up in uniform?"

"I've no idea."

"There's something about men in uniform," said Hazel dreamily. "They always look so handsome."

As she chattered on I began to feel a stirring in me. I could imagine that Lawrence with his film star looks would look especially good in uniform and that he would have a big impact on the family.

Later that evening I wrote to him, inviting him for lunch in a fortnight's time. His answer came back promptly. He would be able to manage Saturday and would be arriving at Paulton station at 11am. My heart fluttered and immediately I began to plan the lunch menu.

Hazel offered to help me and we told Aunty that she was to take the time off and be our guest that day. Reluctantly, she agreed and I suggested she visit her sister Phoebe in the morning and come back in time for lunch. It was not so easy to persuade the boys and Camellia to leave the house. They were very curious about my Air Force friend and wanted to stay around to see him. Instead, I suggested they meet him at the station and escort him to the house. Because neither Hazel nor I were experienced cooks we had decided to have a salad lunch, followed by a light dessert of fruit salad and custard. I took some trouble in setting the table, with the best china and cutlery and a small arrangement of flowers in the centre.

"It looks very nice," said Hazel stepping back to admire the final effect.

Once everything was ready we went upstairs to change. After some thought I selected my latest dress, a simple blue silk and Hazel put on a pretty cotton frock with a floral pattern.

We surveyed each other appreciatively.

"You look lovely, Rhoda,"

"And so do you, little sister. Lawrence will be dazzled."

We laughed and went downstairs to await his arrival.

Promptly at 11.30 the door opened and there he was in our little hallway, towering over everyone. He looked directly into my eyes and I felt suddenly shy of this handsome stranger. He came forward and took my hand warmly in his.

"How pretty you look, Rhoda." Then turning to Hazel he said gallantly, "And you must be Hazel. Good looks certainly run in this family, from the youngest to the eldest," and he chucked Camellia under the chin, making her blush and giggle.

"But where is your aunt?"

"She is coming. We are giving her a break from the kitchen. Oh, here she is now," I said, hearing the door open.

The hall seemed suddenly crowded with young people and Aunty looked diminutive as she entered. I gestured towards Lawrence.

"Aunty, this is Lawrence. Lawrence, this is my aunt, Miss Pritchard."

"How do you do, Miss Pritchard?" and Lawrence proffered his hand. As she took it I was sure Aunty blushed slightly. I smiled to myself. Lawrence was certainly having an effect on the women in our household.

It was the same at lunch. Everyone was vying for his attention and questions came thick and fast.

"Have you flown many planes?" asked Camellia.

"I haven't been in one yet. I've only just joined the Volunteer Reserves but I will be given flying training at weekends over the next five years."

"How is an aeroplane engine different from the average car engine?" This was from Andrew.

"That is what I shall find out once training starts. Afraid I know nothing much at the moment."

"Will you be wearing an Air Force uniform?" asked Hazel.

"Only flying gear, the sort you see pilots wear."

"Are you insured against accidents in the air?" This was David's question.

"Goodness, I hadn't thought about that. Let's hope there are none," said Lawrence laughing.

"Give our guest time to eat," said Aunty, frowning at Camellia who was starting to ask another question.

After that there was silence for a few minutes. Then Hazel said unexpectedly. "Do you think there is going to be another war, Lawrence?"

He put down his knife and fork and looked at her thoughtfully. "That is an interesting question. Germany is certainly becoming strong again under Hitler and he has already taken a major step forward in reoccupying the Rhineland. Churchill said some time back that Germany is on the way to becoming the most heavily armed nation in the world. That is why the RAF is expanding and increasing the number of military aircraft, to match any hostile air force."

"Let's hope it doesn't come to that," said Aunty shuddering. "It was bad enough last time. Now let's drop this talk of war and get on with our lunch."

Later that afternoon Lawrence suggested we go for a walk together, so that I could show him the village. It was his way of making sure that we had some time alone. I took him along Paulto Lane and pointed out the house where my mother had grown up with her brothers and sisters. In response to his questions I filled in more detail about Aunty Nance and her recent illness.

"And now you have decided to stay on in Paulton for a while. Are you not planning to return to Salisbury, Rhoda? It seems rather a pity to give up nursing now that you are fully trained."

"I haven't decided anything definite yet. I just feel the need for a breathing space."

We were nearly at the top of Paulto Hill by then and the fields fell away at our feet. In the distance was the misty outline of hills and a long way below us, the village. It was quite silent, not even a bird sang, and I was very conscious of Lawrence standing beside me.

When he spoke his voice was low. "Rhoda, I've been waiting for a chance to speak to you alone. Now it has come I don't know quite how to put this without sounding like a lovesick schoolboy, but the truth is I'm mad about you and I want to marry you."

He swung around to face me and his face had gone very white. His eyes bored into mine. I was completely taken by surprise and stared back at him.

"Don't feel you have to give me an answer now. If you need time to think, I'll accept that …" His voice tailed off.

I said slowly, "I suppose I've known for some time that you were serious about me, Larry, but I didn't want to have to face it. You see, I don't think I'm ready to be married; I feel too uncertain about the future." I looked away from him and into the distance. "Losing Aunty Nance and leaving Laverton House; there's been so much change in my life all at once. I need time to sort myself out."

"I understand all that," said Lawrence quietly, "You need time to weigh everything up, but please tell me if I can at least hope. Perhaps you will know your mind in three months' time."

I snatched at this. "Yes, I think I will by then. Do you mind waiting for an answer?"

"It won't be easy, but yes, I will wait. Now please, let me kiss you," and he leaned forward and took me in his arms. I found myself responding to him as his lips pressed mine. His body was firm and warm and I felt both excited and safe as he held me. Slowly he disengaged himself and held me at arm's length.

"So you are not an ice maiden, Miss Pritchard," he said, smiling into my eyes. "I shall remember this kiss over the next few months of waiting."

I lowered my eyes.

"And now shall we make our way back down the hill and to normal life again? If we stay up here I will be tempted to kiss you again and there is no telling where that may lead, so come on, Miss Pritchard," and he took my hand, setting off down the road. As we walked hand in hand down the hill I felt strangely happy and lighthearted.

CHAPTER TWENTY-FOUR

The months slipped by and life fell into a regular pattern: the office from Monday to Friday, chapel on Sunday and outings with Helen on Saturday. Lawrence wrote each week and I looked forward to his letters which were always amusing and full of interesting detail. Every weekend he had pilot training at Ternhill, the Training Command Centre, and he described in terms I could understand the various planes he was being taught to fly and the differences between them. I learned about the Wellington bombers, the Tiger Moths and the new Supermarine Model 300 which had made its maiden flight at Eastleigh aerodrome in March, and was later renamed Spitfire.

During that year of 1936 the papers were full of the problems the government was having with the king and his obsession over Mrs. Simpson, the twice divorced American sociallite. The king was determined to marry her, despite the objections of the Prime Minister, Stanley Baldwin, who threatened to resign if the marriage went ahead. There was also opposition from the prime ministers of all the dominions and more importantly from the Church of England, which opposed the remarriage of divorced people. As head of the Church it was hardly consistent for the king to be married to a divorced woman.

The country was divided over the issue and I couldn't help feeling a sneaking sympathy for the man who was prepared to give up his crown to marry the woman he loved. All the same, when the abdication was announced on the 11th December it shook everyone. Lawrence referred to the king slightingly as a man who placed his own selfish desires before his duty and I realised from this that Lawrence had high principles which made me respect him more.

And so we entered the new year of 1937. All through the bitter cold of January I waited for Lawrence to write and renew his offer of marriage, but no letter came. I could not understand it, as Lawrence wrote regularly each week. Then one morning I had a letter from the Major.

Lawrence is in hospital after being in an air crash. He was on a training flight and the engine failed. It was through a technical fault and no fault of his. Lawrence is lucky to have escaped with his life. His leg was broken and he also suffered concussion which is why he was unable to write to you. He is in a private hospital in Surrey.

Then followed the address of the hospital.

I reread the letter, my heart beating fast. All kinds of thoughts raced through my mind. Supposing we had been married and Lawrence were killed. I might even have been left a widow with a young child. Perhaps Lawrence would never be fit to fly an aeroplane again. I noted that there was no mention of particular injuries. Perhaps they were so bad that the Major did not want me to know. Anyway, I decided I must go to visit Lawrence at the first opportunity, which would be the following Saturday.

The train left Paulton very early and arrived at Guildford station shortly after midday. From the station I took a bus to the hospital which turned out to be rather small and homely, although it had the typical hospital smell. My shoes squeaked on the polished linoleum as I made my way along the corridor. A smiling nurse led me into his ward and indicated a bed in the far corner where a man lay in pyjamas, his leg strapped to a pulley.

"He's just having a nap," she whispered, "but I'll be waking him up anyway in ten minutes to bring him his tea."

I tiptoed over to the bed and just as I reached it Lawrence opened his eyes. I had forgotten how blue they were and my heart beat faster.

"Rhoda is it really you or are you a figment of my imagination? I dream of you so often that I can hardly believe you are real."

"I'm real alright. Here's my hand," and I held it out to him. He took it and raised it to his lips. "I was so worried when I didn't hear from you that I wrote to the Major and that is how I learned you were in hospital. What happened, Lawrence?"

"I crashed," he said briefly. "One of those things. Anyway, when I came to I was in this hospital and that is where I've been ever since."

"What's wrong with your leg?"

"Broken in a couple of places but mending quite well. I'll be flying again in a few months they tell me."

"You were lucky to get out alive, your father said in his letter."

"Yes, I managed to land in a field and skidded to a halt instead of rolling. If the plane had caught fire it would have been curtains."

"You're not going to keep flying after this, surely!" I said.

"Of course, the first thing I'll do once I leave here is get back in a plane. Anyway, that's enough about me. Let me look at you, Rhoda. You're a sight for sore eyes. Is that a new hat? It's very becoming. You look like Merle Oberon."

"I've brought you some chocolates," I said, blushing at the compliment.

"Thank you. My favourite food brought by my favourite girl. Now isn't it time you gave me an answer to the question I put to you last year?"

"What question was that?" I asked innocently.

"Shall I give you a clue? It has something to do with the future, yours and mine." He smiled and took both my hands in his, gazing into my eyes.

"I have given it serious thought, Larry, and the answer is yes."

"Really! Do you mean it?"

"Yes."

"Three cheers!" he said boyishly. "This calls for a celebration. Go out and tell that little nurse to fetch us a bottle of wine from somewhere. Tell her I'll pay double what it costs."

"Larry, this is a hospital," I spluttered.

"A private one. You do as I say, Miss Pritchard. The patient is always right," and he gave me a little push.

I found the nurse outside and told her blushingly that we'd just got engaged and Lawrence wanted a bottle of wine to celebrate.

"I think I can manage that," she said smiling. "Leave it to me."

Ten minutes later she returned with wine in a jug and two glasses. "Don't you dare mention this to Matron!" she admonished Lawrence. "I'd be hung drawn and quartered, although Dr. Martin would probably join us. He likes a drop."

Lawrence insisted she fetch a third glass for herself and we stood at his bedside rather self-consciously sipping the wine. I found it a little sour and put my glass on the cabinet.

"I really must go, Larry," I said glancing at my watch, "or I'll miss my train."

The nurse discreetly left the room and Lawrence drew me to him. He kissed me thoroughly then reluctantly let me go. I straightened my hat and stood up.

"Goodbye, Larry. Get better soon. I'll be writing to you."

"Goodbye, darling, you've made me a very happy man."

I left him then, turning round at the door to wave, while he kissed his hand to me.

Going back on the train to Paulton I felt strange, both elated and fearful. In one afternoon I had sealed my fate. I was going to be a married woman. I would never belong to myself again. Had I done the right thing?

I said nothing to the family about my engagement, deciding to wait until Lawrence came out of hospital and we could make it official. He wrote every day, short amusing accounts of day to day incidents and it was only at the end of the letter he would add some ardent little message. His pet name for me was Flo, after Florence Nightingale, and mine for him was Winco, an abbreviation for Wing Commander. I kept my letters to him equally bright and breezy. I still found it awkward to put endearments in writing and got around it by adopting a teasing tone. Lawrence seemed perfectly happy with this, but one day while I was puzzling over how to finish a letter to him I found myself thinking of Harold. *Would I have found it difficult writing to him, supposing we had been engaged*? I pulled myself up short. What treacherous thoughts were these? *I loved Lawrence and I was going to marry him. Surely I should be able to write in the way that lovers do. Perhaps it was just that I was reserved when it came to expressing my feelings in a letter. That was it, I was inhibited.* I picked up my pen and made an effort.

"I do so look forward to seeing you again, darling," I wrote. Well that was true enough, yet it had taken me ten minutes to come up with that one simple sentence. I put the letter into an envelope and stood up, relieved that I did not have to write for another couple of days.

The following Saturday two letters arrived for me. I recognised Lawrence's handwriting immediately but the other was unfamiliar. When I opened it I saw that it was from Dr. Branson. *Why was he writing to me*? As I read the letter my amazement grew. He was offering me a post as his personal secretary. Miss Lewis had resigned suddenly because of family reasons and after consultation with Matron Dunne he had decided that I might be a suitable candidate for the job because of my background of psychiatric nursing and my secretarial qualifications. He asked that I be in touch with him as soon as possible to say whether I was interested or not.

I felt stunned. Now that I had settled into my old job with the Standard Check Book Company I had given up all idea of returning to Laverton House. Then there was my engagement to Lawrence. Once we were married I knew he would not want me to work. Yet now, out of the blue, had come this offer from Dr. Branson. Of course, I would turn it down; circumstances dictated that.

Then I read Lawrence's letter.

Darling Flo,

I have been longing to see you again but something has come up. My firm offered me a post overseas for a year to Hong Kong where they have a branch. They wanted me to manage it and proposed a stupendous salary if I were prepared to make the move. I agonised over this for some days but because it would mean separation from you I turned it down. The upshot was they agreed to transfer me to a branch in Salisbury, at the same salary I am on now. I know that you are living back with your family in Paulton at the moment, but perhaps after we are married you would like to return to Salisbury. If you are agreeable, we could buy a house, perhaps in Laverstock. It seems more sense to own a house rather than rent one.

I reread the letter then got up and walked over to the window. From it I could see our little back garden, with its rows of cabbages, bounded by stone walls on either side. I thought of Salisbury plains stretching into the distance under the open sky and I had a sudden longing to be there. Thoughtfully I made my way downstairs to the kitchen where Aunty Edith was alone.

She looked up and I could see she was annoyed. "Rhoda, when you do your washing please put the soap back in the dish under the sink. I hunted and hunted for it this morning and finally found it in the scullery. I don't know why you can't put things back where you find them. I would have thought with all your training you would be more methodical, but you seem to go around in a dream at home here."

"I'm sorry, Aunty," I said, feeling irritated. *How could she make such a fuss over petty things*?

But she had not finished. "Perhaps Rhoda, you would be happier living somewhere else where you would have more freedom."

I looked at her startled. "It's strange that you should say that, Aunty, because this morning I had a letter from Dr. Branson at Laverton House offering me a job as his personal secretary."

I saw instant relief pass over her face.

"Well, I think you should give it serious thought," she said quietly. "When would he want you to start?"

"I don't know," I said slowly. "I suppose it wouldn't be for another month. Anyway, I would have to give in my notice at the Standard Check Book Company."

"I see," was all she said, but I knew that in her mind the matter was already settled.

I went upstairs after that and sat on the edge of my bed for some time thinking. How strange that the letter from Dr. Branson had arrived on the same day as Lawrence's. This was surely not mere coincidence but an indication that the time had come for me to make a move. I thought of the Good Shepherd and the way He had led me previously. Perhaps this was the new path I should follow. I sat down that evening and wrote my letter of acceptance to Dr. Branson.

CHAPTER TWENTY-FIVE

I left Paulton a month later on a Saturday morning. After saying goodbye to Aunty at the house I walked down to the station accompanied by Hazel and Camellia. Andrew and David were working that morning so could not see me off.

"I wish you weren't going," said Hazel as we hugged each other. "Please write often, Rhoda. I want to know everything that happens to you. I'm going to miss you so much."

"And I will miss you too," said Camellia. "It's been fun having you home,"

I was about to speak, but just then the train rounded the bend with a hiss of steam and so I simply hugged her close.

On the train I thought back to my last day at the Standard Check Book Company. Mr. Sutcliff had been very kind and added a substantial bonus in my final pay packet. He had also written me a glowing reference and as I read it in his office my cheeks grew hot. He was watching me closely.

"I mean every word of it, my dear. Anybody employing you can count himself lucky. I only wish you were staying on here, but I suppose you know what you are doing. Any time you are visiting Radstock remember to call in and see me."

"I will—and thank you for everything, Mr. Sutcliff. Being able to come and work here after my aunt's death got me through a difficult time."

I held out my hand and he clasped it in both of his."Goodbye and good luck," he said huskily.

Sally was waiting for me as I came out of his office. "I wish you weren't leaving, Rhoda. It'll be really dull here without you."

"But you're leaving yourself soon, Sal. Isn't the baby due in a few months?"

"Five months, but I'll stay here as long as I can." She glanced down at her stomach which was only slightly rounded. "We need the money. Bert's not getting full time work at the mine, but I suppose we must be thankful he's still got a job."

Sitting there in the train I thought of her words. It was true, times were hard and the slump had affected most working people. It was fortunate that the Standard Check Book Company was still going because it had seemed touch and go in 1929 after the Wall Street Crash. These last few years had been a grim time for many and often I had gone past places where queues of men had been lining up for the same job. Today, as we steamed through the orderly English countryside, it was hard to believe there could be hardship anywhere.

Dr. Branson was at Salisbury station to meet me. As I climbed into the front seat of his car I felt as though I had come home at last. Salisbury always had this effect on me, especially when I caught sight of the cathedral spire rising above the rooftops, as delicate and ethereal as ever.

Once we were outside the city Dr. Branson said, "I have arranged accommodation for you, Miss Pritchard. Now that you are not on the nursing staff it would be inappropriate for you to live in. Anyway, I thought that you would prefer to be independent, so I have arranged for you to board at a certain Miss Nugent's who lives in Laverstock, not far from the hospital. She has boarded other members of staff and they have all seemed quite satisfied with her."

I felt grateful to him for taking this trouble, but I wondered what this Miss Nugent would be like. I hoped she wasn't a fussy old maid like Aunty Edith or it would be a case of out of the frying pan and into the fire.

All I said was, "Thank you, Dr. Branson. That sounds very suitable."

Soon we reached the outskirts of Laverstock and the doctor drew up outside a brick bungalow, with a spacious front garden full of flowers.

"Well, here we are. I'll come in and introduce you to Miss Nugent," he said, lifting my suitcase from the boot.

As we walked up the path I noticed the flower beds were well weeded and that the flowers were arranged in rows of different colours. Oddly, the effect was artistic rather than regimented. The front door looked freshly painted and the brass door knob shone. Dr. Branson rapped sharply a couple of times and the door was opened by an elderly maid in the traditional black dress with a frilly white apron. He introduced himself and she invited us to step inside. "I'll tell Miss Nugent you are here," she said briefly and went away. Seconds later a very small lady with wispy grey hair and faded blue eyes came into the hallway. She brushed back a stray hair self-consciously when she saw the doctor.

"Dr. Branson, I was expecting you."

"Thank you, Miss Nugent. I've brought Miss Pritchard with me. She is the young lady you offered to give lodgings to."

Miss Nugent looked at me and smiled. She had a very sweet smile that quite transformed her small lined face.

"Welcome, my dear, to my modest abode. I hope you will be happy here. I trust you like cats," she added anxiously, as a large tabby wandered up and rubbed himself against my leg. "That is Walter. He's very friendly but I also have Billy, Fluff and Max. They're around somewhere."

I bent down and stroked Walter, hiding a smile. I had heard of old maids and their cats but I had never met anyone with four of them.

Dr. Branson said hastily. "I think I had better be going, Miss Nugent."

"Won't you stop and have a cup of tea with us?"

"No, thank you all the same. I should be getting along." I wondered whether his swift exit was something to do with the cats.

"Such a dear man," murmured Miss Nugent as he strode down the path. "Always in such a hurry though. Now come inside, Miss Pritchard, and let us get acquainted."

I followed her into the small hallway which smelt of furniture polish and rose petals, with an undercurrent of something else, which I later identified as cat.

The front room was comfortably furnished, although slightly cluttered, with odd pieces of antique furniture that looked as if they had once belonged in a grander house. Miss Nugent invited me to sit down in a chintz armchair and took a chair opposite me. The elderly maid appeared, wheeling a tea trolley on which were a plate of dainty sandwiches and another of tiny cupcakes. My mouth watered because it was some time since I had eaten.

As she poured the tea Miss Nugent asked me about myself. I gave her a very brief history and at the end of it she looked at me shrewdly. "You haven't mentioned whether you have a young man, Miss Pritchard, but I can't imagine an attractive young lady like yourself is without admirers."

I blushed at her forthrightness and decided to tell her about Larry. "Well, as a matter of fact I am unofficially engaged to a man who lives and works in London. He's also an RAF Reserve and is in hospital at the moment, recovering from an air crash."'

"But, my dear, how terrible! What happened?"

She listened intently as I told her about the accident.

"So, if there is another war, he will go straight into the RAF as an officer?" She looked beyond me, as though gazing back into the past. "I lost my brother in the last war and my fiancé also," she said quietly. "War is a terrible thing, Miss Pritchard. I hope there won't be another one, for your sake and for all the women who have loved ones in the forces."

I felt suddenly cold. Her words seemed to have a prophetic ring. I thought of Larry, with his sparkling eyes and his love of life. It was unthinkable that he should die, yet he had just been in an air crash and it was a miracle that he had come out of it alive—and this was not even wartime.

Miss Nugent leaned forward and patted my arm. "Don't be gloomy, my dear. It will probably never happen. Now, if you have finished your tea I will show you to your room."

She took me through the hall to a pretty little bedroom which was simply furnished. The single bed was covered with a primrose yellow quilt which matched the curtains and next to it was a locker with a bedside lamp. A dressing table stood against one wall and in front of the window was a small desk with a chair.

"What a dear little room!" I exclaimed.

"Now remember to keep your door closed, or one of the cats will come in," she said as Walter appeared, as if on cue, and rubbed himself against me.

I bent down and stroked him.

"I think he's taken a fancy to you," Miss Nugent remarked, lifting him up and carrying him firmly from the room.

When she was gone I sank down on the bed feeling weary yet curiously happy. I knew I was going to be at home here with Miss Nugent and her cats and the elderly maid. There was a sense of peace in this house and I was sure that once more the Good Shepherd had guided me to the right place.

The next day being Sunday, I decided to go to the gospel hall. Miss Nugent, as I had guessed, was Church, and went to early communion. I breakfasted on my own in the dining room with Walter for company. It was a cheerful sunny place with a large window overlooking a long back garden. At the end of it was a stone wall and beyond that a field where sheep were grazing. It was all very peaceful.

I allowed myself a good hour to walk to the gospel hall. Previously I had cycled there but I thought I had allowed sufficient time for walking, as there were one or two shortcuts through the fields. It was a perfect morning to be outside; the sun cast dappled patterns across the path and once I startled some rabbits or hares sleeping in the lane. A brightly coloured cock pheasant scuttled out of a hedge and ran in front of me, followed by his modest little mate.

At last I reached the outskirts of the village where the gospel hall stood. When I glanced at my watch I saw it was already a few minutes past eleven. I had underestimated the time it would take me to walk.

I tiptoed into the vestibule and stole into my usual place at the back of the hall. Someone was praying and all the heads were bowed. Then a hymn was given out and everyone stood up.

That was when I saw Harold, two rows in front. My heart lurched and then began beating wildly. *When had he come back? Should I speak to him after the service or hurry away. Why did the sight of him upset me like this? What should I do now*?

I don't know how I got through the remainder of the service. I heard very little of it. At last it was over and everyone stood. This was the moment I was dreading. I felt like running out of the building, but I was trapped by the people standing talking in the aisle. I glanced up and at that very moment Harold looked in my direction, but without recognition. Then his face lit up with surprise and pleasure. He edged past the people blocking the aisle until he stood in front of me.

"Rhoda! What a surprise to see you here! The last I heard was that you had gone back to your folk at Paulton. I felt sure I would never see you again. When did you come back to Salisbury?"

"I was going to ask you the same question."

He grinned. "I can see this is going to be a case of question and answer. Look, why don't you join me for lunch? We could go to the usual place," he added.

"Except that I haven't come by bicycle this morning."

"You mean you walked all the way from Laverstock?"

"Yes."

He thought for a moment. "In that case I'll walk back with you to Laverstock and we can have lunch at the Duck and Swan."

I protested that it was too far and he would have to walk all the way back, but he took no notice. We left the hall shortly afterwards and began the long hike back to Laverstock, but I hardly noticed the distance; there was so much to catch up on. I learned that Harold's father had made a good recovery from his stroke and now was able to carry on his work normally. He was concerned that Harold was not pursuing his art because of the demands on his time at the mission station and he was realistic enough to realise that Harold had no real calling as a missionary, so he insisted Harold come back to England and carry on with his painting.

I told Harold that I had visited Lawrence's art gallery and seen his work exhibited there.

"Yes, and all of the paintings have been sold," said Harold modestly. "Some of them fetched good prices too. I heard from some of the buyers that they would like more bird studies in particular."

"So will you continue to use the studio at Elsie's?" I asked, trying to keep my tone neutral, although I desperately wanted to know how things stood between them.

"Only until I can afford to rent my own. Elsie is very kind but I shouldn't impose on her."

"I'm sure she doesn't see it like that," I said, leading him on.

"Maybe not, but I would like to have everything on a business footing, but she refuses to accept any payment from me. I can't go on like that." His voice was troubled.

We walked on and for the remainder of the way we spoke of inconsequential matters. Harold told me about his time in Malaya and the wild life he had observed over there. He was very interesting but I knew all the time he was talking that neither of us was saying what was uppermost in our minds.

It was over lunch in the pub, where we were seated in a corner screened off from other diners, that there was a pause in the conversation. Harold looked up and said in a rush, "Look, Rhoda, in case you are wondering, there is nothing between me and Elsie. She is a good friend, that is all. Before I went away I had hoped that you and I might … that we might see more of each other, with a view to – er—a more serious attachment."

I looked at him sadly. "It's too late, Harold."

"You mean, there is someone else?"

"Yes, I suppose I should have been patient and waited for you to return, but I did not really know how you felt about me and this other person was keen, and I suppose I was swept along," I finished miserably.

"Are you committed to him?"

"I've promised to marry him."

Harold had gone very white.

"He's a lucky man." He paused. "Just tell me one thing, Rhoda, do you love him?"

"He's a fine man."

"You haven't answered my question."

"I thought I did, or I wouldn't have got engaged to him. I respect and admire him. Yes, I do love him," I said half defiantly.

"In that case, you must keep your promise and marry him and I will take up no more of your time."

"Oh, Harold, I wish it had been different," I burst out.

"I was a fool. I should have spoken up and told you how I felt, but at the time I had nothing to offer you and I had no right to bind you to me. I'm sorry, Rhoda." He held out his hand and I took it. His eyes, as he gazed into mine, were very clear and blue. "I will pray that you find great happiness in your marriage, Rhoda."

I looked away then. I could not trust myself to speak.

"I'll accompany you to your lodgings," he said, "and then I'm afraid it will have to be goodbye."

But once we were outside the pub I said, "Look Harold, I think it would be best if we said goodbye here."

"If you would rather." He took my hand and held it for a long moment. "Goodbye, Rhoda, and God bless you," he said huskily, then mounted his bicycle. As I watched him ride away my eyes filled with tears and I had a bitter taste in my mouth. *Why had God permitted this?* Then I remembered it was I myself who had consciously made the decision to give Harold up because he was out of the country. I could hardly blame God. *Yet, if I loved Harold and he loved me, wasn't it only right that we should marry?* Then I remembered Dad's words to me when I was a little girl, "A promise is a promise, Rhoda. Once given it is binding. The Bible is very definite on that."

I had made a promise to Larry and he loved me and wanted to marry me. I could not go back on it. I might not be in love with him but I did care very deeply about him and that was a good basis for marriage. I had given my word and I must keep it.

CHAPTER TWENTY-SIX

It felt strange arriving at Laverton House on Monday morning as a member of the office staff. The first difference I noticed was that Dr. Branson no longer addressed me as 'Nurse.' I was now 'Miss Pritchard.' His manner too, was brisk and business-like. Without preliminaries he conducted me around the office, showing me where everything was kept and his system of filing. The room was large and well-lit and must have once been a library, judging by the number of shelves lining the walls, most of them filled with medical textbooks. The doctor's desk stood on the opposite side of the room facing the door. It was of solid mahogany and looked antique. By contrast, mine was modern and positioned in front of a bay window commanding a view of the drive.

"That way you can warn me of any visitors coming to the house and I can decide whether I'm at home to them or not," the doctor said with a touch of humour. "Now that you know where everything is I would like you to take some dictation."

He indicated the chair in front of his desk and I sat down ready with my notebook and pencil. Dr. Branson dictated rapidly, but I found it no effort keeping up with him. I was used to Mr. Sutcliff's breakneck speed.

"Now would you read that back?" he said briefly and when I had finished he merely commented, "That is fine. Now type it out, please."

I knew this was by way of being a test but I felt no nervousness. Once I had typed out the letter I took it across to his desk. He scanned it quickly then looked up and smiled.

"That is very good, Miss Pritchard. I can see I made no mistake in asking you to be my secretary."

"Thank you, Doctor, I'm happy to be here," I replied, and it was true. I felt glad to be back in the atmosphere of the hospital once more.

The remainder of the morning passed quickly. Promptly at twelve thirty Dr. Branson stood up. "Lunchtime, Miss Pritchard. No need to come back to the office this afternoon. I'm sure you want to catch up with some of your friends here," and his eyes twinkled behind his glasses.

In the dining room I found Maisie and Joan waiting at a table near the door. They rushed towards me as soon as I came in. Neither of them was in uniform.

"Maisie, Joan, how wonderful to see you! What are you doing out of uniform? Shouldn't you be working?"

"Matron gave us the afternoon off so we could spend time with you," said Joan, "so the first thing we're going to do is take you to the Duck and Swan for lunch."

Laughing and talking we left the hospital and were soon at the pub, sitting in an alcove in a corner, not far from where Harold and I had been the day before.

"Now tell us all your news, Rhoda," began Joan. "Are you engaged yet?"

"Give me a chance to catch my breath," I said laughing.

"Yes, let's order our lunch first," said Maisie, ever practical.

Once our food had arrived I looked across at Joan.

"How are things with you and Jim?"

Without a word Joan held out her left hand. On her third finger was a dainty sapphire ring.

"It's beautiful, Joan. When did you get engaged?"

"Let me see—ten days ago. Now, what about you, Rhoda?"

"My engagement's not official yet."

"But you are going to marry the luscious Larry?" asked Joan.

"Yes."

"This calls for a celebration," said Maisie. "Cider all round, girls?"

The rest of the afternoon passed hilariously. I think we all drank a little too much of the cider which tasted very like lemonade. We seemed to find everything amusing and when we parted at the gate of Laverton House I was feeling a little light-headed. Miss Nugent gave me a quizzical look when she opened the door to me, but she made no comment.

From that day on life settled into a routine. I enjoyed working with Dr. Branson who was a kind and considerate boss. I met Maisie and Joan for lunch whenever they were free and so I felt part of the life of the hospital once more. The patients I spoke to in the dining room all greeted me like old friends and I would often go and sit with them and chat.

A month after I had been at Laverton House Lawrence was due to be discharged from hospital one Saturday morning. I caught an early train to Guildford, where the Major had arranged to pick me up in his car. Together we drove to the hospital and found Lawrence waiting in the foyer balancing on his crutches. He smiled with pleasure when he saw us come in.

"Rhoda! Dad! It's wonderful to see you both!"

I had a momentary twinge of pity when I looked at him. He was as handsome as ever, but the crutches made him seem vulnerable. How glad I was that I had never said a word about breaking our engagement. I could never bear to hurt this man. I went forward to kiss him and he murmured in my ear. "Darling, I've missed you so much."

The journey back to the Major's did not take long and soon we were turning into the drive. Lawrence refused to let us help him from the car but struggled with his crutches while the Major and I stood by. Gladys, the housekeeper, was watching from the door as Lawrence finally heaved himself out of the car and stood up.

"You manage those crutches a treat," she said admiringly as he walked into the house and I felt a surge of pride in him.

Gladys had prepared a splendid lunch for us and in the middle of the table was an opened bottle of champagne. Ceremoniously the Major poured wine into our glasses.

"I wish to propose a toast to Lawrence," he said, raising his glass. "How happy we are to have you home with us today, Son."

Lawrence stood up then, a little awkwardly, and looking towards me said, "And I wish to propose a toast to my fiancée,

Rhoda. We have kept our engagement a secret until now but this seems an appropriate time to announce it."

"Congratulations to you both," said the Major, beaming. "I can't tell you how happy this makes me. Welcome to our family, Rhoda."

"Thank you, Major," I said, blushing slightly.

"And when do you intend to tie the knot?" he asked, turning to Lawrence.

"We haven't discussed it yet. If I had my way it would be next week, but I expect there is a lot to be arranged first." He looked at me. "The first thing I want to do, Rhoda, is buy you an engagement ring, this very afternoon."

The Major drove us into Guildford and we stopped outside an expensive looking jeweller's shop in the high street. We looked at an array of rings and Lawrence urged me to have a large diamond solitaire. Instead, I chose a simple ruby ring with a setting of small diamonds. It was relatively inexpensive, but it was what I wanted and Lawrence agreed that it suited my hand.

"Now we are truly engaged," he murmured, as he fitted it on my ring finger.

"Yes," I replied and when I looked at the ring I knew I was bound to Lawrence as surely as if we were married.

That evening we discussed our wedding.

"I would like to be married at Paulton Baptist Church," I said.

"Not in Salisbury?" Lawrence was surprised.

"No," I said firmly. "My family is in Paulton and I would like Hazel and Camellia to be my bridesmaids."

"And I would like Richard to be my best man. I have no brother, as you know, and over the past few months Richard has been as good as any brother to me. I would also like your brother David to be my groomsman. Do you think he would agree?"

"I'm sure he would be delighted," I said mechanically. I was still recovering from my surprise at Lawrence's choice of Richard as best man.

When Lawrence suggested we be married in a couple of months I demurred.

"I would rather it were August. Also that allows plenty of time for all the things that have to be done."

"I suppose so," said Lawrence reluctantly, "but it seems a dreadfully long way off."

I teased him gently. "You don't want to dot and carry one, all the way to the altar, surely?"

"So long as I marry you nothing else matters," he said stroking my ring finger and I shivered, thinking how nearly I had come to disappointing him.

Lawrence moved to Salisbury a couple of months later and took lodgings near the Close. We did not see much of each other at weekends because he had resumed his flying training and this took up much of his time, especially as he had been promoted to flight officer. We spent most of our time together looking for a suitable house to buy, and when we found a bungalow not far from Miss Nugent's we were delighted. It was very small but I could not imagine that there would be enough to keep me occupied if I gave up my job at Laverton House.

"Larry, I would like to continue working after we are married," I said, once we had signed up for the house.

"I thought most married ladies were content to stay at home and devote their time to keeping house for their husbands," said Lawrence teasingly.

"But what would I find to do all day in such a tiny house?" I said.

"And you would miss all your friends at the hospital."

"That too."

So it was agreed that I should continue working at Laverton House once we were married.

A month before the wedding I went home to Paulton for the weekend. While I was there I took the opportunity to discuss wedding arrangements with the Baptist minister. I also took Hazel and Camellia to Bath to choose their bridesmaids' dresses which were to be pale blue. At the same time I selected my wedding dress.

At Laverton House Maisie and Joan took great interest in my wedding preparations and we spent many an evening discussing all aspects of the event.

One evening Joan looked up and said, "Have you thought about the honeymoon, Rhoda?"

"Of course I have. We are going to Bournemouth for a couple of nights."

"No, that is not what I meant."

"Oh, you are referring to the birds and the bees," I said airily.

"Well, yes, in a manner of speaking." She gave an embarrassed giggle.

"Sister Macnuff in Birmingham was very enlightening on the subject of the human reproductive system and left nothing to the imagination. What else is there to know?" I said with a laugh and the subject was dropped.

But that night in bed I tried to imagine the honeymoon and went hot and cold at the thought of marital intimacy. Finally, I managed to put the subject out of my mind by concentrating on sundry details of the wedding.

The date set was the 1st August. Lawrence booked rooms for his family in one of the central hotels in Bath but I managed to find a cheaper hotel for Maisie and Joan who were to arrive by train the day before. I had invited Miss Nugent, but she declined, saying that she would stay back and look after the cats. I also invited Iris, my friend and roommate from Birmingham days, but she was unable to accept as she was getting married herself the following weekend.

Aunty Edith and Aunty Gladys undertook the flower arrangements for the Baptist chapel and were very busy the day before the wedding, setting them up. David and Andrew had hired suits and they tried them on that very evening. Meanwhile, Hazel and Camellia slipped upstairs and put on their dresses. They appeared in the sitting room looking bashful.

"Now, it's your turn, Rhoda. Please put on your wedding dress and show us."

"Certainly not," I said. "Don't you know that nobody is meant to see the bride's dress until the wedding day? Now you get on upstairs and take those dresses off before they get grubby."

"You sound just like Aunty Edith," grumbled Camellia.

"Well, somebody has to keep you in order!" I retorted. "Anyway, before you go and change I have a little gift for you and Hazel," and I handed them each a box containing a necklace, a single pearl on a gold chain.

"It's for you to wear tomorrow with your bridesmaids' dresses," I said.

"It's beautiful," breathed Camellia and flung her arms around me.

"I'll treasure it all my life," said Hazel.

The boys were looking on.

"Where's ours, Sis? Don't we get a present too?" asked Andrew.

"Don't be a chump," said David. "Didn't you know the bride always gives her bridesmaids a gift?"

"When did you become an authority on brides and weddings?"

"Common knowledge, dear boy," and David pretended to dodge as Andrew picked up a cushion.

"Sh, you two, Aunty will be home any minute," said Hazel pointing at the door.

I laughed, enjoying this family banter. Suddenly the thought occurred to me that as a married woman I would no longer be part of the family in quite the same way.

By the time Aunty came home that evening everyone was sitting demurely in the kitchen drinking cocoa and shortly afterwards we went to bed. I lay awake long after I heard Hazel's regular breathing.

I must have slept finally, because when I woke it was morning. Then I remembered that this was my wedding day. I sprang out of bed and drew back the curtains. There was not a cloud in the sky and outside the birds were singing lustily. I felt a surge of joy.

I seemed to float through the next few hours. I helped Camellia and Hazel get dressed and they assisted me with all the fastenings down the back of my wedding dress. Somehow, we were all ready in time. Uncle Stan was to give me away and had lent his car to take us to the church. Andrew had decorated it with white streamers and was sitting proudly at the wheel.

"None of this tomfoolery of the bride being late," growled Uncle Stan to Andrew. "You get us to the chapel on time, lad."

Andrew turned round and winked at me.

When we arrived at the chapel Uncle Stan helped me from the car. "You look beautiful, lass," he said. "I wish your aunt was here to see you—and your mother," he added.

"Perhaps they are looking down," I replied.

Hazel and Camellia lifted my train and I took Uncle Stan's arm. As we walked through the door the organ struck up the wedding march and we began the slow walk up the aisle. I was not aware of anyone, except Lawrence, who turned his head quickly as I came in.

As the Minister intoned the solemn words of the wedding service, the full significance of the vows I was making took hold of me. "Until death us do part," sounded so final. Then Lawrence placed the ring on my finger and it was all over.

The rest of the day passed in a blur. I smiled and shook hands and said all the appropriate things to the guests, but it seemed as though it were happening to someone else. At the wedding breakfast speeches were made, but I could remember nothing of them afterwards.

Then it was time to change from my wedding dress into my going away outfit. Hazel helped me and just before I went downstairs I turned to her. "It all seems unreal," I said. "I can't believe I'm really married. It feels as though it's happening to someone else."

"You'll always be my sister, even if you are a Mrs.," she said, a catch in her voice.

"Nothing can change that," I said, hugging her.

Everyone stood on the steps of the house waving as Lawrence and I drove off. Some of the neighbours were outside in their front gardens waving too and I had the curious feeling of having done this before. Then I remembered the day, so long ago in New Zealand, when with my brothers and sisters I had driven away from our home in Huntley to begin a new life in England. It all came back to me so clearly: the neighbours standing at their gates waving as we left behind all that was familiar and dear to us. I sighed involuntarily.

Lawrence turned and looked at me, concerned. “You’re not unhappy, are you darling?”

“No, Larry, I was just thinking of the day we left New Zealand when all the neighbours stood in their gardens and waved us off. It felt like that just now.”

“As though you were leaving your old life behind and venturing into the unknown?”

I looked at him, grateful for his understanding.

“And your new life in England was not so bad, was it?”

“No, it was different, that was all.”

“And this new life we are starting out on together will be much better than the old, I guarantee,” he said, taking my hand in both of his.

“Yes, I am sure it will be,” I replied softly.

CHAPTER TWENTY-SEVEN

Our honeymoon in Bournemouth was better than ever I could have imagined. I had heard about the difficulties brides faced on their honeymoon, when the man they married became a stranger, but it was not like that with Lawrence. The more intimately I grew to know him the dearer he became to me. We went for long walks along the beach hand in hand, sometimes talking and sometimes keeping silent. He told me all about his childhood, the way his family had moved from place to place, wherever his father was stationed by the army. I learned about the disruption to his life, when just as he was beginning to call a place 'home', they were moved somewhere completely different.

As he talked I began to catch a glimpse of another Lawrence behind the sophisticated and confident man I had known. He encouraged me to talk about my early life too and I told him of the loneliness I had felt when we left our father in New Zealand after having suffered the loss of our mother such a short while before.

As we walked together our mutual understanding deepened so that by the time evening came it was natural to turn to one another in bed and find comfort in holding each other close; and our lovemaking became a spontaneous overflow of our deep feeling for each other. The intense joy and satisfaction I experienced was like nothing I had known before and I understood then what the Bible meant when it said, "The two shall be one."

The week sped by, but I was not sorry when our honeymoon came to an end, for we were going home to our own little house in Laverstock. I looked forward to seeing it again and walking through the front door, knowing that it was really ours and we were beginning our new life together inside its walls.

My excitement mounted as Lawrence turned into Mansfield Close and stopped outside the tiny brick bungalow with its pocket handkerchief garden. But what was this? The flower bed inside the picket fence was bright with delphiniums, carnations and pansies. Somebody had been busy while we were away and planted a garden. Also, at either side of the door were pots brimming with colour. It was truly a welcome home.

"Miss Nugent," I breathed. "It could only be her."

"It certainly has her stamp," said Lawrence, as he fitted the key into the lock. Without warning he swept me into his arms and carried me laughing into the house. "Our first home together. May we have many long and happy years here." His blue eyes were merry as he looked into mine.

"I do hope so, Larry," yet as I spoke a strange chill went through me. I felt almost too happy at this moment. Could it possibly last?

He took my hand. "Now you've gone quiet. What is on your mind, little Flo?" he asked, using my pet name.

"Nothing, just a stupid idea that nothing lasts forever, not even our happiness."

"What gloomy thoughts! Come on, let's take a tour of our house," he said, catching hold of my hand and together we walked from room to room. We had just finished and were standing in the bedroom when the front doorbell rang.

"Our first visitor!" I exclaimed and hurried through the passage to the front door, where Miss Nugent was standing, holding a wicker cage. A piteous miaow came from it.

"Oh, you've brought Walter."

"Yes, he has been moping since you left and I thought you might like him as a house-warming present," she said, bending down and lifting the lid.

Out jumped Walter, looking a little dishevelled, but he came straight over to me and rubbed himself against my legs purring loudly. Then he pushed past Lawrence and strolled into the house sniffing at the door as he did so.

"You see, he's perfectly at home here," said Miss Nugent beaming.

"Oh, what a lovely homecoming this is! First the garden and all those beautiful flowers and now Walter. Thank you so much, Miss Nugent," and I hugged her. "I would offer you a cup of tea but we haven't got any milk yet."

"I have brought a bottle with me and a cake," said Miss Nugent, indicating the basket she had laid on the ground beside the cage.

"You've thought of everything," I said, tears springing to my eyes at her kindness.

A little while later the three of us were sipping tea in our tiny sitting room and as I looked at these two people who were so dear to me, I remembered that far off day in Birmingham when I was told I could no longer continue with general nursing. That had seemed like the end of everything, yet here I was, sitting in my own house with my darling husband and our kind friend. My heart swelled with gratitude to the Good Shepherd who had led me here.

After this, we had a stream of visitors eager to see our new house. The first was Joan who arrived the next afternoon.

"I just love your little house," she said sighing. "It is exactly what I would like when I am married."

"Have you and Jim decided on a date yet?"

"Not exactly. It all depends on us finding a place of our own. Jim won't consider renting. He says it is a waste of money and we ought to be paying a mortgage."

I thought for a moment. "I think I heard Lawrence say that there was another house in this road coming up for sale. That is what the agent told him when we were finalising this one. Would you like me to find out more for you, Joan?"

Her eyes were shining. "Oh, please do, Rhoda."

I mentioned it to Lawrence that evening and he came home next day with the news that the bungalow two doors from us was definitely for sale.

I passed this on to Joan and a few days later she arrived breathlessly at our door. "We're going to be neighbours, Rhoda! Jim's made an offer on the bungalow and it's been accepted."

"That's wonderful news, Joan. So you will be married very soon."

"Yes, as soon as everything is arranged," and she grabbed me round the waist and waltzed me around the room. Lawrence happened to walk in at that moment.

"Hey, what's all this? Practising for the Salisbury Palais are we?"

"Get a bottle of cider out, Larry. We have to celebrate. Joan and Jim have bought the house along the road and will be getting married soon."

"That is worth celebrating," and he left the room.

"You are lucky having a husband like Larry," whispered Joan. "He's got everything: looks, personality, the lot."

"Sh, here he comes," I said.

"What are you two whispering about?"

"That's our secret," I said winking at Joan.

We spent the next half hour excitedly discussing Joan and Jim's house and when Joan had gone I turned to Lawrence. "I have a feeling that there is something significant about Joan coming to live near us."

Lawrence looked thoughtful, "Well, she will be company for you when I have to be away on flying duties."

"Yes, I suppose so."

"But apart from that, am I not sufficient for you, Flo darling?"

"Of course you are Larry, I was just going to say …" but I got no further as his lips met mine and we clung together for a long time.

Monday morning came around all too soon. When I walked into the office Dr. Branson looked up from his desk, his eyes twinkling behind his glasses, "Well, Mrs. Grantly, I trust you had a good holiday."

"Yes, thank you Doctor. The weather was perfect and our hotel was very comfortable."

"Your time away has certainly done you good. You look blooming, my dear." He said this with so much emphasis that I found myself blushing. It was a relief when his manner became brisk and businesslike as usual.

"Now, I have a pile of letters for you to type. They have been mounting up while you've been away." He leaned back in his chair studying me. "I have been thinking that now you are married you might like a reduction in your hours. What would you say to a working day beginning at nine thirty and finishing at four? I am sure that you would be able to cover all the office work in that time."

"That would suit me perfectly, Doctor," I said gratefully. I could certainly do with the extra time at the end of the day to prepare Larry's dinner. I was an inexperienced cook and even the simplest meals took me ages to prepare.

"Good, that is settled then." He glanced at his watch. " Take your time. I'm going to be out of the office this afternoon. When you have finished typing those letters feel free to go home."

I left him then, thinking how fortunate I was to have such a kind boss. When I arrived at the door of the dining room I paused for a moment feeling suddenly shy. There were bound to be the usual arch comments about the honeymoon. I braced myself.

The first person I met on going into the room was Maisie. "Come and sit down and tell me all about the honeymoon. Not all, but you know what I mean, where you went and what you did."

"Well, we went to Bournemouth." I paused. "The weather was good, the hotel was comfortable and everything was perfect. What more can I say?"

"And now you are back in your own little home. Joan has told me all about it. She says it is like a doll's house."

"So it is and I feel as though I am playing house." I giggled.

"You are so lucky, Rhoda. Joan and I said to each other at your wedding that we felt envious of your lovely family. It made us both wish that we had brothers and sisters like yours. Your sisters made beautiful bridesmaids."

"I suppose I am fortunate. I've always felt sad that I didn't have a mother, and Dad is such a long way away but I do have my brothers and sisters. That is quite truc."

"And now you've got a perfect husband."

"And what about you, Maisie? Who's your latest flame?"

She looked down at the table cloth and her colour rose. "It was when I was at your wedding. I was talking to one of Lawrence's RAF friends, Eric Jameson, and well, things went on from there. He has been writing to me each day and we are going to meet next weekend when he comes down to Salisbury."

"I remember him vaguely. Larry introduced me to some of his friends but …"

"You only had eyes for Lawrence," finished Maisie with a laugh.

"When Eric comes to Salisbury please bring him to our house."

"Yes, I will."

We finished lunch soon after that and Maisie hurried off. When I stood up, several of the nurses came over to the table and there was the usual badinage about my newly married status and requests to see my rings. It was quite a relief to get back to the quietness of the office and settle down to work once more.

It seemed no time at all and I was caught up in the preparations for Joan's wedding. She was married in the little Anglican Church at Woodgreen which she had attended since she was a small child. I think most of the village turned out to wish her well. It was heart-warming to see her on her father's arm as he walked her proudly down the aisle. Jim was a typical bridegroom, rather ill at ease in his smart new suit and inarticulate when it came to making a speech at the wedding breakfast. Through it all Joan looked serene and beautiful at his side. The only sign of emotion she showed was when it came to leaving her parents. She turned to them with tears in her eyes. "Mum and Dad, thank you for all that you've done for me since I was a baby. I love you both very much."

She hugged them and stepped into the car that Jim had borrowed from a friend. It was decorated with a big 'Just Married' sign placed in the back window. Amidst clouds of confetti Jim drove away. When the car had disappeared, Mrs. Russell took my arm.

"Please don't go yet, Rhoda. You and your husband come and have a cup of tea with us. It all seems flat, now that Joanie is gone."

I was feeling it too and was glad to accept the invitation. It seemed very quiet in their sitting room, yet there was a sense of warmth and homeliness here that lapped us around.

Mr. Russell was soon deep in conversation with Lawrence and questioning him about the RAF. Inevitably the subject of war came up.

"I'm so glad we've got a sensible chap like Chamberlain at the helm now. There'll be no more talk of war with Germany with him in charge. After the last show in 1918 the government will keep us out of Europe."

I watched Lawrence's face. I knew he did not want to destroy the old man's faith, but he had talked to me often enough about the preparations the government was making, especially in building up Britain's air defence.

"I'm sure the government will make every effort to stay out of any conflict in Europe, but if the need arises they have to be ready. My father was in the last war and he feels like you, that the last thing we want is to go through it all again."

Mrs. Russell looked up then. "So many of the young men I grew up with lost their lives. George was wounded on the Somme, you know. I'm so thankful they invalided him out or he might not have been here today."

When we got up to leave Mrs. Russell looked at Lawrence and said quietly, "When I meet young men like yourself I feel sure that our country will be safe, whatever happens."

Looking at Lawrence, so tall and smart and confident, I thought he seemed the epitome of all that was fine in English manhood. No force on earth could destroy our nation while we were defended by men like him.

CHAPTER TWENTY-EIGHT

One morning in November I woke up feeling distinctly queasy, yet I had eaten nothing the day before that could have disagreed with me. I did not mention it to Lawrence but fought down the nausea and after a while it passed off. The following morning the same thing happened, only this time I vomited. I managed to go to the office as usual and during the day felt quite normal. After this had occurred three days in succession, I happened to be talking to Matron and mentioned it casually to her. She looked at me knowingly, a little twinkle in her eyes.

"I think you should be making a trip to your doctor, my dear. That sounds to me like a case of morning sickness."

I left her my head reeling. A baby! But we had been married only a few months. Then I calculated. We had actually been married four months, so what was more natural than that I should be pregnant? All the same, it might only be an upset stomach, despite Matron's prognosis, so I would say nothing to Lawrence until I had seen the doctor. I made an appointment with my GP in Laverstock the following day.

He asked me a number of questions and did some tests. Finally, he sat back in his chair and smiled at me. "I am almost one hundred percent sure that you are two months pregnant, Mrs. Grantly."

I left his consulting room feeling both excited and fearful. I couldn't grasp that I was actually going to be a mother. After all, I was only just getting used to being married, but to be a mother. *What a responsibility! How would Lawrence feel about it?* All these questions whirled through my mind.

As soon as Lawrence walked through the door that afternoon he took one look at me and said, "What has happened to you today, Flo, you're all lit up like a firecracker?"

"What a simile, Larry! Well, as a matter of fact I do have news."

"Let me guess. You've had a rise."

"Quite cold."

"What a shame. We could do with some extra dosh."

"Sorry, try again."

The cat's had kittens."

"Oh, Larry, you know it's a male."

"You can't tell with cats. They all look the same. Anyway, it's fat enough."

"I can see I'll have to tell you. I went to the doctor today and, Larry, we're going to have a baby."

"You clever little thing," and he swept me up in his arms and walked round the room with me.

"Put me down, you silly man!" I protested, struggling.

"Oh, sorry, I should be treating you with kid gloves, I suppose, in your interesting condition. Now sit down in this armchair and tell me all about the baby. When is it due?"

"The doctor says I am two months pregnant so that means ...."

"Next June. We'll have to get busy and fit out the spare bedroom as a nursery."

"Then we have to buy a cot and a pram and I will have to start knitting a layette."

"Goodness, this baby will reduce us to poverty," he said teasingly.

I had a sudden thought. "Oh dear, I'll have to let Dr. Branson know and he's sure to say I must stop work."

"But won't you want to anyway?"

"Not if I'm feeling well. Being pregnant doesn't make me an invalid."

"I suppose not, but I thought in novels it was always described as a delicate condition."

"Maybe in Victorian times, but not in the twentieth century."

For the rest of the evening we talked excitedly about the baby.

"I wonder whether it will be a boy or girl," I said.

"Well, it has to be one or the other," grinned Lawrence. "I hope it will be a little girl who looks exactly like you," and he leaned forward gazing at me fondly.

"I don't mind what it is, so long as he or she has all the necessary bits and is healthy."

"Quite right, my darling."

The next day I sought out Matron Dunne to tell her that her diagnosis was correct.

"I'm not often wrong," she said smiling, "and you've been looking particularly blooming lately, another sign of motherhood. Now you will have to let Dr. Branson know. I think he will be sorry to lose you as his secretary."

"I don't intend to leave yet, not until I have to," I said firmly.

I spoke to Dr. Branson soon afterwards and he looked surprised when I said I was willing to stay on.

"Well, that is over to you, my dear, and I must admit that I would be grateful to have some extra time to look around and find a replacement. Good secretaries do not grow on trees and I must say I will be sorry to lose you. So you intend to work for another two months at least?"

"Easily that long," I said confidently.

Over the next few weeks I found it heartwarming to see the interest shown in my baby by everyone at Laverton House. I was particularly amused to watch Joan and Maisie struggling to knit little garments. My own efforts were far from perfect and time after time I had to unpick and start again. Miss Nugent was a great help and I flew to her whenever I was in difficulties.

In this way, the months passed and when I was five months pregnant I reluctantly said goodbye to Dr. Branson. He had found a pleasant middle-aged lady with considerable secretarial experience to replace me. She had been recently widowed and was glad to have a job in a hospital environment rather than in the business world. I liked her immediately and knew that she would fit in with Dr. Branson's little ways.

It was a wrench saying goodbye to the staff at Laverton House and I was touched when several of them presented me with little gifts of booties and matinee jackets that they had knitted for the baby. I did not regret stopping work however, because I found that now I was advanced in my pregnancy I had slowed down and even ordinary little jobs about the house took me longer than usual and I had frequently to sit down and rest.

The doctor had booked me into Salisbury Infirmary, which I was delighted to see was right next to the cathedral and only separated from it by the Avon stream. The maternity ward was on the top floor and from it was a perfect view of the cathedral. Whenever I went shopping in Salisbury I would go and sit on the bank of the stream and look across at the hospital, imagining what it would be like to have my baby there.

Slowly time passed and according to my calculations I was nine months pregnant, yet the baby showed no signs of coming. I made an appointment to see the doctor.

"It's at least five days after the date you said the baby was due," I said anxiously.

"Oh, that is nothing to worry about," he said casually. "Babies come when they are ready, my dear. The baby's in the right position and its heart beat is steady. Your blood pressure is a little higher than normal, but that is nothing to be alarmed about. You should go home and give yourself plenty of rest and take the weight off your legs. You are a healthy young woman and should have no trouble giving birth. No need to be anxious."

I left his surgery feeling reassured.

One morning a week later, I was standing at the sink washing dishes when I felt a tightening of my stomach. I sat down in the nearest chair. So this must be it; I was in labour. I had heard that there was usually quite a long gap between contractions at the start and that I should time them, before ringing for a taxi. Lawrence and I had discussed what I should do once labour started. He wanted me to ring him immediately after I had been in contact with the hospital.

I was shaking with nervousness as I rang through to the maternity ward. The nurse on duty told me to time my contractions and then come in when they were about ten minutes apart. I then phoned Lawrence's office and left a message for him. For the next few hours I carefully noted the frequency of the contractions and when they came steadily at ten minute intervals I rang for a taxi. After I had explained to the receptionist that I was in labour her response was immediate.

"We will have a cab to you in five minutes," she said.

My suitcase was packed ready and as I carried it into the hall Walter came and rubbed himself against my legs. I bent down automatically to stroke him and at that very moment was seized by another excruciating spasm. When it had passed I leaned weakly against the wall. Just then the taxi arrived and the kindly driver took my arm and guided me to the cab.

"Are you comfortable, love?" he enquired as he helped me into the back seat. "I'll go carefully so you'll not have any jolting."

Fortunately, for the whole of the journey I had no more contractions and when we arrived at the hospital I was grateful when the driver took charge of my suitcase and accompanied me in the lift to the maternity ward.

"Good luck, my dear," he said as he stood with me at the reception desk. "My missus has had five. Just like shelling peas," he added cheerfully. "Nothing to worry about."

I noticed the nurse smiling when he said this and as he walked away from the desk she commented, "Men! They simply have no idea what it's like to have a baby."

Just at that moment I was gripped with another pain and she led me to a chair. When it was over a different nurse conducted me to the labour ward.

The next hours were a blur of pain. Never had I experienced anything like it. The intervals between the contractions grew shorter and shorter. Scarcely had I recovered from one than I was hurled into another. I lost all count of time as my body was tossed on a rack of torment.

I was only dimly aware of figures by the bed. Then I heard someone say, "Bear down," and did all I could to obey. "It's coming," I heard the same voice say, and there was another terrible searing pain that seemed to tear my body apart. Then I was suddenly miraculously pain free. I heard a thin cry and opening my eyes saw a tiny form being held in front of me, wet and covered in slime.

"It's a girl," said the doctor. "A fine healthy child," and he brought it closer for my inspection. "Now, I'll just cut the cord and then leave it to you to clean her up," he said briefly to the nurse. Then turning back to me he said, "You've done a good job. I'll see you tomorrow."

I smiled weakly and lay back on the pillow, content to let the nurse do most of the work in cleaning me up while another nurse attended to the baby. "She's a strong baby," the nurse remarked, putting her into my arms, "and she's obviously hungry," as the baby nuzzled against my breast. I looked down at the small head covered with a fuzz of fine dark hair and was full of wonder that this tiny human being was really mine.

Later that evening Lawrence came to visit. He bent down and kissed me fondly. "I'm so proud of you, Rhoda. You did it all on your own—even found your way to the hospital and checked in. By the time I got your message you were already here and in the labour ward."

"Have you seen your daughter, Larry?"

"Not yet. They held up a funny little thing to the glass and said it was mine, but it looked more like a skinned rabbit to me."

"What a thing to say about your own child!" I said laughing.

"What's important is that both of you are alive and well," he said seriously. "It seemed a devil of a long time you were in labour and they would tell me nothing while I was sitting in the waiting room. I don't usually smoke, but I think I used up a whole packet out there."

"Thank goodness it's all over now, anyway," I said. Then I had a sudden thought. "You will remember to feed Walter when you get home, Larry. I left in such a hurry I didn't put any food out for him."

"That cat! You think more about it than you do me! What about my dinner?"

"Don't be silly," I said, reaching across and rumpling his hair. He looked at that moment like a mischievous small boy rather than a father. "I made arrangements with Miss Nugent and she has offered to come and cook for you while I am away. I expect she will look after Walter as well."

"How long are you likely to be here?"

"I think it's a couple of weeks for a first baby."

"Oh, that long! I don't think I can spare you for all that time."

"You will appreciate me all the more when I come home."

Just at that moment a nurse came into the ward and rang a bell.

"Oh visiting time is up already!" I exclaimed.

Lawrence pulled a face and bent down to kiss me. "I'll see you tomorrow, darling. Have a good night," he murmured against my cheek.

When he was gone I lay back against the pillow feeling suddenly deathly tired. *If this was what it was like to have a baby, I would be quite happy with just one,* I thought as I dropped off to sleep.

CHAPTER TWENTY-NINE

Lawrence agreed with me that we should call our baby Hannah, after my mother, and although it sounded slightly old-fashioned, the name seemed to suit her. She was a good little thing and did everything according to the book I had purchased on the bringing up of babies. From the start she slept right through the night and so Lawrence and I scarcely ever had a broken night. She was a contented baby and rarely cried except when she was hungry.

Her christening was held at the local Church of England which we now attended and Joan stood as her godmother and Richard, her godfather. Joan adored her little godchild and popped in to see her nearly every day.

As soon as Hannah was old enough I put her in her pram and wheeled her up to Laverton House to show her off to the staff and the patients. She was dressed in the pink matinee jacket and bonnet that Matron Dunne had given me before she was born and Hannah looked very sweet with her fine brown hair just peeping out at the edges. Her eyes were a deep blue like Lawrence's and her eyelashes long and dark. I thought she was just perfect, but then I was her mother. It was very gratifying to hear others praise her and I was pleased that she would happily go to anyone. In fact, she was passed from one to another like a parcel and she took it in her stride, usually turning to look with interest at the person holding her.

"What an intelligent baby! She's taking everything in," exclaimed Matron Dunne.

"And she's such a little beauty; look at those eyes. How did you produce her, Rhoda? She's not at all like you," said Maisie cheekily.

"She's got her father's looks," I said, gazing down at Hannah; and it was true, she was Lawrence all over again and I was glad.

I could not get over the wonder of her. Each day I noticed some new development and when Lawrence came home I would report it to him. Together we would hang over her cot and take delight in the way she smiled and gurgled up at us. I loved to sit in the morning holding her, after I had given her a bath, brushing her fine downy hair that glinted gold in the sunlight.

Walter, at first, seemed to have his nose out of joint because of all the attention we paid to the new baby, but even he fell under her spell and would sit on a chair with his eyes half slits watching her. When Hannah was able to sit up she would reach for him and he put up with her attempts to grab his tail, dodging her adroitly.

And so the months passed. Hannah's first word was 'Dadda', much to Lawrence's delight and very soon she was crawling everywhere. Every afternoon I put the baby to bed for an hour and then enjoyed the luxury of sitting back and reading the paper. We had two delivered each morning, the Daily Express and the Manchester Guardian and they were diametrically opposed in their political views. I enjoyed the chatty style of the Express and usually picked it up first. One afternoon I opened the paper as usual and was arrested by the huge headline on the front page, Peace in our Time. Underneath it was a photograph of Mr. Chamberlain waving a piece of paper. The report said that the Prime Minister had managed to get Herr Hitler to sign an agreement that he would not go to war with Britain, so long as we agreed to his taking over Sudetenland.

Hitler's argument was that Sudetenland contained more Germans than Czechs and that Germany was in a better position to deal with the unrest in this country on its borders. Hitler's reasons for annexing Sudetenland certainly sounded very plausible, but the fact remained that Sudetenland belonged to Czechoslovakia and the Czech government objected to this territory being handed over to the Germans, on the grounds that other nationalities within the borders of Czechoslovakia might rise up and demand independence.

At first, Mr. Chamberlain told Hitler that Britain, France and the Czech government would not agree to Germany taking over Sudetenland. Then Benito Mussolini stepped in and suggested the way to resolve the issue was to hold a four-power conference of Germany, Britain, France and Italy, and exclude Czechoslovakia.

This meeting was held on the 29th September in Munich, and Sudetenland was handed over to Germany. The editorial of the Daily Express was euphoric. "Be glad in your hearts. Give thanks to your God. People of Britain, your children are safe. Your husbands and your sons will not march to war. Peace is a victory for all mankind. If we must have a victor, let us choose Chamberlain."

My heart lifted as I read this. For so long we had lived under the threat of war and now that fear was removed. My husband and my baby were safe.

I then turned to the Manchester Guardian and read about Mr. Chamberlain's reception when he arrived back to London from Munich. The report said that as Mr. Chamberlain stood on the balcony of Buckingham Palace with the King and Queen, the crowd below roared his name. They acclaimed him as the man of the moment who had rescued the British people from the threat of war.

Then I read the following paragraph which said, "Politically Czechoslovakia is rendered helpless, with all that means to the balance of forces in Eastern Europe. Hitler will be able to advance again, when he chooses, with greatly increased power."

I put both papers to one side. Was this really the solution it seemed? Should Mr. Chamberlain have given in to Hitler and ignored the Czech government? How would we in Britain like it if a foreign power came and claimed part of our country? There seemed something very wrong about the whole deal. I would have to discuss it with Lawrence when he came home this evening.

As soon as Lawrence walked in the door he said, "I feel very ashamed of our country today. We have acted dishonourably and let Czechoslovakia down. We have also lost the support of the Czech army which is one of the best in Europe."

"But surely it is a good thing that Hitler has agreed not to go to war with us?"

"Can you ever believe the words of a dictator? Mr. Chamberlain is living in a fool's paradise if he thinks Hitler will be content with Sudetenland. Before long he'll be marching into Czechoslovakia, and after that Poland. You wait and see, Rhoda." His words had a prophetic ring.

Christmas that year was to be an important event. Hazel was coming to spend it with us and so was the Major. We had only the one spare room and so it was decided that the Major should have it while Hazel would stay with Miss Nugent in my old room.

It was snowing on Christmas Eve when Lawrence went to meet Hazel from the train. Her cheeks were glowing as she came into the house laden with parcels, and my heart leapt with joy to see her.

"Where's Hannah?" were her first words.

"She's in the kitchen, probably giving her dinner to the cat," I said, "Come and meet her."

Hazel followed me into the kitchen and we were just in time to prevent Hannah from lifting her spoon over the side of the chair while Walter waited beneath ready to receive whatever bounty was coming his way. I lifted Hannah out of the chair and handed her to Hazel.

Hannah crowed and reached up to grab a handful of hair, while Hazel held her at arm's length and inspected her.

"This is Aunty Hazel," I said to Hannah and much to our amazement she repeated the name.

From that moment Hazel took her over and for the whole of her stay I had hardly to do anything for the baby. Hazel fed, bathed and dressed her.

When the Major arrived a little later on Christmas Eve he too was entirely captivated by Hannah and Lawrence and I looked on as Hazel and he took it in turns to entertain her.

"That child is going to be thoroughly spoilt by her grandfather and her aunt," said Lawrence gazing fondly at Hannah as she played on the hearth rug with a toy rabbit while we sat talking around the fire.

At nine o'clock Lawrence accompanied Hazel down the road to Miss Nugent's. It was snowing hard and I was sorry that they both had to turn out in the cold, but I knew there would be a warm welcome for them there.

"Come as early as you can in the morning, Haze," I said as I kissed her goodnight.

Christmas Day was bright but cold. Snow lay on the ground and sparkled in the wintry sunshine. When Hazel and Miss Nugent arrived in the middle of the morning, they crunched up the path leading to the front door, their cheeks glowing and their arms full of parcels. Lawrence led them into the sitting room which he had decorated with streamers and paper chains early that morning. In the corner was a tiny fir tree in a tub, lit with fairy lights.

"It's beautiful," breathed Hazel and Lawrence looked gratified.

While he poured a glass of sherry for everybody I took myself off to the kitchen to attend to the last minute preparations for dinner. Miss Nugent insisted on helping me and supervised the vegetables. Hazel looked after Hannah and so I was able to concentrate on the food. I still found cooking a bit of an ordeal and it was the first time I had put on a Christmas dinner. Miraculously everything came together and we sat down to the meal promptly at one o'clock. The Major said grace for us and after that we pulled crackers, donned party hats and read the jokes in time honoured fashion. As I looked around the table at the happy faces I thought how blessed I was.

Hazel left us on Boxing Day and the Major stayed for the week until after New Year. I could see that he and Lawrence had plenty to talk about, but a lot of it went over my head. Neither of them believed that the Munich Agreement held much weight and, like Churchill, they mistrusted Hitler. They agreed that it was only a matter of time and Germany would take the rest of Czechoslovakia and then there would be no stopping Hitler.

On New Year's Day we were sitting by the fire after tea.

"Well, here it is the first day of 1939," began the Major. "I'm afraid I don't feel very optimistic about this year. I don't see how we can avoid war with Germany. Chamberlain is a fool not to be preparing for it. It's as plain as the nose on your face that Hitler is building up the army. He's had conscription since 1935."

"Yes and the Luftwaffe is getting steadily stronger. We can't compete with Germany in the air," said Lawrence. "Chamberlain's policy of disarmament is downright stupid."

I entered the discussion at this point. "You men and your talk of war. I'm thankful that back in September Chamberlain got a guarantee from Hitler that Germany would not fight with us. I can't believe our government will let us in for another war after the last one."

A glance passed between Lawrence and his father and to my relief they dropped the subject.

After the Major had returned home I made a point of reading the papers. Each day the reports became gloomier and full of foreboding about Germany. Then it happened, just as Lawrence had predicted months beforehand, Hitler marched into Czechoslovakia on March 15th.

I read with horror in the Manchester Guardian of the 17th March: "Prague's streets were jammed with silent pedestrians wandering about, looking out of the corners of their eyes at German soldiers carrying guns, at armoured cars and at other military precautions."

I put the paper down and tried to imagine what it would feel like to have the quiet streets of Salisbury full of soldiers with guns, and I shivered. Surely it could not happen here in England. We were not part of Europe anyway, but supposing we did go to war with Germany and were invaded. It did not bear thinking about.

I read on. "Suicides have begun. The fears of the Jews grow. The funds of the Jewish community have been seized, stopping Jewish relief work. The Prague Bar Council has ordered all its 'non-Aryan' members to stop practising at once. The organisation for Jewish emigration has been closed. Hundreds of people stood outside the British Consulate shouting, "We want to get away!"

I thought of the times my father had read to us from the Old Testament and said that the Jews were God's chosen people, yet here they were being victimised. I couldn't understand it.

That evening when Hannah was in bed Lawrence came into the kitchen where I was doing the dishes. "I need to talk seriously to you, darling," he began. "Leave the dishes and come into the sitting room."

Once we were seated he gazed at me without speaking for a few moments. "You know what this means, don't you, the invasion of Czechoslovakia? It is the end of the Munich Agreement. Hitler has broken his word and now there is nothing to stop him from advancing into Europe. It is the end of our appeasement policy and from now on we will have to prepare for war. Chamberlain has promised Poland that we will go to their support if they are attacked."

"So it is really only a matter of time?" I said slowly.

"Yes, and because I am in the Reserve Service of the RAF I will probably be called up right away."

I could only gaze at him dumbly. I knew how important our air defences were and inevitably Lawrence would be in the front line.

"We need to be prepared for whatever might happen," said Lawrence. "If the worst comes to the worst I have made provision for you and Hannah."

"Oh, don't say such things, Larry," I cried. "I can't bear to think of anything happening to you."

"All right, I'll say no more about it and we will live each day as it comes—the way you always have, my darling," and he smiled at me half teasingly. "I know that whatever happens to you, you will always come through smiling."

"Oh Larry, I do love you so," I said springing out of my seat and throwing myself into his arms.

CHAPTER THIRTY

Each weekend Lawrence was away on intensive training with the RAF. He was already a Flight Lieutenant but we both knew he was being groomed for a position of greater responsibility, possibly as Squadron leader. He was based at Andover which was the headquarters of RAF Maintenance command and I became accustomed to seeing him briefly on a Friday night before he drove off to the airbase. He did not return until Sunday afternoon and it was always a joyful reunion for us. We would take Hannah and go for a quiet drink at the Duck and Swan. It was very pleasant sitting outside in the sunshine and sometimes Joan and Jim would join us.

During that summer of 1939 the sun seemed to shine constantly and it was hard to imagine that war was on the horizon. Yet already over Europe the clouds were gathering and on the first day of September the storm broke. Hitler marched into Poland and Chamberlain gave him an ultimatum: withdraw his troops from Poland within two days or we would declare war on Germany.

That very afternoon a phone call came for Lawrence from government headquarters telling him that, as a member of the RAF Voluntary Reserve, he was now ordered to go into permanent service. We had been expecting this so it did not come as a surprise, but all the same I felt heavy-hearted as I packed Lawrence's suitcase that Friday afternoon.

"I have to report to Andover on Sunday afternoon so let us make the most of the little time we have left together," said Lawrence, placing his hand on my shoulder as I bent over the case. "Leave the packing and let's plan what we shall do tomorrow. I suggest that we go for a good long walk in the direction of Stonehenge and stop for lunch in that little country pub you showed me once."

"And what about Hannah?"

"I'm sure Miss Nugent would be delighted to look after her, or even Joan."

"If she can bear to give up the time. All this week she's been busy sewing blackout curtains. She's convinced the Germans will bomb us as soon as war is declared."

"They'll hardly bother about a small place like Laverstock and I shouldn't think they'll even target Salisbury. No, their aim will be to cripple our air force. They'll be out to bomb all the airfields."

"Oh, Larry, really! Then you will be at risk in Andover."

"That is war, my darling. Anyway, you can be sure we will be ready for them. Our squadron is on alert already."

"I do hope that Hitler takes notice of our ultimatum and withdraws from Poland."

"I wouldn't be too optimistic, Rhoda. He's been planning this for years, ever since he put troops into the Rhineland in 1936. That is when we should have put a stop to his little game, but our government was too obtuse to see that he had grander ambitions. Only Churchill saw the writing on the wall."

"You should be in Parliament," I said laughing. "You'd tell them."

"Dad knew this would happen," said Lawrence thoughtfully. "I remember him talking to me about it at the time." He shrugged. "Still, we can't turn the clock back now. Let's forget about Hitler and make the most of this weekend," and he kissed me tenderly.

Miss Nugent was delighted to take charge of Hannah for the day and on Saturday morning we took our daughter down to the little bungalow and left her playing happily in the garden. Hand in hand, Lawrence and I set off along country lanes fragrant with the scent of many kinds of wild flowers. Lawrence laughed at me when I stopped to pick poppies and cornflowers growing in profusion beside the hedges. He twisted some buttercups and wild violets together and made a little circlet then placed it on my hair.

"Now you really look like the gypsy you are, with your black hair and dark complexion," he teased. "I can just see you sitting on the steps of your caravan in the sun inviting passing strangers to have their fortunes told."

"You do talk nonsense, Larry," I giggled, then shivered suddenly. "I'm so glad we can't see into the future. I would hate to know what is going to happen over the next few years. I'm just thankful that God has it all under control."

"It's hard to see where God is in all this mess. Why does He let evil men like Hitler have their way?"

"I suppose it's because He gave us free will. People can choose to do evil rather than good."

"And it's up to us to prevent evil men having their way, which is why we have to go to war," said Larry thoughtfully.

"Yes, but it does seem dreadful that men have to die who would rather lead peaceful lives going about their business." I paused, looking at the fields spread out before us, sprinkled with wild flowers, where cows stood lazily in the sunshine chewing the cud. "It just seems all so unreal, Larry. I wish we could hold on to this present moment and nothing need change."

After that, we said very little, stopping now and again to listen to bird song. There was a hush over everything as though this were an enchanted world and we were the only human beings in it.

This perfect day came to an end finally and when we went to pick up Hannah Miss Nugent brought us back to reality.

"You will be going to church tomorrow, won't you? Mr. Chamberlain is making his broadcast to the nation at eleven o'clock, to tell us whether or not we are at war."

"Do you really think the vicar will arrange for us to listen to the wireless in church?" I said, trying to imagine our rather staid vicar allowing such a modern invention as a wireless to be used in his church.

"I'm sure he will. Ever since Hitler invaded Czechoslovakia he's been warning us to expect war. Have you noticed the increased numbers at church recently? Anyway, he will want to hear the broadcast as much as we do," said Miss Nugent confidently.

She was right. On Sunday morning the little Anglican Church at Laverstock was crowded. We arrived early and sat in our usual pew with Hannah between us. I was glad when Miss Nugent came and sat next to us. There was an expectant hush as the vicar mounted the steps to the lectern.

"My dear fellow Christians," he began. "This is a momentous day, when our country stands on the brink of war. I hope for all our sakes that even at this eleventh hour we will hear good news. I have arranged that the wireless broadcast by Mr. Chamberlain will be played this morning at eleven o'clock. This will take place during the usual time allotted for the sermon. After the broadcast I will pray and then the service will close."

I glanced at my watch. It was just after ten thirty. *How would we get through the next half hour?*

It seemed the vicar had put a great deal of thought into the service. He selected as the lesson, a reading from Psalm 91, where I was particularly struck by the words, "You will not fear the terror of night, nor the arrow that flies by day," and I thought of bombs dropping from the sky at night or even in the daytime. Then came the words, "A thousand may fall at your side and ten thousand at your right hand, but it will not come near you," and I felt comforted. Even if Lawrence were in the thick of battle he would be protected.

Then we sang the hymn, "Abide with me" and I felt the peace of God descend on me. I knew that whatever was about to happen God would be there with us. The Good Shepherd would be leading us as He had done all along and there was nothing to fear.

The hands of the clock on the wall stood at a couple of minutes before eleven. The vicar said, "I will now turn on the wireless."

He walked over to the table where the set had been placed and turned a knob. Some quiet classical music came through the speakers, then there was a pause and the voice of Mr. Chamberlain said clearly:

"I am speaking to you from the Cabinet Room at 10, Downing Street. This morning the British Ambassador in Berlin handed the German Government a final note stating that unless we heard from them at 11 a.m. that they were prepared at once to withdraw their troops from Poland, a state of war would exist between us. I have to tell you that no such undertaking has been received, and that consequently this country is at war with Germany."

Lawrence reached across Hannah and gripped my hand tightly. I heard muffled sobs behind me and I noticed Miss Nugent take her handkerchief from her bag and wipe her eyes. This declaration of war was reviving bitter memories in those people in the congregation who had lived through the Great War. I looked around the walls of the church at the faded flags and the names engraved on stone tablets of those who had died serving their country. I wondered which names would be added to them after this war was over.

At the end of the broadcast the vicar asked us all to stand. Then he prayed, not from the prayer book this time, but fervently in his own words. He asked God to keep our minds and hearts at peace and trusting in His almighty power to protect us.

We filed out of the building sombrely, some of the older women weeping, their husbands supporting them as they stumbled along the path. Most people hurried away, although groups of younger people stood talking together in subdued tones.

"Miss Nugent, will you come home to lunch with us?" I said, as we walked along the path between the rows of ancient graves.

"No, thank you, Rhoda, I think I will spend the day quietly with my memories," she said, turning a pale and tearstained face towards me. "You and Lawrence need time on your own, my dear, but thank you for your kind thought," and she hurried away from us.

Lawrence took my arm and I held out my hand to Hannah who was clutching her doll under her arm and chattering happily to herself. I was glad at that moment she was too young to be aware of what was about to happen to us all.

CHAPTER THIRTY-ONE

Lawrence had to report to RAF Andover at 7 o'clock that evening. After lunch we sat in the garden in the sunshine making the most of our last few hours together. Hannah played happily in her little sandpit while Walter sunned himself on the garden wall. The sky was a cloudless blue and a gentle breeze rustled the leaves of the apple tree. It was hard to believe that we were at war. Neither Lawrence nor I wanted to talk about the coming separation and instead, we recalled the happy times we had spent together before we were married, and our honeymoon in Bournemouth.

Suddenly Lawrence looked across at me, "Do you know what I would like to do on my first leave, my darling? I would like us to go back to Bournemouth for a couple of days and spend the time totally together."

"Not even take Hannah with us?"

"No, just the two of us together."

"So we can recapture our first fine careless rapture," I said smiling.

"With apologies to Shelley, yes, something like that."

"I think that is a wonderful idea, Larry, and it will give us something to look forward to."

I think we were both cheered at the thought of this and so, when it came to saying goodbye that afternoon, the parting was not as painful as it might have been. I stood on the doorstep with Hannah beside me and watched Lawrence, in his smart blue uniform, get into his car and drive away.

With a sigh I walked indoors and went straight to the kitchen to make a cup of tea. The kettle had only just boiled when there was a knock on the door. I went to open it and there stood Joan and Maisie.

"We thought you might like some company this evening," explained Joan, "so here we are."

"You're just in time for a nice cup of tea!" I exclaimed.

"And some cake as well," smiled Maisie, holding out a paper bag.

As we sat chatting around the kitchen table about the difference war would make in each of our lives, Joan looked across at me and said, "Rhoda, what are you going to do with yourself each day now that you are on your own?" She glanced around the room. "This is such a small house you can't have much in the way of housework, and Hannah is not much trouble. Why don't you get a part-time job?"

"Maybe they would give you back your secretarial post at Laverton House," said Maisie. "I happen to know that Dr. Branson's secretary is thinking of leaving to look after her sister in Fordingbridge."

"I couldn't possibly think of working while Hannah is so young," I said emphatically.

"It would do her good to mix with others her own age. I know some nurseries take children as young as two and even though Hannah is not two yet, she is very advanced," said Joan lifting my daughter onto her lap.

"I'll have to think about it," I said, wishing they would drop the subject. I did not feel ready to make decisions so soon.

When they had gone I put Hannah to bed and shortly afterwards went myself. I lay for hours in our double bed, poignantly aware of the empty space beside me. My mind was too active for sleep and try as I might, I could not rid myself of anxiety about Lawrence. He had told me that No 107 squadron at Andover, to which he was attached, was a bomber squadron and that he would be flying Bristol Blenheims. These were light bomber aircraft designed and built by the Bristol Aeroplane Company and were used as long-range and night fighters. I had asked him how successful they would be against the German Messerschmitts and he admitted that they would not stand much chance during daylight operations. At the time, I had not taken much notice of his answer, but now I went hot and cold as I envisaged him being chased across the sky by faster German planes. Finally, I fell into an uneasy sleep and woke unrefreshed several hours later, to find that it was seven o'clock and time to get up and feed Hannah.

The day passed slowly and I found myself looking at the clock every hour, wondering what Lawrence would be doing. As soon as it was six o'clock I switched on the wireless to hear the news from the BBC. I sat down at the kitchen table and gave it my full attention, but there seemed little of real importance they could add after yesterday. They reported that in one Cambridgeshire church the service had been abandoned and everybody hurried home, but also that in other places churches were full. I thought of our own service and how many people had turned up yesterday morning. Apparently at 11.28 am on Sunday morning all around the country air raid sirens had been set off and many people panicked.

As soon as the news was over I switched off the wireless and concentrated on Hannah. It was a relief to be able to bathe her and watch her splashing around in the warm soapy water, crowing with pleasure as she played with her duck. As I rubbed her down I thanked God for her and all the other little children and prayed that they should be protected from the effects of war.

Lawrence's first leave came a month later and we drove to Bournemouth as we had planned, leaving Hannah with Miss Nugent. We even managed to stay in the same hotel in Boscombe where we had spent our honeymoon. But nothing felt the same. Already, there was a sense of wartime stringency and the blackout curtains at every window were depressing. Along the whole length of the beach from Boscombe to Sandbanks, rolls of barbed wire were being laid as a hindrance to any enemy landing craft. Everywhere we went were reminders of war.

Even between Lawrence and myself there was tension. His old light-heartedness was gone and I noticed lines on his face that had not been there before. He seemed to have aged during the short time he had been away. When I tried to question him about his activities at the base, he lifted my chin and said, "I'm sworn to secrecy, my darling. Anyway, what you don't know can't harm you," and I had to be content with that.

I was glad when it was time to go home and as we walked through the door of Miss Nugent's little bungalow Hannah came running to meet us and reached up her arms to Lawrence. He swung her into the air and she laughed delightedly. I looked at Lawrence and saw that, for the first time, he was relaxed and happy as he lifted Hannah above his head.

"She's been so good," said Miss Nugent, "but she's been running to the door every time she heard a car when I told her Mummy and Daddy were coming back today. I think Walter's been missing you too, though it hasn't put him off his food."

"Thank you so much, Miss Nugent," I said. "It's good to be home again."

"Didn't you enjoy Bournemouth then?" she asked, surprised.

"It's not the same in wartime. Anyway, we both missed Hannah."

I realised as I spoke, that we could never be just a couple again; that we were a family now and Hannah was part of us.

The remainder of Lawrence's leave we spent quietly at home and these were happy days. The sun still shone and we sat in the garden enjoying being together. When it came time for Lawrence to go I asked when he would have his next leave.

"Nothing is certain, Rhoda. Everything is quiet at the moment, but we have to be ready. Any day the enemy could attack, and now that I am Squadron Leader I have to be on the spot. When I get the chance I will ring you."

"Do you have to go out on bombing missions, Larry? I lie awake and worry about you most nights, wondering if you are in the air."

"There is no need to worry, Flo. We don't take unnecessary risks and I'm responsible for the safety of the men in my squadron. Anyway, a lot of my work is administrative these days."

"Thank goodness for that," I said, relieved.

I waved him off from the door, Hannah at my side, and after the car had disappeared went back indoors. The house seemed very quiet and lonely without him and I knew it would take a few days to adjust once again to being on our own. Even Hannah was listless and Walter seemed to sense our sadness because he rubbed himself comfortingly against my legs.

Time passed slowly over the next few weeks and months, although I kept myself busy around the house. Each afternoon when Hannah was having her rest I sat down and wrote at length to Lawrence, telling him about all the little humdrum details of our life. I watched eagerly for the post but his letters were brief and contained no reference to his activities. He wrote lovingly about our times together in the past and asked many questions about Hannah, but he told me next to nothing about life on the base.

And so the months passed and 1939 gave way to 1940. I lived for the times that Lawrence came home on leave, but it was doubly hard when he went back on duty. I had stopped worrying about him because he assured me that there was very little action going on at the base. The papers called this the 'phony war' because for a few months the enemy was silent, but I think we all knew that they were building up to something.

Then In April Hitler invaded Norway and shortly after that Denmark fell. The following month Germany occupied Holland, Belgium and Luxembourg, as well as attacking French positions in Western France. Hitler's advance across Europe was rapid. Then came the announcement that Mr. Chamberlain had resigned as Prime Minister and Mr. Winston Churchill was replacing him as Head of a coalition government. On the 13th May I heard him make his memorable speech:

> *"We have before us many, many long months of struggle and of suffering. You ask, what is our policy? I will say: It is to wage war, by sea, land and air, with all our might and with all the strength that God can give us; to wage war against a monstrous tyranny, never surpassed in the dark and lamentable catalogue of human crime. That is our policy. You ask, what is our aim? I can answer in one word: victory; victory at all costs, victory in spite of all terror, victory, however long and hard the road may be; for without victory, there is no survival.*

I was sitting at my kitchen table as I listened to these stirring words and my attitude to the war changed. I realised that we were fighting for something that was above and beyond ourselves, something I had always taken for granted, justice and freedom. From that moment I was determined I would do all I could to support this war. We had to win at all costs.

As I looked around my little kitchen, at Hannah trying to pick up a struggling Walter and the sun slanting across the table, where the remains of breakfast were waiting to be cleared away, this 'monstrous evil' Churchill spoke about, seemed unreal and remote, yet nevertheless it existed and we must resist it.

I ceased to feel sorry for myself because I was on my own. Instead, I thought of all those other women whose husbands had been called up to the services and like me, were facing days of loneliness and uncertainty. I knew it was essential to keep going and preserve a cheerful and positive outlook, not to complain about shortages and wartime cutbacks, but to make the best of what we had. I must learn to feel thankful for little things.

The next day we were told that the German army had reached the Channel coast and were threatening to capture the ports. The British and French forces were concentrated at Dunkirk and it looked as if they would be trapped there and unable to evacuate. Mr. Churchill said in a speech to Parliament that the "whole root and core and brain of the British Army" had been stranded at Dunkirk and it was absolutely urgent that they came back to Britain, or we were defenceless.

Then the unexpected happened. The German army halted for three days and this gave space for the Allies to make plans for the evacuation.

On the 26th May, King George called for a national day of prayer, urging the people of Britain to pray for our soldiers in dire peril in France. All around the country churches were filled with people praying for a miraculous deliverance. I went to our little Anglican church at Laverstock with Miss Nugent in the morning and was surprised to see people there I had never seen before, on their knees praying fervently. Later that evening I went with Maisie and Joan after they came off duty and once again the little church was full.

The next day, the 27th May, the order came for the evacuation from Dunkirk. As well as the destroyers and other large ships, hundreds of little ships were hastily assembled, fishing boats and pleasure craft as well as lifeboats. Over the next nine days thousands of troops were ferried across the channel and the weather remained miraculously calm, so that the smallest ships were able to cross without difficulty. By the 4th June 330,000 Allied troops had been rescued. Churchill hailed the evacuation as a 'miracle of deliverance.'

It was then I knew that God was in control of this war. I knew that however bleak the situation might appear, we would come through and win. I knew that evil would never triumph. The British people were standing together and trusting God to deliver them. The evacuation of Dunkirk had proved to us that miracles did happen. As I listened to Churchill speaking tears of thankfulness welled up in my eyes.

After Dunkirk there was a sense that we were all in this together, and whenever I took Hannah out in her pushchair, neighbours would stop and chat to me and soon I came to know everyone in our road. Gone were the barriers of pre-war life when neighbours kept themselves to themselves. I did not even bother to lock the door anymore. It was simply not necessary. I particularly enjoyed my trips into Salisbury on the bus, when complete strangers would chat to me like old friends. The ancient city took on a homely atmosphere and although the shops had empty shelves and the clothing on display was more utilitarian than attractive, everyone was helpful and obliging. I no longer minded queuing in the food shops because everyone was so friendly.

At the end of a shopping expedition I would wheel Hannah in her pushchair to the park near the cathedral and while she played on the swings I would gaze in wonder at the cathedral, with its barrage balloons floating around the spire. Over the centuries it had stood pointing upwards to God in the midst of turmoil and it would survive still. I knew it in my bones. One day this war would be over and people would once more stroll around the cathedral close, enjoying the peace and quiet of the ancient sanctuary.

CHAPTER THIRTY-TWO

I was never sure when Lawrence would be on leave. Generally it was every six weeks but I never knew the exact day. He would ring me the day before and I would scramble to have everything ready so that we could spend all our time together. About six weeks after the evacuation of Dunkirk he rang to say that he would be home the next day. As soon as he walked through the door he threw his bags into a corner and seized me in his arms. There was a kind of desperation in his embrace. When I had a chance to look at him I noticed lines of fatigue in his face.

"Larry, you look as though you haven't slept for days," I exclaimed.

"That's about it, Rhoda," he said soberly. "And I think for the next few months there won't be rest for any of us. There are reports coming through that Jerry is going to start bombing airfields. Hitler wants to cripple our air force so he can get on with the invasion."

I was horrified. "Does that mean you could be a target at Andover?"

"Of course, but we're in the process of setting up a decoy airbase to fool the Luftwaffe into bombing it and not us. They'll also be going for aircraft factories and any places to do with the RAF."

"So you could be in considerable danger, darling," I said slowly.

"No more than the rest of the country. You'll see, the Germans will also go for places like Portsmouth, to destroy the navy, and probably London. I'm just thankful that Salisbury is not a strategic centre, although there is the army base on Salisbury Plain."

For the rest of his leave we made no further mention of the war but there was an underlying feeling that our time together might be short. I sometimes caught Lawrence looking at Hannah wistfully and I guessed what was passing through his mind.

Just before the end of his leave I asked him diffidently, because I did not really want to know the answer. "Larry, what happens after a bombing raid by the Luftwaffe? Does the RAF do the same thing to their air bases in Germany?"

"Yes."

"It must be very dangerous flying over enemy territory."

"There are dangers but we travel in tight formation with our fighter planes keeping close to the bombers."

"You told me once that your work is mainly administrative so that means you wouldn't be going out on that kind of operation, would you?" I looked at him hopefully.

There was a long pause. Finally he spoke, choosing his words carefully. "Things are a little different now, Rhoda. As Squadron Leader it is important for me to lead my men from the front and so I do go out on most of the sorties. But you can be sure our Spitfires and Hurricanes are a match for the German Messerchmitts and we are well protected by our fighters."

I asked no further questions but as I said goodbye to Lawrence that afternoon, standing with Hannah beside me, my heart was heavy.

In July Portsmouth was bombed. Lawrence was right. The main targets were coastal shipping convoys and shipping centres. Then on the 24th August bombs fell on London. The Battle of Britain had begun. We heard that forty-three aircraft from Bomber Command had retaliated by bombing Berlin the following night. I prayed that Lawrence's squadron would not be called on to fly into enemy territory. After this, came an intense period of daylight bombing from the Luftwaffe. I would lie awake at night hearing the crump crump of the German bombers as they passed over us on their way to London and pray for those poor people in the capital who were about to be blitzed.

Every day over the wireless we were given the figures of enemy planes that were shot down and our own losses. It seemed that we were holding our own against the enemy although so many young RAF pilots had to sacrifice their lives.

Now it was September and the attacks from the air showed no sign of letting up. Our most vulnerable time in Salisbury was when the Luftwaffe were returning from a raid and dropped any surplus bombs before crossing the channel. Lawrence had dug an Anderson shelter in our back garden and had made it as comfortable as he could for Hannah and me. When the air raid warning was given I would bundle her into a rug and within minutes we would be in the safety of our dug-out, together with Walter who followed us into it and curled up on the end of my bed. Hannah slept soundly but I would lie sleepless waiting for the all-clear. During these times I prayed earnestly for Lawrence's safety and all those young pilots battling it out in the skies over England.

The reports that come over the wireless each day are very heartening. It seems we are holding our own against the Luftwaffe and the number of Messerschmitts shot down, far exceed our losses in the air. We are definitely winning the war in the air, but my constant prayer is the Larry will be kept safe.

That was my diary entry yesterday, the 24th September 1940.

I closed the exercise book and dropped it on the floor beside my chair then stood up, feeling stiff and cramped. Glancing at my watch I saw it was half past one. I had been sitting here for over four hours. I tiptoed to Hannah's room and saw that she had thrown the covers off and was lying with one arm around her dolly and the other stretched back behind her head. I covered her up and stole back to my own room.

For many hours I lay in the darkness reliving the events of the past few weeks and thinking of Lawrence. The word "missing" seemed to be stamped across every picture of him in my mind. I knew the likelihood of his being alive was very remote. If he had been shot down over enemy territory there was only a ten percent chance of his survival. It might be many days before I would know definitely from the War Office and in the meantime I must come to terms with the possibility that I would never see him again. The thought made me feel icy cold. *Never to hear his voice again and feel his arms around me. It was too dreadful to think of. I must keep hoping.* Yet deep within me I knew he was gone.

I lay huddled in bed unable to cry, or even to pray. I felt panic rising within me. I was utterly and completely alone. How could I survive without Larry? As I was lying there, feeling chilled to the bone and despairing I felt a warm presence above me and love radiating down over me. I felt like a small child in the arms of a loving father and all the tension ebbed away. I relaxed and within seconds was sound asleep. When I awoke it was full daylight. For a few moments I lay, my mind completely blank. I even wondered what day it was. Then Walter leaped on my bed and in the next room I could hear Hannah calling, "Mummy, Mummy."

Gradually the events of yesterday came back to me. Lawrence was missing, but the thought no longer horrified me. Wherever he was, he was happy. I knew that now. Last night I had experienced God's love in a tangible way and I knew there was nothing to fear in the future. I got up and went into Hannah's room. She was playing happily with her toys on her bed and looked up with a smile, Lawrence's smile. I gathered her in my arms and hugged her. "Come on, time for breakfast, Han, and Walter's looking hungry; we'd better feed him first."

In the kitchen the sun was streaming through the window and outside I could hear a robin carolling. Suddenly there was a knock at the door. Goodness, I was still in my dressing gown. I went to the door and opened it a crack.

"Oh, Miss Nugent, thank goodness it's only you, with me not dressed and it's gone nine."

"It's not like you to sleep in, Rhoda. Is everything all right?"

"Well, yes and no, but do come in and have a cup of tea and I'll explain."

When we were sitting comfortably at the kitchen table I told her about the telegram and my experience of the night before. She listened carefully and then said, "Something similar happened to me when I lost Jack, my fiancé. I had a very vivid dream in which he appeared to me and told me not to grieve for him because he was very happy where he was. Somehow that helped me over that terrible time." She looked at me thoughtfully. "I think you will come through this experience too, Rhoda, and be a stronger person for it. And you have Hannah to think about," she added looking across at my little daughter who was on the floor trying to catch hold of Walter's tail. We both laughed and I got up to fill her mug with warm milk.

Miss Nugent did not stay long and when she had gone I busied myself about the house with various chores.

A week later I had a letter from the Wing Commander at RAF Andover. He said that Lawrence had been shot down when leading his squadron on a mission to protect British ships in the coastal waters near Portsmouth. *Your husband was a courageous man and was not willing to let his men go into battle unless he led them from the front. We have lost a very fine man and a great leader. My heartfelt sympathy goes out to you.*

So that was it. Larry was dead. Now I knew it for certain I experienced a kind of relief. The waiting was over but I had a constant ache in my heart that lessened only when I was busy. An idea was taking shape in my mind. I would do what Joan and Maisie had suggested to me a while ago. I would go to Laverton House and offer my services in the office. There was a possibility that they might need some extra help and if I could work part-time, Hannah would be well looked after in the War Nursery.

That afternoon I dressed carefully and put Hannah in her pushchair. It was a mellow autumn afternoon and I was reminded of the first day I had seen Laverton House. It still reminded me of a gracious country mansion with the Virginia creeper, now a vivid red, covering half the front of the house. A few patients were strolling in the grounds and they smiled at me as I pushed Hannah along the drive.

As it happened I met Matron Dunne in the lobby, coming out of her office. "Why, Rhoda. How lovely to see you and Hannah too! My word, she's growing. Do come and have a cup of tea with me and tell me all your news." I followed her into her small office and sat down in one of the chairs in front of her desk. She gave the bellpull a tug and one of the maids appeared. I did not recognise her.

"Bring us in some morning tea, Alice, and extra milk for the little girl," said Matron Dunne, adding after she had gone, "Alice is new. She came over from Ireland to marry one of our gardeners. It's very hard to get maids now. So many have gone to work in the factories. I suppose it's better money for them. Anyway, what is your news, Rhoda? How is that handsome husband of yours?"

"Well, it's really about him I came to see you." The breath caught in my throat and tears sprang to my eyes. I struggled for some seconds before I was able to speak the words that sounded so dreadfully final. "He was shot down a week ago; I've just had confirmation that he is dead."

"Oh, Rhoda, how terrible for you! So he was one of our gallant RAF fighters who put up such a marvellous show against the Luftwaffe on the 17th."

"Anyway, Matron, that is why I have come to see you. I would like to go back to work. It's awful being in the house all day long." I saw Matron's eyes glance towards Hannah. "And I know Hannah will be fine in the War Nursery playing with the other children."

Matron looked thoughtful. "I have a feeling that Dr. Branson's secretary might be glad of some extra time off. She is looking after her invalid sister at the moment and is finding it quite hard fitting that in with a full-time job. After you've had your tea we'll go along to Dr. Branson's office and see how the land lies."

When we walked into his office a short time later I felt as though I were coming home. Everything was comfortingly familiar. Dr. Branson greeted me warmly then introduced me to his secretary whom I had met briefly once before. Matron Dunne quickly outlined my situation and both the doctor and his secretary looked at me sympathetically.

The secretary spoke first. "I would welcome the chance to work part-time so that I could have more time with my sister. As a matter of fact, Doctor," and she turned to him, "I was about to hand in my resignation, but perhaps after all that won't be necessary, if Mrs. Grantly can take on some of my days."

The doctor beamed. "Well, that seems the perfect solution then, Mrs. Grantly. When can you start?"

"As soon as you like," I said promptly.

"Let's say the day after tomorrow then, and that gives us time to sort out your hours."

And that is how I came to get my old job back at Laverton House. Each day I took Hannah on the back of my bicycle and left her at the War Nursery before going into the office. I worked in the mornings from nine until one, then collected Hannah to take her home for lunch. It was a pleasant routine and gave me sufficient time to do my housework or go shopping. Hannah enjoyed playing with the other children and chattered happily about all that she had done during the day. Her vocabulary widened but I was rather horrified to hear her speaking to Walter one day. She told him to hurry up and eat his " bloody breakfast". Another time she looked up and said, "That's a bugger of a thing."

"Hannah, those are bad words," I exclaimed, shocked. She simply looked at me.

"What am I to do about her swearing?" I asked Joan and repeated to her what Hannah had said.

Joan giggled.

"It's serious," I said reprovingly.

"I know it is, but I think the more notice you take of it, the more she'll do it. You're probably best to play it down, because Hannah knows she can get a reaction from you when she uses those words."

"I'm wondering whether to take her away from that War Nursery because it's obvious she's picking up bad language from the other children."

"You can't protect her from everything," said Joan practically. "She's going to have to go out and mix with all types later on, but at least you've given her a good example to follow. Don't be too much of a mother hen, Rhoda."

I decided to change the subject. "How does Jim like the navy?" I asked. He had volunteered a couple of months earlier.

"He moans about it but I think he really enjoys the life. You know he's on mine sweepers?"

"That's pretty dangerous work. Do you worry, Joan?"

"I used to, but now I'm quite fatalistic. If the bullet's got your name on it, it'll find you. Jim told me about a chap who was working in the safest part of one of the ships, in a steel plated room right below deck. A bullet was fired from an enemy boat and it bounced from side to side of the companionway then hit the wall opposite the room and went straight to this chap's heart. That bullet certainly had his name on it. When Jim told me that story I stopped worrying."

I repeated this to Miss Nugent. "I think there's a lot of truth in that, Rhoda. It helps one to live through times of war."

"So you think that Larry was always going to die in the way he did?"

"That's the best way to think, Rhoda," said Miss Nugent quietly. "He accomplished what he was sent here to do. Even if he had lived for another fifty years he might never have done anything more worthwhile than he did in this war. He is one of those who have died to save our country from a terrible evil. Hannah and all her generation will be able to grow up in a free country because of his sacrifice."

Her words gave me a lump in my throat and I thought of them many times during that autumn of 1940 when the Luftwaffe pounded us from the air and the RAF fought back with every last ounce of strength.

At last in October we heard that Hitler had changed his mind about an amphibious attack on Britain. We had won victory in the air against Germany. Churchill warned us that this was only the beginning of a long hard struggle. When I listened to his speech about what we owed to the RAF I felt a thrill of pride. Lawrence was one of those brave airman to whom we owed so much.

Whenever I was swept with feelings of grief I reminded myself of this and the ache of loss would subside. Nevertheless, those remaining months of 1940 were difficult and if it hadn't been for Hannah and my job at Laverton House I might have given in to loneliness and depression. Evenings were the hardest time. When Lawrence was alive I used to spend the evening writing long letters to him but now I did not even have that to fill in the time. One night after I had put Hannah to bed I drew out my writing pad and wrote to the Major. I had received a brief letter of condolence from him which I had acknowledged. I sat and thought for a few minutes. I would tell him about our short but happy marriage and what Lawrence had meant to me. I knew the Major would be grieving for his only son and in sharing my memories he might find comfort as well.

I started to write and very soon had filled several pages. As memories came flooding back I found I was reliving those golden days and alternately laughing and crying. Something was released in me that night and the dreadful ache in my heart began to ease. When I posted the letter next day I hoped the Major would not mind this outpouring of my personal feelings. I need not have worried. His reply came by return of post.

"*My dearest Rhoda,*" he wrote. "*You have no idea how much your letter meant to me. I was very moved by the things you wrote of my precious boy. I am so glad that you made his last months on this earth such a joyful time. I happen to know that he was not your first choice of a husband. Although you said nothing at the time all the signs were there that you were in love with Harold. I said nothing to Lawrence because I knew that he had fallen heavily for you by then and selfishly I wanted you for my daughter-in-law. Then Harold went abroad and Lawrence got his chance. You agreed to marry him and I was delighted. Then Harold returned and I knew you were faced with a major decision, to go ahead and keep your promise to Lawrence or break the engagement. You made the right choice and how glad I am that you did because it gave my boy great happiness in the final months of his life. But now, my dear, you are a free woman. Once this time of grieving is over you must press forward with your life. You are young and, God willing, have many more years ahead of you. You also have a little daughter who needs not only a mother but a father. Please, Rhoda, do not hesitate to seek happiness with another man. This is what Lawrence would have wanted and it is what I want for you. You will always be my beloved daughter-in-law whatever happens and I will always be here to support you.*

Your loving friend and father-in-law,

Robert Grantly

I came to the end of this letter in wonderment. I had no idea that the Major knew of my feelings for Harold, nor that I had made a sacrifice in giving him up. How understanding he was and how clear-sighted. He had given his blessing to any other relationship I might form with another man. Still, it was too soon even to consider such a thing. I had not the slightest interest in anyone at present and as for marriage that was unthinkable. Carefully, I folded the Major's letter and put it back in its envelope, then placed it in the top drawer of my bureau where I kept all Lawrence's letters.

CHAPTER THIRTY-THREE

It was now September 1941 and we had been at war nearly two years. I had almost forgotten what peace time was like. Somehow rationing and queuing had become a way of life and I had even grown accustomed to air raids.

I heard regularly from Hazel and she kept me up to date with family news. She told me that she was now working in the Rolls Royce factory at Filton making parts of aeroplanes. David had failed the fitness test for the army because of his poor eyesight and instead was firefighting in Bristol and Andrew was in the RAF on ground duties as a mechanic. I was thankful that he was not a fighter pilot and in danger of being shot down. It was bad enough to have lost one of my loved ones that way. Camellia was still at school and according to Hazel couldn't wait to leave, while Aunty Edith grumbled about food shortages but was still able to make a good cake using margarine instead of butter.

I was very reliant on Miss Nugent as a baby-sitter. She was willing to look after Hannah whenever I asked her, but I did not like to take advantage of her kindness and tried to take Hannah with me wherever I went.

"Look upon me as Hannah's substitute grandma," said Miss Nugent one day. "If I had ever had grandchildren I would have loved a little girl like her. It's a joy to me to spend time with her." She looked at me shrewdly. "And you need some time off, my dear. You are looking very peaky these days. I would like to see you going out to the pictures sometimes with Joan and Maisie. I know Joan has asked you a few times and you have refused because of Hannah."

I thought about her words and decided that the next time Joan mentioned there was a good film on in Salisbury I would go with her.

The following week we went to see Marlene Dietrich in Blue Angel and after the film, when we were sitting in a café having a cup of tea, Joan said unexpectedly, "I bumped into Mrs. Forster in Salisbury the other day and she mentioned that Harold was in the army and had been promoted to captain. I think he's been sent abroad somewhere. Mrs. Forster asked about you and I told her you were back working at Laverton House. She said she had heard about Lawrence and to let you know they have all been thinking about you. She also said that they would love to see you back at the gospel hall."

Joan looked at me curiously. "Do you ever think of going there, Rhoda? I know you grew up attending the gospel hall."

"When I married Lawrence naturally I went with him to the Church of England, but in a way I do miss the gospel hall. Perhaps I will go one day and take Hannah with me. I'll have to give it some thought."

I did think about it and one Sunday morning I put Hannah in her seat on the back of my bike and set off along the country roads to the gospel hall. It was a quiet sunny morning and I heard a skylark singing above us as I toiled along the uneven road which had been neglected since the war and now had grass growing between the cracks.

We arrived a few minutes early and as I lifted Hannah from her seat I heard a familiar voice behind me. "Rhoda, is that really you?"

I swung around and there was Harold in army uniform smiling down at me.

"I thought you were overseas," I stammered, feeling suddenly weak.

"I've just finished a stint in Egypt but I'm home on leave for a few days before they post me somewhere else. Is this your little daughter? What age is she?"

"Yes, this is Hannah," I said, glad to have a few moments to recover my equilibrium. "She's three and a half."

"Hello, Hannah," Harold said smiling at her. "Have you enjoyed your ride this morning on the back of Mummy's bike?"

"Yes," she replied looking at him and smiling. "Mummy always takes me on her bike."

"Is that right? Then I suggest that after the service we cycle into the country and have lunch all together somewhere," said Harold turning to me.

My heart was thumping but I managed to thank him and taking Hannah by the hand went into the building. Mr. Forster happened to be on the door that morning and he shook my hand warmly.

"So this is your little girl," he said, beaming down at Hannah. "I do hope you will both join us for lunch today. We've been given a ham by some kind friends who own a butcher's shop and we would love to share it with you." He looked over my shoulder at Harold. "And you will join us too, Harold?"

"If Rhoda doesn't mind a sudden change of plan," said Harold smiling at me.

"Of course not," I said quickly.

"In that case we all accept your invitation, Mr. Forster," said Harold.

In the warm atmosphere of the Forsters' home the awkwardness I had felt on first meeting Harold dropped away and soon we were talking freely. He told us of his duties in the platoon, where because of his teaching background, he had been given the job of teaching illiterate young soldiers how to read and write.

"It's amazing how many come through the state system and never pick up even the basics," he said. "I suppose some of them have got away with playing truant or their parents have kept them home for various reasons. Quite a few are Londoners and have spent their lives on the streets. They are very conscious of being illiterate and want to learn to read and write. It's amazing how quickly they pick it up." We then went on to discuss Hannah's progress at the War Nursery and the difference early education made to children.

Time passed quickly and Harold seized the moment while Mr. and Mrs. Forster were out of the room, to speak to me urgently. "Rhoda, I've only a few more days left to this leave and

I would dearly like to see more of you, if that's possible. Are you free this coming week?"

"I work every morning but I finish at one thirty." I thought quickly. "Would you like to come to lunch on Tuesday? I'll give you my address." I wrote it down for him on the back of an envelope and he tucked it into his pocket book.

I spent most of Monday afternoon preparing for his visit, even baking a cake, using all our sugar ration for the week.

When I told Dr. Branson I was having a visitor for lunch he insisted that I leave early. I was glad to have the extra time to put the finishing touches to lunch and to change Hannah. I put on a pretty summer frock and touched up my makeup, so that when Harold knocked at the door I felt more or less ready. Nevertheless, I still had flutterings of nervousness especially when I saw him standing on the doorstep smiling down at me.

As he followed me into the house he looked around him with frank interest. "What a lovely home you have, Rhoda."

"It's only small," I said pleased.

"But that doesn't matter. You've furnished it tastefully and not cluttered it up, like so many people in England."

Hannah came running forward and smiled delightedly up at him. "Hello, Hannah, I have something for you," said Harold, producing a brown paper parcel which he had concealed behind his back. She took it from him, her eyes large.

"Can I open it now?"

"Of course," and Harold knelt beside her as she tugged at the string.

"Here, let's save that string. It might come in handy for something later on."

I watched him as he patiently worked at the knot, admiring the trouble he took to preserve even a little bit of string. He must have had a lifetime of frugality. At last the parcel was free and Hannah impatiently tore at the paper. Harold glanced at her tolerantly and smiled up at me. I noticed how clear and blue his eyes were and my heart thumped.

Inside, wrapped in tissue, was a china doll, dressed in a pretty cotton frock with little frilled panties. Hannah took it in her arms and hugged it ecstatically.

"Say thank you to Uncle Harold," I prompted.

"Thank you, Uncle Harold," she said obediently, still eyeing the doll. "I'm going to put her to bed."

"You can do that later, dear," I said. "Put her in the chair for now so she can watch us having our lunch."

As the three of us sat around the table with the doll in one of the kitchen chairs I couldn't help thinking we seemed like a real family.

While I was cutting the cake Harold said appreciatively. "It's a long time since I had home baked food and this tastes marvellous, quite different from anything they serve up in the mess."

"How long is your leave, Harold?"

"I've got another six days but I am going up to London to stay with my parents in Richmond for the last two."

"I thought they were in Singapore."

"They managed to get out just before the Japanese invaded. It was a close call and they were on the last ship to leave."

"They must feel terribly upset at the state of things in Singapore now."

"Yes." Harold looked wistful. "They've been working out there for thirty years among the Chinese and Malays."

"Their life's work, in fact."

"But that's what this war is about, isn't it, Rhoda, trying to preserve the things that are worthwhile in our civilization? I believe we will win through eventually, although it will be a long hard struggle and many people will die first." He lowered his voice. "I was sorry to hear about your husband. He fought in the Battle of Britain didn't he?"

"Yes, and he died for what he believed in. That is what I hang on to."

"We all have to face the possibility of death, Rhoda," Harold said quietly.

"I suppose so." There was a long silence. At last I asked, "What have you done with your paintings, Harold? Have you stored them somewhere?"

"As a matter of fact they are still in the shed at Elsie's. She very kindly said they could stay there indefinitely. She joined the Wrens, you know, and is stationed in Portsmouth."

"What about her mother? I thought Elsie looked after her."

"She went to live with her sister somewhere near Bournemouth and the house is shut up for the duration."

I thought of the gracious Elizabethan manor house deserted and the beautifully tended grounds neglected and running to weeds.

I said, "You know that Lawrence closed the studio in Guildford, I suppose."

"Yes, I did hear that, but what happened to Richard and his family?"

"Richard was not strong enough to go into the services because of his weak chest. Instead he does warden duties in Guildford. He and his family still live in the flat above the shop."

We were both silent for a few moments thinking of how different times were during those happy days before the war.

"Can I get down now?" asked Hannah. "I want to put dolly to bed."

When she was gone I said to Harold. "That was the perfect gift for Hannah. She just loves her doll and I have a feeling it will go with us everywhere."

"I tried to think what a little girl would like best. I've had so little to do with girls but when I saw the doll in a toyshop it seemed just the right thing."

The rest of the afternoon passed all too quickly. We sat in the garden while Hannah played in her sandpit. Harold showed her how to make a castle using her bucket and spade, and looking at their two heads bent over it I caught myself thinking how like a father and daughter they were. I told myself not to be silly and to put all such thoughts out of my head; all that was past for me now.

When we said goodbye to Harold that evening Hannah reached up to him and putting her arms around his neck she planted a wet kiss on his cheek. "Thank you for Rosalie," she said. "That's my dolly's name."

Harold gave me the ghost of a wink then looked seriously back at Hannah and said, "Mind you put some warm blankets on her tonight so she doesn't catch cold." Then he turned to me. "Is it possible for us to go for a walk tomorrow afternoon, Rhoda?"

"That sounds lovely, but I will have to check with Miss Nugent first to see if she is free to take care of Hannah."

After Harold had gone I went round to Miss Nugent's.

"Of course I'd be delighted to look after Hannah," she said. "Harold hasn't got much leave left has he, and who knows when you will see each other again? You need to make the most of the next few days," she added meaningfully. I found myself growing hot under her gaze, so I thanked her and left a short time later.

At Harold's suggestion we walked out to Stonehenge the next day, following the same paths we had taken long ago. A skylark poured out its song above us and we both stopped to listen.

'It's as though nothing has changed since we were last here," I said. "It's hard to believe there's a war on."

"Places like this are timeless. Stonehenge will be here long after we are gone."

I shivered. I did not want to think about the future. It all seemed so uncertain. Harold sensed my mood and said practically. "I think we had better be getting back now so you can fetch Hannah for tea."

That became our pattern for the next couple of days, a walk in the country, then arriving back at Miss Nugent's in time to collect Hannah for tea.

On our last afternoon together Harold suggested we go to the Duck and Swan for a drink. As we were sitting outside at one of the wooden tables in the mellow autumn sunshine with our glasses of cider in front of us, Harold looked across at me and his eyes were very clear and blue. "Rhoda, do you remember the last occasion we were here?" I nodded. *How could I ever forget*?

"I realised then that you were a woman of character because when I asked you to marry me you said you had promised yourself to somebody else and you would not go back on your word. I admired you for that and though I wanted you desperately I knew you were doing the right thing." He paused and gazed deeply into my eyes. "Now things are different, Rhoda. You are a free woman and I would like to put the same question to you today. Will you marry me?"

I looked back at him and felt my heart growing large within my breast. I longed with all my being to say yes, but it was as though a cool clear voice was telling me to pause and consider. Finally, I heard myself saying, "I would love to marry you, Harold, but this is the wrong time. We could not enjoy a normal married life in the midst of all this uncertainty. You are going away now and I don't know when I shall see you again. I promise you though, that I will marry you—when this war is over."

He put his hand over mine and said, gazing into my eyes. "When this war is over, Rhoda, we will build a home together and with God's help we will make of it a lovely place where happiness and love abide and nothing will destroy its peaceful atmosphere."

I thought about those words many times over the ensuing months and I prayed earnestly that Harold would be kept safe wherever he was. From time to time a letter arrived from him with no indication of where he was stationed, but at least I knew he was alive.

Then at last the war was over and even in Salisbury VE Day was celebrated in the streets of the old city. Joan, Maisie and I crowded into the back of one of the cars that was setting off from Laverton House and joined the revellers in the market square. Everyone seemed to be dancing and singing and we were swept along by the excited crowd. Suddenly, above the din, all the church bells of the city rang out, and chime after chime filled the air while people listened rapt. All through the war the church bells had been silent. A great cheer went up from the crowd and tears came to my eyes. I looked at my friends and I could see that they too were moved.

"Let's go to the cathedral," I said, as a great longing took possession of me, to be inside those hallowed walls and giving thanks for our deliverance.

"Yes, let's," said Joan and Maisie together, and joining hands so that we would not be separated, we set off in the direction of the cathedral. We passed under the stone arch at the entrance to the Close and walked along the narrow alleyway that was closed in on both sides by tall stone houses. Coming out from the darkness I was quite unprepared for the sight before me. The breath caught in my throat. The cathedral was floodlit and stood before us like a tangible presence, solid yet ethereal, firmly grounded yet soaring upward. In that moment I saw it as the symbol of victory, not ours but God's; the triumph of good over evil and light over darkness. We had fought a long hard battle but we had won with God's help. This monument in stone, raised for the glory of God, had stood for a thousand years and would continue to stand as a reminder of the permanence of God's presence among us.

Later, as we took our places inside the cathedral my heart was full. I had lost Lawrence, but God had given me Hannah and I thanked Him for her. I prayed that Harold might return safely from whatever distant battlefield he had been posted. When we got up to leave the cathedral I felt completely at peace.

Some weeks later I was preparing tea while Hannah was playing in the front garden. She came running into the kitchen.

"Mummy, there's a man at the door and he wants to speak to you."

Probably just another travelling salesman, I thought irritated, as I wiped my floury hands on my apron and followed Hannah to the door. A man in a blue suit was standing framed in the doorway and with the light behind him I could not see his features.

"Rhoda," he said gently. Then I knew him.

"Harold!" I exclaimed. "I'd almost given up hope of seeing you again and here you are." Tears sprang to my eyes yet at the same time I laughed, from sheer relief and joy. Harold took both my hands in his and gazing into my eyes, said huskily. "Yes, I've come home at last, to you and Hannah, and now we can build a home together."

"Where happiness and love abide and nothing will destroy its peaceful atmosphere. That is what you said the last time we were together and I have clung to those words during my darkest moments."

Harold drew Hannah and me close to his side and said quietly, "Now this war is over, and with God's help we will never be separated again."

Printed in Australia
AUOC01n0830280813
257595AU00002B/1/P

9 781625 169303